About the Author

Terry Pratchett was the acclaimed creator of the global bestselling Discworld® series, the first of which, *The Colour of Magic*, was published in 1983. In all, he was the author of over fifty bestselling books. His novels have been widely adapted for stage and screen, and he was the winner of multiple prizes, including the Carnegie Medal, as well as being awarded a knighthood for services to literature. He died in March 2015.

www.terrypratchett.co.uk

About the Illustrator

When she's not trying to take over the world or fighting sock-stealing monsters, **Laura Ellen Anderson** is a professional children's book author and illustrator who lives in north London. The creator of *Evil Emperor Penguin* for the *Phoenix* comic, she is also the illustrator of Sibéal Pounder's Witch Wars series and CBeebies presenter Cerrie Burnell's picture books and Harper fiction series. Laura's first author/illustrator picture book, *I Don't Want Curly Hair*, was published by Bloomsbury in 2017. She has also created new cover illustrations for Enid Blyton's Famous Five series.

www.lauraellenanderson.co.uk

@Lillustrator

TERRY PRATCHETT

The Shepherd's Crown

A TIFFANY ACHING NOVEL

CORGI BOOKS

CORGI BOOKS

UK | USA | Canada | Ireland | Australia
India | New Zealand | South Africa

Corgi Books is part of the Penguin Random House group of companies
whose addresses can be found at global.penguinrandomhouse.com.

www.penguin.co.uk
www.puffin.co.uk
www.ladybird.co.uk

 Penguin
Random House
UK

First published in Great Britain by Doubleday 2015
Published by Corgi Books 2016
This edition published 2017

001

Typeset in Minion 12/14.5pt by Falcon Oast Graphic Art Ltd
Printed in Great Britain by Clays Ltd, St Ives plc

A CIP catalogue record for this book is available from the British Library

ISBN: 978–0–552–57634–5

All correspondence to:
Corgi Books
Penguin Random House Children's
80 Strand, London WC2R 0RL

 MIX
Paper from
responsible sources
FSC
www.fsc.org   FSC® C018179

Penguin Random House is committed to a
sustainable future for our business, our readers
and our planet. This book is made from Forest
Stewardship Council® certified paper.

For Esmerelda Weatherwax
– mind how you go.

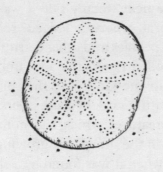

PROLOGUE

A Crown in the Chalk

It was born in the darkness of the Circle Sea; at first just a soft floating thing, washed back and forth by tide after tide. It grew a shell, but in its rolling, tumbling world there were huge creatures which could have cracked it open in an instant. Nevertheless, it survived. Its little life might have gone on like this for ever until the dangers of the surf and other floating things brought an end, were it not for the pool.

It was a warm pool, high on a beach, replenished by occasional storms blown in from the Hub, and there the creature lived on things even smaller than itself and grew until it became king. It would have got even bigger if it were not for the hot summer when the water evaporated under the glare of the sun.

And so the little creature died, but its carapace remained, carrying within itself the seed of something

1

sharp. On the next stormy tide it was washed away onto the littoral, where it lodged, rolling back and forth with the pebbles and other detritus of the storms.

The sea rolled down the ages until it dried and withdrew from the land, and the spiky shell of the long-dead creature sank beneath layers of the shells of other small creatures which had not survived. And there it lay, with the sharp core growing slowly inside, until the day when it was found by a shepherd minding his flock on the hills that had become known as the Chalk.

He picked up the strange object which had caught his eye, held it in his hand and turned it over and over. Lumpy, but not lumpy, and it fitted in the palm of his hand. Too regular a shape to be a flint, and yet it had flint in its heart. The surface was grey, like stone, but with a hint of gold beneath the grey. There were five distinct ridges spaced evenly, almost like stripes, rising from a flattish base to its top. He had seen things like this before. But this one seemed different – it had almost jumped into his hand.

The little piece tumbled as he turned it around and about, and he had a feeling that it was trying to tell him something. It was silly, he knew, and he hadn't had a beer yet, but the strange object seemed to fill his world. Then he cursed himself as an idiot but nevertheless kept it and took it to show his mates in the pub.

'Look,' he said, 'it looks like a crown.'

Of course, one of his mates laughed and said, 'A crown? What would you want with one of them? You're no king, Daniel Aching.'

But the shepherd took his find home and placed it carefully on the shelf in his kitchen where he kept the things he liked.

And there, eventually, it was forgotten and was lost to history.

But not to the Achings, who handed it down, generation to generation . . .

CHAPTER 1

Where the Wind Blows

It was one of those days that you put away and remember. High on the downs, above her parents' farm, Tiffany Aching felt as though she could see to the end of the world. The air was as clear as crystal, and in the brisk wind the dead leaves from the autumn swirled around the ash trees as they rattled their branches to make way for the new spring growth.

She had always wondered why the trees grew there. Granny Aching had told her there were old tracks up here, made in the days when the valley below had been a swamp. Granny said that was why the ancient people had made their homes high up – away from the swamp, and away from other people who would like to raid their livestock.

Perhaps they had found a sense of refuge near the

5

old circles of stones they found there. Perhaps they had been the ones who built them? No one knew for certain where they had come from . . . but even though they didn't really believe it, everyone knew that they were the kind of thing it was probably better to leave alone. Just in case. After all, even if a circle did hide some old secrets or treasure, well, what use was *that* when it came to sheep? And although many of the stones had fallen down, what if the person buried underneath didn't want to be dug up? Being dead didn't mean you couldn't get angry, oh no.

But Tiffany herself had once used one particular set of stones to pass through an arch to Fairyland – a Fairyland most decidedly not like the one she had read about in *The Goode Childe's Booke of Faerie Tales* – and she knew the dangers were real.

Today, for some reason, she had felt the *need* to come up to the stones. Like any sensible witch, she wore strong boots that could march through anything – good, sensible boots. But they did not stop her feeling her land, feeling what it told her. It had begun with a tickle, an itch that crept into her feet and demanded to be heard, urging her to tramp over the downs, to visit the circle, even while she was sticking her hand up a sheep's bottom to try and sort out a nasty case of colic. Why she had to go to the stones, Tiffany did not know, but no witch ignored what could be a summons. And the circles stood as protection. Protection for her land – protection from what could come through . . .

She had headed up there immediately, a slight

frown on her face. But somehow, up there, on top of the Chalk, everything was right. It always was. Even today.

Or was it? For, to Tiffany's surprise, she had not been the only one drawn to the old circle that day. As she spun in the crisp, clean air, listening to the wind, the leaves dancing across her feet, she recognized the flash of red hair, a glimpse of tattooed blue skin – and heard a muttered 'Crivens' as a particularly joyful surge of leaves got caught on the horns of a rabbit's-skull helmet.

'The kelda hersel' sent me here to keep an eye on these stones,' said Rob Anybody from his vantage point on a rocky outcrop close by. He was surveying the landscape as if he were watching for raiders. Wherever they came from. *Particularly* if they came through a circle.

'And if any of them scuggans wants to come back and try again, we're always ready for them, ye ken,' he added hopefully. 'I'm sure we can give them oor best Feegle hospitality.' He drew his wiry blue frame up to its full six inches and brandished his claymore at an invisible enemy.

The effect, Tiffany thought, not for the first time, was quite impressive.

'Those ancient raiders are all long dead,' she said before she could stop herself, even though her Second Thoughts were telling her to listen properly. If Jeannie – Rob's wife and the kelda of the Feegle clan – had seen trouble a-brewing, well, it was likely that trouble was on the way.

'Dead? Weel, so are we,' said Rob.*

'Alas,' Tiffany sighed. 'In those long-ago days, mortals just died. They didn't come back like you seem to do.'

'They would if they had some of our brose.'

'What's that?' asked Tiffany.

'Weel, it's a kind of porridge with everything in it and, if possible, ye ken, a dram of brandy or some of your old granny's Sheep Liniment.'

Tiffany laughed, but that uneasiness remained. I need to speak to Jeannie, she thought. Need to know why she and my boots are both feeling the same thing.

When they arrived at the large grassy mound nearby that housed the intricate warren of the Feegle dwelling, Tiffany and Rob made their way over to the patch of briars which concealed the main entrance and found Jeannie sitting outside, eating a sandwich.

Mutton, Tiffany thought with just a tinge of annoyance. She was well aware of the agreement with the Feegles that they could have the occasional old ewe in exchange for the fun of fightin' off the corbies that would otherwise swoop down on the young lambs, who were doing their best to do what lambs did best: get lost, and get dead. The lost lambs up on the Chalk had a new trick now – heading at speed across the downs, sometimes *backwards*, with a Feegle under each tiny foot, as they were returned to the flock.

---

* The Feegles believed to a man that they had to be dead, as the world they now lived in was grand, filled as it was with so many opportunities for stealin' and fightin' and boozin'. A land fit for dead heroes.

A kelda needed a big appetite, for there was only one kelda in a Nac Mac Feegle clan, and she had a lot of sons, plus the occasional lucky daughter popping out.* Each time Tiffany saw Jeannie, the little kelda was a bit wider and a bit rounder. Those hips took *work*, and Jeannie was certainly working hard at getting them bigger right now as she tackled what looked like half a sheep's leg between two bits of bread. No mean feat for a Feegle only six inches high, and as Jeannie grew to become a wise old kelda, the word 'belt' would no longer signify something to hold up her kilt but just something to mark her equator.

Young Feegles were herding snails and wrestling. They were bouncing off each other, off the walls, and sometimes off their own boots. They were in awe of Tiffany, seeing in her a kind of kelda, and they stopped brawling and looked at her nervously as she approached.

'Line up, lads, show oor hag how hard ye ha' been workin',' their mother said with pride in her voice, wiping a smear of mutton fat off her lips.

Oh no, Tiffany thought. What am I going to see? I hope it doesn't involve snails . . .

But Jeannie said, 'Let yon hag hear your ABC now. Come on, you start, Slightly-more-wee-than-wee-Jock-Jock.'

The first Feegle in the line scratched at his spog and flicked a small beetle out. It seems to be a fact of

---

* Sometimes literally, since a kelda usually gave birth to about seven Feegle babies at a time. Jeannie herself had produced a daughter in amongst her first brood.

life that a Feegle's spog will always be itchy, Tiffany thought, possibly because what is kept in it might still be alive. Slightly-more-wee-than-wee-Jock-Jock swallowed. 'A is for . . . *axe*,' he bellowed. 'To cut yer heid off, ye ken,' he added with a proud boast.

'B is for *boot!*' shouted the next Feegle, wiping something that looked like snail slime down the front of his kilt. 'So as to *stamp* on yer heid.'

'An' C is for *claymore* . . . and crivens, I'll gi'e ye sich a guid kickin' if'n you stick that sword intae me one muir time,' shouted the third, turning and hurling himself at one of his brothers.

A yellowing crescent-shaped object fell to the ground as the brawl spun off into the brambles, and Rob snatched it up and tried to hide it behind his back.

Tiffany narrowed her eyes. That had looked suspiciously like . . . yes, a bit of old toenail!

'Weel,' said Rob, shuffling his feet, 'ye is always cuttin' these little chunks off'n them old gentl'men you goes to visit most days. They fly out o' the winders, jus' waitin' for a body to pick 'em up. An' they is hard as nails, ye ken.'

'Yes, that's because they *are* nails—' Tiffany began, then stopped. After all, maybe someone like old Mr Nimlet would like to know that parts of his body were still ready for a scrap. Even if he himself couldn't get out of a chair without help these days.

The kelda drew her to one side now, and said, 'Weel, hen, your name is in the soil. It talks to you, Tir-far-thóinn, Land Under Wave. Do you talk to it?'

'Yes,' said Tiffany. 'Only sometimes though. But I do *listen*, Jeannie.'

'Not every day?' said the kelda.

'No, not every day. So much to do, so much to do.'

'I ken that,' said the kelda. 'Ye know that I watch over you. I watch ye in my heid, but I also see ye whizzing aboot *over* me heid. And ye must remember ye are a long time deid.'

Tiffany sighed, weary to her bones. Going around the houses – that was what you did if you were a compassionate witch, what she and all the other witches did to fill in the gaps in the world, doing things that had to be done: carrying logs in for an old lady or popping on a pot of stew for a dinner, bringing a herbal remedy for a sore leg or a troublesome ache, fetching a basket of 'spare' eggs or second-hand clothes for a new baby in a house where money was scarce, and listening, oh yes, always listening to people's troubles and worries. And the toenails . . . those toenails, they seemed to be as hard as flint, and sometimes an old boy without friends or family would have his toenails twisting inside his boots.

But the reward for lots of work seemed to be lots more. If you dug the biggest hole, they just gave you a bigger shovel . . .

'Today, Jeannie,' she said slowly, 'I *did* listen to the land. It told me to go to the circle . . . ?' There was a question hanging in the air.

The kelda sighed. 'I dinnae see it clear yet, but there is . . . something not right, Tiffan,' she said. 'The veil between oor worlds is thin and can be easily brake, ye ken. The stones stand, so the gateway is nae open – and the Quin of the Elves will nae be strong after ye sent her back to Fairyland afore. She will nae be in a hurry to get past ye agin, but . . . I am still a-feared. I can feel it noo, like a fog driftin' oor way.'

Tiffany bit her lip. If the kelda was worried, she knew she should be too.

'Dinnae fash yesel',' Jeannie said softly, watching Tiffany closely. 'Whin ye need the Feegles, we will be there. And until that time, we will keep a watch for ye.' She took a last bite of her sandwich, and then gave Tiffany a different sort of look as she changed the subject. 'Ye ha' a young man – Preston, I think you call him. Do ye see him much?' Her gaze was suddenly as sharp as an axe.

'Well,' said Tiffany, 'he works hard, just like I do. Him in the hospital and me in the Chalk.' To her horror, she felt herself begin to blush, the kind of blush that begins in your toes and works its way up to your face until you look like a tomato. She couldn't blush! Not like a young country girl with a beau. She was a witch! 'We write to each other,' she added in a small voice.

'And is that enough? Letters?'

Tiffany swallowed. She had once thought – everyone had thought – that she and Preston might have an Understanding, him being an educated boy, running the new school at the barn on the Achings' farm until he had enough saved to go study in the big city to be a doctor. Now everyone *still* thought they had an Understanding, including Tiffany and Preston.

Except . . . did she have to do what everyone expected her to do? 'He is very nice and tells wonderful jokes and is great with words,' she tried to explain. 'But . . . we like our work, both of us, in fact you might say we *are* our work. Preston is working so hard at the Lady Sybil Free Hospital. And I can't help thinking about Granny Aching and how much she liked her life, up on the downs, just her and the sheep and her two dogs, Thunder and Lightning, and . . .' She tailed off and Jeannie laid a small nut-brown hand on her arm.

'Do ye think this is the way to live, my girl?'

'Well, I do like what I am doing and it helps people.'

'But who helps you? That broomstick of yours flies everywhere and I think sometimes it might burst into flames. Ye look after everybody – but who looks after ye? If Preston is away, weel, there's your friend the Baron and his new wife. Surely they care about their people. Care enough to help.'

'They do care,' said Tiffany, remembering with a shudder how everyone had once also thought that she and Roland, now the Baron, had an Understanding. Why were they so keen to try and find her a husband? Were husbands *that* difficult to find if she wanted one? 'Roland is a decent man, although not yet as good as his father became. And Letitia . . .'

Letitia, she thought. Both she and Letitia knew that Letitia could do magic but right now was just playing the role of the young Baroness. And she was good at it – so good that Tiffany wondered if the Being a Baroness might come to win over Being a Witch in the end. It certainly involved a lot less mess.

'Already ye have done such things other folk wouldnae credit,' Jeannie continued.

'Well,' said Tiffany, 'there's too much to be done and not enough people to do it.'

The smile that the kelda gave her was a strange one. The little woman said, 'Do ye let them try? Ye mustn't be afraid to ask for help. Pride is a good thing, my girl, but it will kill you in time.'

Tiffany laughed. 'Jeannie, you are always right. But I am a witch so pride is in the bones.' That brought to mind Granny Weatherwax – the witch all the other witches thought of as the wisest and most senior of them all. When Granny Weatherwax said things, she never *sounded* proud – but she didn't need to. It was just there, built right into her essence. In fact, whatever a witch needed in her bones, Granny Weatherwax had it in great big shovelfuls. Tiffany hoped, one day, that she might be that strong a witch herself.

'Weel, that's guid, so it is,' said the kelda. 'Ye're oor hag o' the hills and we need oor hag to ha' some pride. But we'd also like ye to have a life of your ain.' Her solemn little gaze was fixed on Tiffany now. 'So off ye gae and follow where the wind blows ye.'

The wind down in the Shires was angry, blowing everywhere as if it was upset, howling around the chimneys of Lord Swivel's mansion, which stood surrounded by acres of parkland and could only be reached by a long drive – ruling out visits by anyone not in possession of at least a decent horse.

That put paid to the majority of the ordinary

people thereabouts, who were mostly farmers, and who were too busy to do any such thing anyway. Any horse they had was generally large and hairy-legged and usually seen attached to carts. The skinny, half-mad horses that pranced up the drive or pulled coaches up it were normally conveying a very different class of man: one who always had land and money, but often very little chin. And whose wife sometimes resembled his horse.

Lord Swivel's father had inherited money and the title from his father, a great master builder, but he had been a drunkard and had wasted almost all of it.* Nevertheless young Harold Swivel had wheeled and dealed, and yes, swivelled and swindled, until he had restored the family fortune, and had added two wings to the family mansion which he filled with expensively ugly objects.

He had three sons, which pleased him greatly in that his wife had produced one extra over and above the usual 'heir and spare'. Lord Swivel liked to be one up on everyone else, even if the one up was only in the form of a son he didn't overly care for.

Harry, the eldest, didn't go to school much because he was now dealing with the estate, helping his father and learning who was worth talking to and who wasn't.

---

* Lord Swivel's father reckoned it was no waste, and that he had thoroughly enjoyed drinking the family fortune. At least, he thought this until he drank so much he fell over and met a gentleman with a decided lack of flesh on his bones and the definitive addition of a scythe a good few years earlier than he should have done.

Number two was Hugh, who had suggested to his father that he would like to go into the church. His father had said, 'Only if it's the Church of Om, but none of the others. I'm not having no son of mine fooling around with cultic activities!'* Om was handily silent, thereby enabling his priests to interpret his wishes how they chose. Amazingly, Om's wishes rarely translated into instructions like 'Feed the poor' or 'Help the elderly' but more along the lines of 'You need a splendid residence' or 'Why not have seven courses for dinner?' So Lord Swivel felt that a clergyman in the family could in fact be useful.

His third son was Geoffrey. And nobody quite knew what to make of Geoffrey. Not least, Geoffrey himself.

The tutor Lord Swivel employed for his boys was named Mr Wiggall. Geoffrey's older brothers called him 'Wiggler', sometimes even to his face. But for Geoffrey Mr Wiggall was a godsend. The tutor had arrived with a huge crate of his own books, only too aware that some great houses barely had a single book in them, unless the books were about battles of the past in which a member of the family had been spectacularly and stupidly heroic. Mr Wiggall and his wonderful books taught Geoffrey about the great philosophers Ly Tin Weedle, Orinjcrates, Xeno and

---

* He knew, too, that gods could sometimes make inconvenient requests. He had an associate who had chosen to follow the crocodile god Offler and then found he had to keep an aviary of tooth-cleaning birds handy to fulfil his god's dental whims.

Ibid, and the celebrated inventors Goldeneyes Silverhand Dactylos and Leonard of Quirm, and Geoffrey started to discover what he might make of himself.

When they weren't reading and studying, Mr Wiggall took Geoffrey to dig up things – old bones and old places – around the Shires, and told him about the universe, which he previously had not thought about. The more he learned the more he thirsted for knowledge and longed to know all about the Great Turtle A'Tuin, and the lands beyond the Shires.

'Excuse me, sir,' he said to his tutor one day. 'How did you become a teacher?'

Mr Wiggall laughed and said, 'Someone taught me, that's how it goes. And he gave me a book, and after that I would read any book that I could find. Just like you do, young sir. I see you reading all the time, not just in lessons.'

Geoffrey knew that his father sneered at the teacher, but his mother had intervened, saying that Geoffrey had a star in his hand.

His father scoffed at that. 'All he's got in his hand is mud, and dead people, and who cares where Fourecks is? No one ever goes there!'*

His mother looked tired, but took his side, saying, 'He's very good at reading and Mr Wiggall has taught him three languages. He can even speak a bit of Offleran!'

Again his father sneered. 'Only handy if he wants

---

* Very true, but a lot of people *came from* Fourecks, as is often the case with a Place-That-Nobody-Has-Ever-Heard-Of. They just never bothered to go back again.

to be a dentist! Ha, why waste time on learning languages. After all, everyone speaks Ankh-Morpork these days.'

But Geoffrey's mother said to him, 'You read, my boy. Reading is the way up. Knowledge is the key to everything.'

Shortly afterwards, the tutor was sent away by Lord Swivel, who said, 'Too much nonsense around here. It's not as if the boy will amount to much. Not like his brothers.'

The walls of the manor could pick up voices a long way away and Geoffrey had heard that and thought, Well, whatever I do choose to become, I am *not* going to be like my father!

With his tutor gone, Geoffrey wandered about the place, learning new things, hanging around a lot with McTavish, the stable-lad who was as old as the hills but somehow still was known as a 'lad'. He knew all the bird songs in the world and could imitate them too.

And McTavish was there when Geoffrey found Mephistopheles. One of the old nanny goats had given birth, and while she had two healthy kids, there was a third kid hidden in the straw, a little runt which its mother had rejected.

'I'm going to try and save this little goat,' Geoffrey declared. And he spent all night labouring to keep the newborn alive, squeezing milk from its mother and letting the little kid lick it off his finger until it slept peacefully beside him in a broken-up bale of hay, which kept them both warm.

He is such a small thing, Geoffrey thought,

looking into the kid's letterbox eyes. I must give him a chance.

And the kid responded, and grew into a strong young goat with a devilish kick. He would follow Geoffrey everywhere, and lower his head and prepare to charge anyone he thought threatened his young master. Since this often meant anyone within reach, many a servant or visitor found themselves skipping rather smartly out of the way when faced with the goat's lowered horns.

'Why did thee call that hell-goat Mephistopheles?' asked McTavish one day.

'I read it in a book.* You can tell it is a very good name for a goat,' Geoffrey replied.

Geoffrey grew older, turning from a little boy into a young lad and then a bigger lad, wisely catching his father's eye only occasionally.

Then one day McTavish saddled a horse for him and they rode over to the fields at the edge of Lord Swivel's estate and crept quietly to a fox's earth in the woods. There, as they had done many times before, they watched the vixen play with her cubs.

'Nice to see 'un like so,' whispered McTavish. 'A fox mun eat and feed yon cubs. But they has too much of a taste for me chickens for my liking. They kill things as matter to us, an' so we kill them. 'Tis the way of the world.'

'It shouldn't be,' said Geoffrey, sorrow in his voice as his heart went out to the vixen.

* Thus proving that books can teach you much, if only to give you a good name for a devilish smart goat.

'But we needs the hens and mun protect 'em. That's why we hunts foxes,' said McTavish. 'I brings you here today, Geoffrey, for the time is coming when your father will want you to join the hunt. Of yon vixen mebbe.'

'I understand,' Geoffrey said. He knew about the hunt, of course, as he had been made to watch them ride out every year since he was a baby. 'We must protect our hens, and the world can be cruel and merciless. But making a *game* of it is not right. That's terrible! It's just execution. Must we kill everything? Kill a mother who is feeding her cubs? We take so much and we give back nothing.' He rose to his feet and went back to his horse. 'I do not want to hunt, McTavish. My word, I do not like to hate – I don't even hate my father – but the hunt I would like to see put in a dark place.'

McTavish looked worried. 'I think thee needs to be careful, young Geoffrey. You knows what your father is like. He's a bit of a stick-in-the-mud.'

'My father is not a stick-in-the-mud; he is the mud!' Geoffrey said bitterly.

'Well then, if you tries talking to him – or your mother – mebbe he might understand that you are not ready to join the hunt?'

'No point,' said Geoffrey. 'When he has made up his mind, you cannot get through to him. I hear my mother crying sometimes – she doesn't like to be seen crying, but I know she cries.'

Then it was, as he looked up to watch a hawk hovering, that he thought to himself: There is freedom. Freedom is what I want.

'I would like to fly, McTavish,' he said, adding, 'Like the birds. Like Langas.'*

And almost immediately, he saw a witch flying overhead on a stick, following the hawk, and he pointed up and said, 'I want one of those. I want to be a witch.'

But the old man said, 'It's not for thee, boy. Everybody knows men can't be witches.'

'Why not?' asked Geoffrey.

The old man shrugged and said, 'Nobody knows.'

And Geoffrey said, 'I want to know.'

On the day of Geoffrey's first hunt he trotted out with the rest, pale-faced but determined, and thought, This is the day I must try to stand up for myself.

Soon the local gentry were galloping across the countryside, some taking it to the extreme by careering into ditches, through hedges or over gates, often minus their mounts, while Geoffrey carefully held his position well to the back of the throng, until he could slip away unnoticed. He circled the woods in the opposite direction to the hunt, his heart aching, especially when the baying of the hounds turned to joyous yelps as the prey was brought down.

Then it was time to return to the house. There,

* The legend of Pilotus and his son Langas, who wanted to fly like the birds, was known by every well-educated boy. They did indeed build themselves wings by sewing together feathers and thistledown. The boy at least flew a little way, but his elderly and portly father crashed. The moral of the story is: understand what you are doing before you do it.

everyone was at that happy stage of a hunt where 'tomorrow' is a word that still means something and you have a mug of hot beverage that is liberally laced with something not too dissimilar to Tiffany's grandmother's Special Sheep Liniment. A reward for the returning heroes! They had survived the hunt. *Huzzah!* They swigged and swilled and the drink ran over their non-existent chins.

But Lord Swivel looked at Geoffrey's horse – the only animal not to be lathered in sweat with its legs besplattered in mud – and his wrath was unquenchable.

Geoffrey's brothers held him while his mother looked on imploringly, but to no avail. She averted her face as Lord Swivel smeared vixen's blood on Geoffrey's face.

His lordship was almost incandescent in his rage. 'Where *were* you? You should have *been* there at the kill!' he roared. 'You will do this, young man – and like it! I had to do it when I was young, and so did my father before me. And so will you. It is a tradition. Do you understand? Every male member of our family has been blooded at your age. Who are you to say it's wrong? I'm ashamed of you!'

There it came, the swish of the crop, across Geoffrey's back.

Geoffrey, his face dripping with the vixen's blood, looked to his mother. 'She was a beautiful thing! Why kill her in such a way? For fun?'

'Please don't upset your father,' his mother pleaded.

'I see them in the woods, and you just hunt them.

Can you eat them? No. We – the unspeakable – chase and kill what we cannot eat, just for the blood. For fun.'

Swish.

It hurt. But Geoffrey was suddenly full of . . . what? All at once he had the amazing feeling that things could be *made* right, and he told himself, I could do it. I know I can. He drew himself up to his full height and shook himself free of his brothers' grasp.

'I must thank you, Father,' he said with unexpected vigour. 'I have learned something important today. But I won't let you hit me again – never – and nor will you see me again unless you can change. Do you understand me?' His tone was oddly formal now, as if befitting the occasion.

Harry and Hugh looked at Geoffrey with a kind of awe and waited for the explosion, while the rest of the hunt, which had given Lord Swivel space in which to deal with his son, stopped pretending that they weren't watching. The world of the hunt was out of kilter, the air frozen but somehow contriving also to seem to hold its breath.

In the charged silence, Geoffrey led his horse off to the stables, leaving Lord Swivel standing there like a stone.

He gave the horse some hay, took off its saddle and bridle, and was rubbing the beast down when McTavish walked up to him and said, 'Well done, young Geoffrey.' Then, surprisingly outspoken, the stable-lad added under his breath, 'You stood up for yourself, right enough. Don't let that bastard grind thee down.'

'If you talk like that, McTavish, my father could turn you out,' Geoffrey warned. 'And you like it here, don't you?'

'Well, lad, you're right there. I'm too old to be changing my ways now, I reckon,' McTavish replied. 'But you stood your ground and no man could do better nor that. I expect thee'll be leaving us now, Master Geoffrey?'

'Alas, yes,' said Geoffrey. 'But thank you, McTavish. I hope my father doesn't take it out on you for talking to me.'

And the oldest stable-lad in the world said, 'He won't do that, no, never, not while I'm still useful like. Anyways, after all these years, I know him – like one of them volcanee things, he is. Powerful dangerous explosions for a while, and no care for who gets caught by the red-hot boulders spewing every which way, but it still blows out in the end. Smart folks just keep out of sight until it's over. You've been very pleasant and respectful to me, Master Geoffrey. I reckons you take after your mother. A lovely lady, always so good to me and so helpful when my Molly was dying. I remember that. And I'll remember you too.'

'Thank you,' said Geoffrey. 'And I will remember you.'

McTavish lit up a most enormous pipe and the smoke billowed. 'I reckon you'll be wanting to take away that dratted goat of yourn.'

'Yes,' said Geoffrey. 'But I don't think I have any say in the matter – Mephistopheles will make up his own mind. He usually does.'

McTavish gave him a sideways look. 'Got any food, Master Geoffrey? Got any money? I reckon you won't want to go into the house now. I tell you what, I'll loan thee a bit o' cash till you finds out where you wants to be.'

'No!' said Geoffrey. 'I can't possibly!'

'I'm your friend, Master Geoffrey. Like I said, your mother has been good to me and I owes her a lot. You come back and see her sometime. And when you do that, just make sure you look up old McTavish.'

Geoffrey went to fetch Mephistopheles and hitched him up to the little cart McTavish had made for him. He loaded a few things into the cart, picked up the reins, clicked his tongue and they set off out of the stable yard.

As the goat's dainty hooves echoed down the drive, McTavish said to himself, 'How does the boy do it? That hell-goat kicks the arse of everybody who comes here. But not Geoffrey.'

If Geoffrey had looked back, he would have seen his mother's beseeching look as she sobbed, while his father still stood there like a statue, amazed at such defiance. His brothers made as if to follow, but halted when they saw the rage in their father's eyes.

And so Geoffrey and his goat went off to find a new life. Now, he thought, as they rounded the first of the drive's many bends and he rode into his future, I've got nowhere to go.

But the wind whispered, 'Lancre.'

*

In Lancre, it hadn't been a good day for Granny Weatherwax. A young lumberjack at work higher up in the Ramtop mountains had nearly severed his own foot. And on a day when the resident Igor was elsewhere so unable to patch him up. When Granny arrived at the camp on her rickety old broomstick she immediately saw that the lad was in an even worse mess than she had expected. He had been doing his best to look brave in front of his mates, who were clustered around him trying to cheer him up, but she could see the pain in his face.

As she examined the damage, he cried out for his mother.

'You, lad,' Granny said sharply, turning a piercing look on the nearest of his mates. 'You know where this lad's family live?' And at the boy's scared nod – a witch's pointy hat often seemed to make young lads suddenly very scared – she went on, 'Go then. Run. Tell the lady I'm bringing her son back and she'll need hot water on and a clean bed. *Clean*, mind.' And as the boy raced off, Granny glared at the others standing sheepishly around. 'You others,' she said sharply, 'don't just stand around. Make a stretcher from some of that there wood lying about so's I can take your friend there.'

The lad's foot was all but hanging off and his boot was full of blood. Granny gritted her teeth, and set to with everything in her armoury and all the knowledge accumulated over many years, quietly, gently, taking his pain away from him, drawing it into herself to hold until she could release it.

His face came alive and his eyes sparkled and he started chatting to the witch like an old friend. She cleaned and she stitched, all the while telling the lad what she was doing in a cheerful and calm voice before giving him what she called 'a little tincture'. To the onlookers it looked like the boy was almost himself again when they brought to her a rather makeshift stretcher and found the lad dreamily telling Granny how to get to his home.

The habitations of the lumberjacks up in the mountains were often no better than sheds and it turned out the boy – a lad by the name of Jack Abbott – and his mother lived in one of these. It was a rickety little hut held together more with dirt than with anything else, and when Granny Weatherwax arrived outside with the stretcher lashed underneath her broomstick, she frowned, wondering how this lad's injury could possibly be kept clean in such surroundings. The mother ran out to her boy and flapped around as the lad who had run down to her with the news helped Granny carry the stretcher inside and move the boy onto a pallet onto which the mother had heaped blankets to create a bed fit for an invalid.

Granny Weatherwax said quietly to the injured boy, 'You lie right there and don't get up.' And to the distraught mother, who was wringing her hands and making noises about paying something, she said, 'No payment necessary, mistress – that's not how we witches work – and I'll come back to see him in a few days, and if I can't make it then send for Mrs Ogg. I know boys, and your son'll want to be up and doing as soon as possible, but mark my words, bed rest is the thing for him now.'

The boy's mother stared at Granny and said, 'Thank you so much, Mrs . . . um . . . well, I ain't never had need to call on a witch before, and I've heard some folks round here say witches do nasty things. But I can tell 'em now as I ain't seen nothing of that sort.'

'Really?' said Granny, struggling to keep her temper. 'Well, I would like to do some nasty things to the overseer for not keeping an eye on these lads, and don't you let that man tell your boy to get up until I do. If he does, tell him that Granny Weatherwax will be after him for using these young men who don't really know how to climb trees. I'm a good witch, as it happens, but if I find your boy working before that foot is healed there will be a reckoning.'

As the mother waved Granny away she said, 'I will pray to Om for you, Mrs Weatherwax.'

'Well, do tell me what he says,' said Granny sharply. 'And that's *Mistress* Weatherwax, thank you. But if you've got some old clothing I could take back with me when I come again – well, that *would* help. I'll see you in a day or so, along with your boy. And mind you keep that wound *clean*.'

You, Granny's white cat, was waiting for her when she arrived back at her cottage, along with several people wanting potions and poultices. One or two were looking for advice but generally people were careful not to ask Granny Weatherwax, as she had a tendency to dish out advice whether wanted or not, such as the wisdom of not giving little Johnny hand-made soldiers until he was old enough to know not to stuff them up his nose.

She bustled around for another hour, dishing out medicaments to person after person, and it was only much later that she realized that although she had fed the cat, obviously, she herself had had nothing to eat or drink since the dawn. So she heated up some pottage – not a great meal, but it filled her up.

Then she lay on her bed for a while, even though sleeping in the daytime was something that only very grand ladies did, and so Granny Weatherwax allowed herself not forty winks but just the one. After all, there were always more people to see and things to do.

Then she pulled herself up, and despite it being now quite late she went out and cleaned the privy. And she scrubbed it. She scrubbed it so hard that she could see her face in it . . .

But somehow, in the shimmering water, her face could also see her, and she sighed and said, 'Drat, and tomorrow was going to be a much better day.'

CHAPTER 2

A Voice in the Darkness

It was a bright sunny day, thought Granny Weatherwax, a perfect day in fact. She had been up all night and cleaned the hall and kitchen in her cottage until everything that could shine was shining – the stove polished, the rag rug shaken and the flagstones scrubbed.

She moved up her corkscrew staircase and concentrated next on the floor in the bedroom. She had made some very good soap this year,* and the jug and little wash basin by the bed were gleaming. The spiders in the corners, who had thought they had tenure unto Doomsday, were carefully shown the window, webs and all. Even the mattress looked clean and wholesome. Every so often You, her cat, appeared to

---

* Granny's soap was like her advice: strong and sharp and it stung a bit at the time, but it worked.

see what was going on, and to lie on the patchwork quilt that was so flat it looked like someone had trodden on a huge tortoise.

Then Granny cleaned the privy once again, just for good measure. Not an errand for a fine day, but Esmerelda Weatherwax was meticulous in these things and the privy yielded to her efforts and, yes, it shone. Amazingly so.

Watching her, the intensity that showed on her cat's face was remarkable. This was a different day, You sensed. A day not yet experienced. A day that bustled as if there would never be another day, and with the inside of the cottage up to scratch, You now followed Granny into the scullery.

A bucket of water, filled from the pump by the well, did the trick there. Granny smiled. She had always liked the scullery. It smelled of hard work being done properly. Here there were also spiders, mostly hiding around the bottles and jars on the shelves, but she thought scullery spiders didn't really count. Live and let live.

She went outside next, to the walled paddock at the back of the cottage, to check on her goats. The itinerary of her thinking was declaring that once again all things were in their rightful place.

Satisfied, or as satisfied as a witch ever could be, Granny Weatherwax went to her beehives.

'You are my bees,' she said to them. 'Thank you. You've given me all my honey for years, and please don't be upset when someone new comes. I hope that you will give her as much honey as you have given me.

And now, for the last time, I will dance with you.' But the bees hummed softly and danced *for* her instead, gently pushing her mind out of their hive. And Granny Weatherwax said, 'I was younger when I last danced with you. But I am old now. There will be no more dances for me.'

You kept away from the bees, but stalked through the garden, following Granny as she moved through the herbs, touching a frond or a leaf as she passed, and the whole garden seemed to answer her, the plants almost nodding their heads in respect.

You narrowed her eyes and looked sideways at the plants with what might be called feline disfavour. An onlooker might swear Granny's herbs were sapient, as they often moved without the wind blowing. On at least one occasion, to the cat's horror, they had actually turned round to watch her as she sneaked past on a hunting expedition. She preferred plants that did what they were told, which was mostly to stay dead still so that she could go back to sleep.

At the far end of the herbs, Granny came to the apple tree old Mr Parsons had given her only last year, planting it roughly where anyone else would have a fence around their garden – for no witch's cottage ever needed an actual fence or wall. Who would cross a witch? The wicked old witch in the woods? Sometimes stories can be useful for a witch without, it must be said, any fence-building skills. Granny eyed the tiny apples appearing on the bough – they had only just begun to grow and, well, time was waiting. And so she walked again back to her cottage door, acknowledging every root, stem and fruit she passed.

She fed the goats, who looked at her askance with their slotted eyes. Their gaze followed her as she turned to the chickens, who always squabbled over their feed. Today, however, they didn't squabble, but looked at the old witch as if she wasn't there.

With the animals fed, Granny Weatherwax went into the scullery and came back with a switch of willows. She got to work, teasing every piece of resilient willow into the right place. Then, when the thing she had made was clearly excellent and fit for purpose, Granny Weatherwax left it near the foot of the stairs where it would be noticed, for those with eyes to see.

She tidied the remnants of her work back to the scullery and came out again with a small bag. A white one. And a red ribbon coiled in her other hand. She looked to the sky. Time was wasting.

She walked briskly into the woods, You trailing behind, curious as only a cat can be until at least the first eight of its lives have been used up. Then, her task completed, Granny Weatherwax retraced her steps towards the little stream which ran through the woods close by. It gurgled and tinkled.

She knew the woodlands. Every log. Every bough. Every creature that lived in there. More intimately than anyone not a witch could ever know. When her nose told her there was no one around apart from You, she opened the bag, took out a bar of her soap and undressed.

She stepped into the stream, getting as clean as could be. And now, drying herself off and wrapping just her cloak around her washed body, she went back to the cottage, where she gave You an extra meal, stroked her head, and climbed the squeaking staircase to her bedroom, humming an old dirge as she went.

Then Esmerelda Weatherwax brushed out her long grey hair and repinned it into its usual bun with an army of pins, and dressed again, this time choosing her best witch's dress and least-mended pair of drawers. She paused to open the little wooden window to the soft evening air and carefully placed two pennies on the small bedside table, beside her pointy witch's hat festooned with unused hatpins.

The last thing she did before she lay down was to pick up a familiar card she had written on earlier.

And a little later, when the cat jumped up onto the bed, it appeared to You that something strange was happening. She heard an owl hoot, and a fox barked in the darkness.

And there was just the cat, You. All alone.

But if cats could smile, this one did.

It was a strange night; the owls hooted almost nonstop, and the wind outside for some reason made the wicks of the candles inside wobble with a vengeance and then blow out; but Granny Weatherwax was dressed in her best and ready for anything.

And now in the deep warm darkness, as dawn began to stealthily steal the night, her soul had a visitor, an individual with a scythe – a scythe with a blade so shadow-thin that it could separate a soul from a body.

Then the darkness spoke.

ESMERELDA WEATHERWAX, YOU KNOW WHO COMES, AND MAY I SAY IT'S A PRIVILEGE TO DEAL WITH YOU.

'I know it is you, Mister Death. After all, we witches always knows what's coming,' said Granny, looking down at her body on the bed.

Her visitor was no stranger, and the land she knew she was going to was a land she had helped many others to step through to over the years. For a witch stands on the very edge of everything, between the light and the dark, between life and death, making choices, making decisions so that others may pretend no decisions have even been needed. Sometimes they need to help some poor soul through the final hours, help them to find the door, not to get lost in the dark.

And Granny Weatherwax had been a witch for a long, long time.

ESMERELDA WEATHERWAX, WE HAVE MET SO MANY TIMES BEFORE NOW, HAVEN'T WE?

'Too many to count, Mister Reaper. Well, you've finally got me, you old bugger. I've had my season, no doubt about it, and I was never one for pushing myself forward, or complaining.'

I HAVE WATCHED YOUR PROGRESS WITH INTEREST, ESMERELDA WEATHERWAX, said the voice in the dark. He was firm, but oh so polite. But now there was a question in his voice. PRAY TELL ME, WHY WERE YOU CONTENT TO LIVE IN THIS TINY LITTLE COUNTRY WHEN, AS YOU KNOW, YOU COULD HAVE BEEN ANYTHING AND ANYBODY IN THE WORLD?

'I don't know about the world, not much; but in

my part of the world I could make little miracles for ordinary people,' Granny replied sharply. 'And I never wanted the world – just a part of it, a small part which I could keep safe, which I could keep away from storms. Not the ones of the sky, you understand: there are other kinds.'

AND WOULD YOU SAY YOUR LIFE BENEFITED THE PEOPLE OF LANCRE AND ENVIRONS?

After a minute the soul of Granny Weatherwax said, 'Well, not boasting, your willingness, I think I have done right, for Lancre at least. I've never been to Environs.'

MISTRESS WEATHERWAX, THE WORD 'ENVIRONS' MEANS, WELL, THEREABOUTS.

'All right,' said Granny. 'I did get about, to be sure.'

A VERY GOOD LIFE LIVED INDEED, ESMERELDA.

'Thank you,' said Granny. 'I did my best.'

MORE THAN YOUR BEST, said Death. AND I LOOK FORWARD TO WATCHING YOUR CHOSEN SUCCESSOR. WE HAVE MET BEFORE.

'She's a good witch, to be sure,' said the shade of Granny Weatherwax. 'I have no doubts whatsoever.'

YOU ARE TAKING THIS VERY WELL, ESME WEATHERWAX.

'It's an inconvenience, true enough, and I don't like it at all, but I know that you do it for everyone, Mister Death. Is there any other way?'

NO, THERE ISN'T, I'M AFRAID. WE ARE ALL FLOATING IN THE WINDS OF TIME. BUT YOUR CANDLE, MISTRESS WEATHERWAX, WILL FLICKER FOR SOME TIME BEFORE IT GOES OUT – A LITTLE REWARD FOR A LIFE WELL LIVED. FOR I

CAN SEE THE BALANCE AND YOU HAVE LEFT THE WORLD MUCH BETTER THAN YOU FOUND IT, AND IF YOU ASK ME, said Death, NOBODY COULD DO ANY BETTER THAN THAT . . .

There was no light, no point of reference except for the two tiny blue pinpricks sparkling in the eye sockets of Death himself.

'Well, the journey was worth taking and I saw many wonderful things on the way, including you, my reliable friend. Shall we go now?'

MADAM, WE'VE ALREADY GONE.

In the early morning light, in a village pond near Slice, bubbles came to the surface, followed by Miss Tick, witchfinder. There was no one there to observe this remarkable occurrence, apart from her mule, Joseph, grazing steadily on the river bank. Of course, she told herself sadly as she picked up her towel, they all leave me alone these days.

She sighed. It was such a shame when old customs disappeared. A good witch-ducking was something she had liked doing in the bad old days – she had even *trained* for it. All those swimming lessons, and practice with knots at the Quirm College for Young Ladies. She had been able to defeat the mobs under water if necessary. Or at least work at breaking her own record for untying the simple knots they all thought worked on the nasty witch.

Now, a bit of pond-dipping had become more like a hobby, and she had a nasty feeling that others were copying her after she passed through their villages.

She'd even heard talk of a swimming club being started in one small hamlet over by Ham-on-Rye.*

Miss Tick picked up her towel to dry herself off and went back to her small caravan, gave Joseph his breakfast nosebag and put the kettle on. She settled down under the trees to have her snap – bread and dripping, a thank-you the day before from a farmer's wife for an afternoon's knowledge of reading. Miss Tick had smiled as she left because the eyes of the rather elderly woman had been sparkling – 'Now,' she had said, 'I can see what's in those letters Alfred gets, especially the ones that smell of lavender.' Miss Tick wondered if it might be a good idea to get moving soon. Before Alfred got another letter anyway.

Her stomach filled, ready for the day ahead, she sensed an uneasiness in the air, so there was nothing for it but to make a shamble.

A shamble is a witch's aid to inner concentration and always has to be made right there and then, when needed, to catch the moment. It could be made of pretty much anything, but had to include something alive. An egg would do, though most witches would prefer to save the egg for dinner, in case it exploded on them. Miss Tick dug in her pockets. A woodlouse, a dirty handkerchief, an old sock, an ancient conker, a stone with a hole in it, and a toadstool which Miss Tick couldn't quite identify and so couldn't risk eating. She expertly strung them all together with

* A popular idea among the young lads, since they felt that everyone – and 'everyone' definitely included the young ladies – should swim without their clothes.

a bit of string and a spare length of knicker elastic.

Then she *pulled* at the threads. But there *was* something wrong. With a *twang* that reverberated around the clearing, the tangle of objects threw itself into the air and spun, twisting and turning.

'Well, that's going to complicate things,' Miss Tick groaned.

Just across the woods from Granny Weatherwax's cottage, Nanny Ogg nearly dropped a flagon of her best home-made cider on her cat, Greebo. She kept her flagons of cider in the shady spring by her cottage. The tomcat considered a growl, but after one look at his mistress he tried to be a good boy, for the normally cheerful face of Nanny Ogg was like thunder this morning.

And he heard her mutter, 'It should have been me.'

In Genua, on a royal visit with her husband Verence, Queen Magrat of Lancre, former witch, discovered that even though she might think she had retired from magic, magic had not retired from her. She shuddered as the shock wave was carried across the world like a tsunami, an intimation that things were going to be . . . otherwise.

In Boffo's Novelty and Joke Emporium in Ankh-Morpork, all the whoopee cushions trumpeted in a doleful harmony; while over in Quirm, Agnes Nitt, both witch and singer, woke with the sinking feeling known to many that she might have made a fool of herself at the previous evening's first-night party.* It certainly still seemed to be going on behind her eyeballs. Then she suddenly heard her inner Perdita wail . . .

Over in the great city of Ankh-Morpork, at Unseen University, Ponder Stibbons had just finished a lengthy breakfast when he entered the basement of the High Energy Magic Building. He stopped and gaped in amazement. In front of him, Hex was calculating at a speed that Ponder had never seen before. And he hadn't even entered a question yet! Or pulled the Great Big Lever. The ant tubes that the ants crawled through to make their calculations were blurred with their motion. Was that . . . was that an *ant crash* by the cogwheel?

Ponder tapped a question into Hex: What do you know that I don't? Please, Hex.

There was a scuffling in the anthills and the answer spat out: *Practically everything.*

Ponder rephrased his question more carefully with the requisite number of IF and BEFORE clauses. It was wordy and complicated, a huge ask for a wizard with only one meal in him, and no one else would have understood what Ponder even meant, but after a big hiccough of ants, Hex shot out: *We are dealing with the death of Granny Weatherwax.*

And then Ponder went to see the Archchancellor,

---

* Though Agnes does have the very handy excuse that if she behaves badly, it might not be *Agnes* doing the Devil-Amongst-the-Pictsies dance on the table, but her other personality, Perdita, who is much more outgoing and, incidentally, a lot thinner.

Mustrum Ridcully, who would definitely want to hear this news . . .

In the Oblong Office of the Patrician of Ankh-Morpork, Lord Vetinari watched amazed as his *Times* crossword filled itself in . . .

High above the Ramtops, in the monastery of Oi Dong, the Abbot of the History Monks licked his mystic pencil and made a note of it . . .

The cat called You purred like a kind of feline windmill.

And in the travelling now, Eskarina, a woman who had once been a wizard, held the hand of her son and knew sorrow . . .

But in a world shimmering just the other side of the Disc, a world where dreams could become real – where those who lived there liked to creep through to other worlds and hurt and destroy and steal and poison – an elf lord by the name of Peaseblossom felt a powerful quiver shoot through the air, as a spider might feel a prey land on his web.

He rubbed his hands in glee. A barrier has gone, he whispered to himself. They will be weak . . .

Back on the Chalk the kelda of the Wee Free Men watched her fire flicker and thought, The witch of witches is away to the fair lands.

'Mind how ye go, Hag o' hags. Ye'll be sore missed.' She sighed then called to her husband, the Big Man of the clan. 'Rob, I'm afeared for oor big wee hag. She is going to ha' need of ye. Gae to her, Rob. Take a few of the lads and get ye awa' to her.'

Jeannie bustled into her chamber to fetch her cauldron. The edges of oor world will nae be as strong, she said to herself. I need to ken what may be comin' oor way . . .

And far away, in some place unthinkable, a white horse was being unsaddled by a figure with a scythe with, it must be said, some sorrow.

CHAPTER 3

An Upside-down World

In a small cottage in a little hamlet on the rolling fields of the sheep-haunted Chalk, Tiffany Aching had her sleeves rolled up and was sweating just as much as the mother-to-be – a young girl only a few years older than she herself was – who was leaning on her. Tiffany had already helped more than fifty babies into the world, plus lots and lots of lambs, and was generally held to be an expert midwife.

Unfortunately, Miss Milly Standish's mother and several other women of varying ages, who had all claimed to be relatives and asserted their right to a place in the very small room, thought they were experts themselves and were generously telling Tiffany what she was doing wrong.

Already one or two of them had given her old-fashioned advice, wrong advice and possibly dangerous advice, but Tiffany kept her calm, tried not to shout at anybody and concentrated on dealing with the fact that Milly was having twins. She hoped that people couldn't hear her teeth grinding.

It was always going to be a difficult birth with two boisterous babies fighting one another to be the first out. But Tiffany was focused on the new lives, and she would *not* allow Mr Death a place in this room. Another sweating push from the young mother, and first one and then another baby came yelling into the world to be handed to their grandmother and a neighbour.

'Two lads! How wonderful!' said Old Mother Standish with a distinct note of satisfaction.

Tiffany wiped her hands, mopped her brow and continued to look after the mother while the crowd cooed over the new arrivals. And then she noticed something. There was another child in that capacious young woman. Yes, a third baby was arriving, hardly noticed because of the battling brothers ahead of it.

Just then, Tiffany looked down and in a slight greenish-yellow haze saw a cat, pure white and as aloof as a duchess, staring at her. It was Granny Weatherwax's cat, You – Tiffany knew the cat well, having given her to Granny Weatherwax herself only a few years ago. To her horror one of the older ladies went to shoo You away. Tiffany almost screamed.

'Ladies, that cat belongs to Granny Weatherwax,' she said sharply. 'It might not be a good idea to make a *very senior* witch angry.'

Suddenly the gaggle backed away. Even here on

the Chalk, the name of Mistress Weatherwax worked a treat. Her reputation had spread far and wide, further and wider than Granny Weatherwax had been in the habit of travelling herself – the dwarfs over in Sto Plains even had a name for her that translated as 'Go Around the Other Side of the Mountain'.

But Tiffany, sweating again, wondered why Granny's cat was *here*. Usually You would be hanging around Granny Weatherwax's cottage back in Lancre, not all the way down here on the Chalk. Witches saw omens everywhere, of course. So was it some kind of omen? Something to do with what Jeannie had said? Not for the first time, she wondered how it was that cats seemed to be able to be in one place one moment, and then *almost at the same time*, reappear somewhere else.*

There was a cry of pain from the young mother and Tiffany gritted her teeth and turned her attention back to the job in hand. Witches do the task that is in front of them and what was in front of her right at that moment was a struggling young mother and another small head.

'One big push, Milly, please. You're having triplets.'

Milly groaned.

'Another one. A small one,' said Tiffany cheerfully, as a girl child arrived, unscathed, quite pretty for a newborn and small. She handed the baby girl to

---

* She did not know it, but a keen young philosopher in Ephebe had pondered exactly that same conundrum, until he was found one morning – most of him, anyway – surrounded by a number of purring, and very well fed, cats. No one had seemed keen to continue his experiments after that.

another relative, and then reality was back again.

As Tiffany began clearing up, she noticed – because noticing was the ground state of her being as a witch – that there was a lot more cooing over the two boys than there was for their sister. It was always good to recognize those things and put them away and keep them in mind, so that a little trouble wouldn't, one day, become a larger trouble.

The ladies had produced the family groaning chair for Milly, so that she could sit in state to receive the congratulations of the throng. They were also busy congratulating each other, nodding sagely about the advice given which had, clearly, been the *right* advice since here was the evidence. Two strapping boys! Oh, and a little girl.

Bottles were opened, and a child was fetched and told to go across the fields to find Dad, who was working on the barley with *his* dad. Mum was beaming, especially since young Milly was very soon to be *Mrs* Robinson, because Mum had put her foot down very, very hard about that and made certain that young Mister Robinson was definitely going to do his duty by her girl. There hadn't been a problem about this; this was the country after all, where boy would meet girl, as Milly had met her beau at Hogswatch, and nature would eventually take its course, right up until the moment when the girl's mother would notice the bump. She would then tell her husband and her husband, over a convivial pint of beer, would have a word with the boy's father, who would then talk to the boy. And usually it worked.

Tiffany went over to the old lady holding the little girl. 'Can I see her for just a moment, please, just to see if she's, you know, if she's all right?'

The rather toothless old crone handed over the little girl with alacrity. After all, she knew that Tiffany, apart from being a midwife, was a witch, and you never knew what a witch might do if you got on the wrong side of one. And when the old granny went to get her share of the drink, Tiffany took the child in her arms and whispered a promise to her in a voice so low that no one could have heard. This little girl would clearly need some luck in her life. And with luck, now, she would get some. She took her back to her mother, who didn't seem very impressed with her.

By now, Tiffany noticed, the little boys had names, but the girl didn't. Worried about this, Tiffany said, 'What about your girl? Can't she have a name?'

The mother looked over. 'Name her after yourself. Tiffany is a nice name.'

Tiffany was flattered, but it didn't take the worry away about baby Tiffany. Those big, strapping boys were going to get most of the milk, she thought. But not if she could do something about it, and so she decided that this particular family was going to be visited almost every week for a time.

Then there was nothing for it, but to say, 'Everything looks fine, you know where to find me, I'll pop in and see you next week. And if you'll excuse me, ladies, I have other people to see.'

She kept on smiling, right up to the time when she came out of the cottage, picked up her broomstick and the white cat leaped onto the handle of it like a figurehead. The world is changing, Tiffany thought – I can feel it.

Suddenly she caught a flash of the red that showed a Feegle or two lurking behind a milk churn. Tiffany had, if only for a few days, once been the kelda of the Nac Mac Feegle, and this created a bond between them that could never be broken. And they were *always there* – always, watching over her, making sure no harm came to their big wee hag.

But there was something different today. This lurking was somehow not like their usual lurking, and . . .

'Oh, waily waily,' came a voice. It was Daft Wullie, a Feegle who had been somewhere else when the brains of a Feegle – small enough to begin with – had been handed out. He was shut up suddenly with a 'whmpf' as Rob slapped a hand over his mouth.

'Shut yer gob, Wullie. This is hag business, ye ken,' he said, stepping out to stand in front of Tiffany, shuffling his feet and twiddling his rabbit-skull helmet in his hands. 'It's the big hag,' he continued. 'Jeannie tol' me to come fetch ye . . .'

All the birds of the day, the bats and the owls of the night knew Tiffany Aching and didn't fly in her way when she was busy, and the stick ploughed on through the air to Lancre. The little kingdom was a long flight from the Chalk and Tiffany found her mind filling up with an invisible grey mist, and in that thought there was nothing but grief. She could feel herself trying to push back time, but even the best witchcraft could not do that. She tried not to think, but it's hard to stop your brain working, no matter how much you try. Tiffany was a witch, and a witch learned to respect her forebodings, even if she hoped that what she feared was not true.

It was early evening by the time she settled her broomstick down quietly outside Granny Weatherwax's cottage, where she saw the unmistakable rotund shape of Nanny Ogg. The older witch had a pint mug in one hand and looked grey.

The cat, You, jumped off the broomstick instantly and headed into the cottage. The Nac Mac Feegles followed, making You scuttle just a little faster in that way cats scuttle when they want to look like, oh yes, it was *their* decision to speed up and, oh no, *nothing* to do with the little red-haired figures melting into the shadows of the cottage.

'Good to see you, Tiff,' said Nanny Ogg.

'She's dead, isn't she?' said Tiffany.

'Yes,' said Nanny. 'Esme's gone. In her sleep, last night, by the looks of it.'

'I knew it,' said Tiffany. 'Her cat came to tell me. And the kelda sent Rob . . .'

Nanny Ogg looked Tiffany in the face and said, 'Glad to see you're not cryin', my dear; that's for later. You knows how Granny wanted things: no fuss or shoutin', and definitely no cryin'. There's other things as must be done first. Can you help, Tiff? She's upstairs and you know what them stairs is like.'

Tiffany looked and saw the long, thin wicker

basket that Granny had made, waiting by the stairs. It was almost exactly the same size as Granny. Minus her hat, of course.

Nanny said, 'That's Esme for you, that is. Does everything for 'erself.'

Granny Weatherwax's cottage was largely built of creaks, and you could play a tune with them if you wanted to. With accompaniment from the harmonious woodwork, Tiffany followed Nanny Ogg as she huffed and puffed up the cramped little staircase that wound up and round like a snake – Nanny always said that you needed a corkscrew to get through it – until they arrived at the bedroom and the small, sad deathbed.

It could, Tiffany thought, have been the bed of a child, and there, laid out properly, was Granny Weatherwax herself, looking as if she was just sleeping. And there too, on the bed by her mistress, was You the cat.

There was a familiar card on Granny's chest, and a sudden thought struck Tiffany like a gong.

'Nanny, you don't suppose Granny could just be Borrowing, do you? Do you think that while her body is here, her actual self is . . . elsewhere?' She looked at the white cat curled upon the bed and added hopefully, 'In You?'

Granny Weatherwax had been an expert at Borrowing – moving her mind into that of another creature, using its body, sharing its experiences.* It was dangerous witchery, for an inexperienced witch

---

* And its meals. It's amazing how a night as an owl, snacking on voles, can *really* leave a nasty taste in your mouth.

risked losing herself in the mind of the other and never coming back. And, of course, whilst away from one's body, people could get the wrong idea . . .

Nanny silently picked up the card from Granny's chest. They looked at it together:

Nanny Ogg turned it over as Tiffany's hand crept towards Granny Weatherwax's wrist and – even now, even when every atom of her witch being told her that Granny was no longer there – the young girl part of her tried to feel for even the slightest beat of life.

On the back of the card, however, there was a scrawled message that pretty much put the final strand in the willow basket below.

Quietly Tiffany said, 'No longer "probably".' And then the rest of the note rocketed into her mind. 'What? What does she mean by "All of it goes to Tiffany..."?' Her voice tailed off as she looked at Nanny Ogg, aghast.

'Yes,' said Nanny. 'That's Granny's writing, right enough. Good enough for me. You gets the cottage and the surroundin' grounds, the herbs and the bees an' everything else in the place. Oh, but she always promised me the pink jug and basin set.' She looked at Tiffany and went on, 'I hopes you don't mind?'

Mind? Tiffany thought. Nanny Ogg is asking *me* if I mind? And then her mind rattled on to: *Two* steadings? I mean, I won't need to live with my parents ... But it will be a lot of travel ... And the main thought hit her like a thunderbolt. *How can I possibly tread in the footsteps of Granny Weatherwax? She is ... was ... unfollowable!*

Nanny didn't get to be an old senior witch without learning a thing or two along the way. 'Don't get your knickers in a knot just yet, Tiff,' she said briskly. 'It won't solve anything an' will just make you walk odd. There's plenty of time later to talk about ... all of that. Right now, we needs to get on with what must be done ...'

Tiffany and Nanny had dealt with death many times. Out in the Ramtops, witches did the things that had to be done to make the departed presentable for the next world – the slightly messy things that weren't talked about, and other little things like opening a window for the soul to get out. Granny Weatherwax had, in fact, already opened the window, though her soul, Tiffany thought, could probably get out of anywhere and go anywhere she chose.

Nanny Ogg held up the two pennies from the bedside table and said, 'She left 'em ready for us. Just like Esme, thoughtful to the end like. Shall we begin?'

Unfortunately Nanny had brought Granny Weatherwax's bottle of triple-distilled peach brandy – for medicinal use *only* – from the scullery; she said it would help her as she went through the rites for their sister in the craft, and although they dealt with Granny Weatherwax as if she were a precious gem, Nanny Ogg's drinking was not helping.

'She looks good, don't she?' said Nanny after the nasty bits – and, thank goodness, Granny had still had all her own teeth – were over and done with. 'It's a shame. Always thought as I'd be the first to go, what with my drinkin' and suchlike, especially the suchlike. I've done a lot o' that.' In fact, Nanny Ogg had done a great deal of *everything*, and was commonly held to be so broad-minded that you could pull her mind out through her ears and tie a hat on with it.

'Is there going to be a funeral?' asked Tiffany.

'Well, you know Esme. She wasn't one for that kind of thing – never one to push herself forward* – and we witches don't much like funerals. Granny called them fuss.'

Tiffany thought of the only other witch's funeral

* She hadn't ever needed to. Granny Weatherwax was like the prow of a ship. Seas parted when she turned up.

she had been to. The late Miss Treason, for whom she had worked, had wanted a lot of fuss. She hadn't wanted to miss the event herself either, so she had sent out invitations in advance. It had been . . . memorable.

As they put Granny Weatherwax to bed – as Granny had called it – Nanny said, 'Queen Magrat has to be told. She's away in Genua at the moment with the King, but I daresay as she'll be along soon as possible, what with all these railways and whatnot. Anyone else as needs to know will probably know already, you mark my words. But first thing tomorrow, before they get here, we'll bury Esme the way she wanted, quiet-like an' no fuss, in that wickerwork basket downstairs. Very cheap, wickerwork baskets are, and quick to make, Esme always said. An' you know Esme, she's such a frugal person – nothing goes to waste.'

Tiffany spent the night on the truckle bed, a tiny thing which was usually pushed away when it wasn't needed. Nanny Ogg had settled for the rocking chair downstairs, which squeaked and complained every time she rocked back. But Tiffany didn't sleep. There were a series of half-sleeps as the light of the moon filtered into the room, and every time she looked up there was You, the cat, asleep at the foot of Granny's bed, curled up like a little white moon herself.

Tiffany had watched the dead before many times, of course – it was the custom for a departing soul to have company the night before any funeral or burial, as if to make a point to anything that might be . . . lurking: this person *mattered*, there is someone here to make sure nothing evil creeps in at this time of danger. The night-time creaking of woodwork filled the room now and Tiffany, fully awake, listened as Granny Weatherwax began making sounds of her own as her body settled down. I've done this often, she told herself. It's what we witches do. We don't talk about it, but we do it. We watch the dead to see that no harm comes to them out of the darkness. Although, as Nanny said, maybe it's the *living* you have to watch – for despite what most people thought, the dead don't hurt anybody.

What do I do now? she thought in the small hours of the night. What's going to happen tomorrow? The world is upside down. I can't replace Granny. Never in a hundred years. And then she thought, What did young Esmerelda say when Nanny Gripes told her that her steading was the whole world?

She twisted and turned, then opened her eyes and looked up suddenly to see an owl gazing in at her from the windowsill, its huge eyes hanging in the darkness like a lantern to another world. Another omen? Granny had liked owls . . .

Now her Second Thoughts were at work, thinking about what she was thinking. You can't say you're not good enough – no witch would ever say that, they told her. I mean, you know you are pretty good, yes; the senior witches know that you once threw the Queen of the Fairies from our world, and they saw you go through the gate with the hiver. They all saw you return too.

But is that *enough*? her First Thoughts butted in. After . . . after we have done what we need to do, I could just put on my number-two drawers and go home on my broomstick. I have to go anyway, even if I take on the steading. I have to tell my parents. And I'm going to need help on the Chalk . . . it's going to be a nightmare if I have to be in two places at once. I'm not like a cat . . .

And as she thought that, she looked down, and there was You looking at her, but not just looking – a penetrating stare of the kind that only cats can achieve, and it seemed to Tiffany that this meant: Get on with your job, there is a lot of work to be doing. Don't think of yourself. Think for all.

Then tiredness was finally her friend, and Tiffany Aching had a few hours' sleep.

The clacks rattled as the news of Granny Weatherwax went down the lines in the morning, and people who got the message faced it in their various ways.

In the study of her manor house, Mrs Earwig* got the news while she was writing her next book on 'Flower Magick' and there was a sudden sense of wrongness, of the world going askew. She put the right expression of grief on her face and went to tell her husband, an elderly wizard, trying to keep her joy hidden as she realized what this could mean: she, Mrs Earwig,

* Pronounced Ah-wij.

was going to be one of the most senior witches in Lancre. Perhaps she could get her latest girl into that old cottage in the woods? Her sharp face went even sharper as she thought how *magickal* she could make it look with the help of a few curse-nets, charms, runic symbols, silver stars, black velvet drapes and – oh yes, the *essential* crystal ball.

She called to her latest young trainee to fetch her cape and broomstick, and pulled on her very best pair of black lacy gloves, the ones with the silver symbols stitched over each fingertip. She would need to Make an Entrance . . .

In Boffo's Novelty and Joke Emporium, 4 Tenth Egg Street, Ankh-Morpork – '*Everything for the Hag in a Hurry*' – Mrs Proust said, 'What a shame, but the old girl had a good innings.'

Witches don't have leaders, of course, but everyone knew that Granny Weatherwax had been the best leader they didn't have, so now someone else would need to step forward to generally *steer* the witches. And to keep an eye too on anyone prone to a bit of cackling.

Mrs Proust put down an imitation cackle she had taken from her *Compare the Cackle* display, and looked towards her son Derek and said, 'There's going to be an argument now, or my name's not Eunice Proust. But it will surely be young Tiffany Aching who gets that steading. We all saw what she can do. My word, we did!' And in her mind, she said, Go to it, Tiffany, before somebody else does.

*

In the palace, Drumknott the clerk hurried with the *Ankh-Morpork Times* to the Oblong Office where Lord Vetinari, the Patrician of the city, had been waiting for his daily crossword to arrive.

But Vetinari already knew the news that mattered. 'There will be some trouble. Mark my words, I expect squabbling on the distaff side.' He sighed. 'Any ideas, Drumknott? Who will rise to the top of the brew, do you think?' He tapped the top of his ebony cane as he considered his own question.

'Well, my lord,' said Drumknott, 'the rumour on the clacks is that it's likely to be Tiffany Aching. Quite young.'

'Quite young, yes. And any good?' asked Vetinari. 'I believe so, sir.'

'What about this woman called Mrs Earwig?'

Drumknott made a face. 'All show, my lord, doesn't get her hands dirty. Lot of jewellery, black lace, you know the type. Well-connected, but that's about all I can say.'

'Ah yes, now you tell me, I've seen her. Pushy and full of herself. She's the kind who goes to soirees.'

'So do you, my lord.'

'Yes, but I am the tyrant, so it's the job I have to do, alas. Now, this Aching young lady – what else do we know about her? Wasn't there some bother the last time she was in the city?'

'My lord, the Nac Mac Feegles are very fond of her and she of them. They consider themselves an honour guard to her on occasions.'

'Drumknott.'

'Yes, my lord?'

'I'm going to use a word I've not used before. Crivens! We don't want Feegles around here again. We can't afford it!'

'Unlikely, my lord. Mistress Aching has them in hand and she's unlikely to want to repeat the events of her last visit, which after all had no long-lasting damage.'

'Didn't the King's Head become the King's Neck?'*

'Yes indeed, my lord, but it has in fact proved a welcome change to many, most of all to the publican, who is still getting wealthy because of the tourists. It's in the guide books.'

'If she has the Nac Mac Feegles on her side, she is a force to be reckoned with,' Vetinari mused.

'The young lady is also known to be thoughtful, helpful and clever.'

'Without being insufferable? I wish I could say the same of Mrs Earwig. Hmm,' said Vetinari, 'we should keep a careful eye on her . . .'

Mustrum Ridcully, Archchancellor of Unseen University, stared at his bedroom wall, and cried again, and once he'd pulled himself together he sent for Ponder Stibbons, his right-hand wizard.

'The clacks confirms what Hex told you, Mr Stibbons,' he said sadly. 'The witch Esme Weatherwax

---

* The only known instance of the Feegles rebuilding a pub they had drunk dry and demolished. The rebuilt version, however, turned out back to front. Complete with a big ripe boil on the neck in question.

of Lancre, known to many as Granny Weatherwax, has died.' The Archchancellor looked slightly embarrassed. There was a bundle of letters on his lap, which he was turning over and over. 'There was a bond, you see, when we were both young, but she wanted to be the best of all witches and I hoped one day to be Archchancellor. Alas for us, our dreams came true.'*

'Oh dear, sir. Would you like me to arrange your schedule so that you can attend the funeral? There will *be* a funeral, I assume . . .'

'Mr Stibbons, schedules be damned. I am leaving now. Right now.'

'With respect, Archchancellor, I must tell you, sir, that you promised to go to a meeting with the Guild of Accountants and Usurers.'

'Those penny-pinchers! Tell them that I have got an urgent matter of international affairs to deal with.'

Ponder hesitated. 'That is not strictly true, is it, Archchancellor.'

Ridcully riposted with, 'Oh yes, it is!' Rules were for other people. Not for him. Nor, he thought with a pang, had they been for Esme Weatherwax . . . 'How long have you been working for the University, young man?' he boomed at Stibbons. 'Dissembling is our stock in trade. Now I am going to get on my broomstick, Mr Stibbons, and I will leave the place in your very capable hands.'

---

* Thus proving that dreams that come true are not always the *right* dreams. Does wearing a glass slipper lead to a comfortable life? If everything you touch turns into marshmallows, won't that make things a bit . . . sticky?

*

And in that . . . other world, that parasite with its evil little hooks in the gateways of stone, an elf was hatching his plans. Plotting to seize Fairyland from the control of a Queen who had never fully recovered her powers after her humiliating defeat at the hands of a young girl named Tiffany Aching. Plotting to pounce, to spring through a gateway that – for a time, at least – would be gossamer-thin. For a powerful hag no longer stood in their way. And those in that world would be vulnerable.

The Lord Peaseblossom's eyes gleamed and his mind filled with glorious images of victims, of the pleasures of cruelty, the splendours of a land where the elves could toy once more with new playthings.

When the moment was right . . .

CHAPTER 4

A Farewell – and a Welcome

Getting Granny Weatherwax's corpse down the winding stair with its tiny little steps in the tiny little cottage the following morning was not helped by the big jug of cider which Nanny Ogg was emptying speedily, but nevertheless they got it done without a bump.

They laid Granny's body carefully in the wicker casket, and Tiffany went out to the barn to fetch the wheelbarrow and shovels while Nanny Ogg caught her breath. Then, together, they gently lifted the basket into the wheelbarrow, and placed the shovels on either side of her.

Tiffany picked up the handles of the barrow. 'Ye stay here now, Rob,' she said to the Feegle as he and his little band appeared from their varied hiding places and lined up behind her. 'This is a hag thing, ye ken. Ye cannot help me.'

Rob Anybody shuffled his feet. 'But ye are oor hag, and ye ken that Jeannie—' he began.

'Rob Anybody.' Tiffany's steely gaze pinned him to the ground. 'Ye remember the chief hag? Granny Weatherwax? Do ye want her shade to come back and . . . *tell ye what tae do for ever and ever?*' There was a group moan and Daft Wullie backed away, whimpering. 'Then *understand this*: this is something we hags must do by ourselves.' She turned to Nanny Ogg, resolute. 'Where are we going, Nanny?'

'Esme marked a spot in the woods, Tiff, where she wanted to be planted,' Nanny replied. 'Follow me, I know where it is.'

Granny Weatherwax's garden was cheek by jowl with the woodland beyond, but the journey felt a long way to Tiffany before they arrived at the heart of the forest where a stick was pushed into the ground, a red ribbon tied to the top of it.

Nanny passed Tiffany a shovel and the two of them started digging in the cool early morning air. It was hard work, but Granny had chosen her place well and the soil was soft and friable.

The hole finally dug – mostly, it has to be said, by Tiffany – Nanny Ogg, sweating cobs (according to her), rested on the handle of her shovel and took a swig from her flagon as Tiffany brought the wheelbarrow over. They laid the wicker basket gently in the hole and then stood back for a moment.

Without a word being said, together, solemnly, they bowed to Granny's grave. And then they picked up the shovels again and started to fill it back in.

Ker-thunk! Ker-thunk! The earth built up over the wicker until all that could be seen was soil, and Tiffany watched it flow in until the last crumb had stopped moving.

As they smoothed the fresh mound of earth, Nanny told Tiffany that Granny had said she wanted no urns, no shrines and definitely no gravestone.

'Surely there should be a stone,' said Tiffany. 'You know how badgers and mice and other creatures can lift the earth. Even though we know the bones are not her, I for one would want to be sure that nothing is dug up until . . .' She hesitated.

'The ends of time?' said Nanny. 'Look, Tiff, Esme tol' me to say, if you wants to see Esmerelda Weatherwax, then just you look around. She is here. Us witches don't mourn for very long. We are satisfied with happy memories – they're there to be cherished.'

The memory of Granny Aching suddenly shone in Tiffany's mind. Her own granny had been no witch – though Weatherwax had been very interested in hearing about her – but when Granny Aching had died, her shepherding hut had been burned and her bones had gone down into the hills, six feet deep in the chalk. Then the turf had been put back with the spot marked only by the iron wheels of the hut. But it was a *sacred* spot now, a place for memories. And not only for Tiffany. No shepherd ever passed without a glance at the skies and a thought for Granny Aching, who had tramped those hills night after night, her light zigzagging in the darkness. Her nod of approval had meant the world on the Chalk.

This spot in the woods, Tiffany realized, would be the same. Blessed. It had been a nice day for it, she thought, if there ever was such a thing as a good day to die, a good day to be buried.

And now the birds were singing overhead, and there was a soft rustling in the undergrowth, and all the sounds of the forest which showed that life was still being lived blended with the souls of the dead in a woodland requiem.

The whole forest now sang for Granny Weatherwax.

Tiffany saw a fox sidle up, bow and then run away because a wild boar had arrived, with its family of piglets. Then there was a badger, paying no heed to those who had come earlier, and it remained, and Tiffany was astounded when creature after creature settled down near the grave and sat there as if they were domestic pets.

Where is Granny now? Tiffany wondered. Could a part of her still be . . . here? She jumped as something touched her on the shoulder; but it was just a leaf. Then, deep inside, she knew the answer to her question: *Where is Granny Weatherwax?*

It was: *She is here – and everywhere.*

To Tiffany's surprise, Nanny Ogg was weeping gently. Nanny took another swig from her flagon and wiped her eyes. 'Cryin' helps sometimes,' she said. 'No shame in tears for them as you've loved. Sometimes I remember one of my husbands and shed a tear or two. The memories're there to be treasured, and it's no good to get morbid-like about it.'

'How many husbands have you actually had, Nanny?' asked Tiffany.

Nanny appeared to be counting. 'Three of my own, and let's just say I've run out of fingers on the rest, as it were.' But she was smiling now, perhaps remembering a *very* treasured husband, and then, bouncing back from the past, she was suddenly her normal cheerful self again. 'Come on, Tiff,' she said, 'let's go back to *your* cottage. Like I always says, a decent wake don't happen by itself.'

As they made their way back to the cottage, Tiffany asked Nanny the question which had been burning in her mind. 'What do you think will happen next?'

Nanny looked at Tiffany. 'What do you mean?'

'Well, Granny wasn't exactly the head witch . . . except that most people thought she was . . .'

'There ain't no such thing as a head witch, Tiff, you know that.'

'Yes, but . . . if Granny's not here any more, do you become the not-head-witch?'

'Me?' Nanny Ogg laughed. 'Oh no, dear, I've had a very good life, me, lots of children, lots of men, lots of fun and, yes, as witches go, I'm pretty good. But I never thought of steppin' into Esme's shoes. Ever.'

'Well, who is, then? Someone's got to.'

Nanny Ogg scowled and said, 'Granny never said as she was better than others. She just got on with it and showed 'em and people worked it out for themselves. You mark my words, the senior witches will get together soon enough to talk about this, but I know who Granny would choose – and it's as I would too.' She stopped and looked serious for a moment. 'It's you, Tiff. Esme's left you her cottage. But more'n that. You must step into the shoes of Granny Weatherwax or else'n someone less qualified will try an' do it!'

'But— I can't! And witches don't have leaders! You've just *said* that, Nanny!'

'Yes,' said Nanny. 'And you must be the best damn leader that we don't have. Don't look at me sideways like that, Tiffany Aching. Just think about it. You didn't try to earn it, but earn it you has, and if you don't believe me, believe Granny Weatherwax. She tol' me that you was the only witch who could seriously take her place, she said that on the night after you run with that hare.'

'She never said anything to me,' said Tiffany, feeling suddenly very young.

'Well, she wouldn't say nothing, o' course she wouldn't,' said Nanny. 'That's not Esme's way, you know that. She would have given a grunt, and maybe said, "Well done, girl." She just liked people to know their own strengths – and your strengths are formidable.'

'But, Nanny, you are older, more experienced, than me – you know lots more!'

'And some of it I wants to forget,' said Nanny.

'I'm far too young,' Tiffany wailed. 'If I wasn't a witch, I'd still just be thinking of *boyfriends*.'

Nanny Ogg almost jumped on her. 'You're not too young,' she said. 'Years ain't what's important here.

Granny Weatherwax said to me as you is the one who's to deal with the future. An' bein' young means you've got a lot of future.' She sniffed. 'Lot more'n me, that's for sure.'

'But that's not how it works,' Tiffany said. 'It ought to be a senior witch. It has to be.' But her Second Thoughts then leaped up in her head, challenging her. Why? Why not do things differently? Why should we do things how they have always been done before? And something inside her suddenly thrilled to the challenge.

'Huh!' Nanny retorted. 'You danced with the hare to save the lives of your friends, my girl. Do you remember being so . . . angry that you picked up a lump of flint and let it dribble between your fingers as if it was water? All the senior witches were there, and they took their hats off to you. You! Hats!' She stomped off towards the cottage, with just one parting shot. 'And remember, You chose you. That cat there, she went to *you* when Esme up and left.'

And there the white cat was, sitting on the stump of an old birch, preening herself, and Tiffany wondered. Oh yes, she wondered.

Just as they got back to the cottage, a dishevelled but very large wizard was trying to land his broomstick by the goat shed.

'It is good of you to come, Mustrum,' Nanny Ogg shouted across the garden, as the gentleman smoothed down his robes, trod carefully past the herbs and doffed his hat to them – Tiffany noticed with glee that he had tied it onto his head with string. 'Tiff, this is Mustrum Ridcully, Archchancellor of Unseen University.'

Tiffany had only met one or two wizards, and they had mostly been of the type that relied on the robes, pointy hat and staff to make their point, hoping that they never had to actually *do* anything magical. On the face of it, Ridcully looked exactly the same – beard, big staff with a knob on the top, a pointy hat . . . wait, a pointy hat with a *crossbow* tucked into the hatband? The witch side of her stepped back and watched carefully. But Ridcully was not interested in her at all. To her astonishment, the Archchancellor actually appeared to be *crying*.

'Is it true, then, Nanny? Has she really gone?'

Nanny gave him a handkerchief and as he blew noisily into it, she whispered to Tiffany, 'He and Esme were, well, you know, good friends when they were younger.' She winked.

The Archchancellor seemed to be overcome. Nanny handed him her flagon. 'My famous remedy, your worship. Best to drink it down in one great gulp. Works a right treat for melancholy, it does. Whenever I'm a bit unsure of myself I drinks a lot of it. Medicinal use only, o' course.'

The Archchancellor took the flagon, swigged down a couple of gulps in one go and then flourished it at Nanny. 'Here's to Esmerelda Weatherwax and lost futures,' he said in a voice choked with sorrow. 'May we all go round again!' He removed his hat, unscrewed the pointy bit and brought out a small bottle of brandy and a cup. 'For you, Mrs Ogg,' he boomed. 'And now, may I see her, please?'

'We have laid her down already, where she wanted to rest,' said Nanny. 'You know how it is. She didn't want no fuss.' She looked at him, and continued, 'I'm very sorry about that, Mustrum, but we'll take you to the spot where she is now. Tiffany, why don't you lead the way?'

And thus the most important wizard in the world respectfully followed Tiffany and Nanny Ogg through the woods to the last resting place of the most important witch in the world. The trees surrounding the little clearing were full of birds, singing their souls out. Nanny and Tiffany held back to allow the wizard a private moment by the grave. He sighed. 'Thank you, Mistress Ogg, Mistress Aching.'

Then the Archchancellor turned to Tiffany and looked at her properly.

'For the sake of Esmerelda Weatherwax, my dear, if you ever need a friend, you can call on me. Being the most important wizard in the world must mean *something*.' He paused. 'I have heard of you,' he said, and at her gasp, he added, 'No, don't be surprised. You must know that we wizards keep an . . . eye on what you witches do. We know when the magic is disturbed, when something . . . *happens*. And so I heard about the flint. Was it true?' His voice was brusque now – a man who did not do small talk, only big talk, and in a big voice too.

'Yes,' said Tiffany. 'All of it.'

'My word,' said Ridcully. 'And now I feel certain

that your future is going to be, let us say, very speck-led. I can see the signs in you, Mistress Tiffany Aching – and I know many people of power, people who have so much power that they don't have to wield it. You are hardly into your prime, yet I see this in you, and so I live in wonder about what you might do next.' His face now fell and he continued, 'Would you ladies now leave me alone with my feelings. I am sure I can find my way back to the cottage.'

Later on, the Archchancellor walked back to his broomstick and Tiffany and Nanny Ogg watched him disappear in the general direction of Ankh-Morpork. The broomstick itself was wobbling about as he rose over the woods in a final salute.

Nanny smiled. 'He is a wizard. He can be sober when he likes, and if he ain't, well, he can fly a broom-stick well enough with a brandy or two inside him. After all, there's not much to bump into up there!'

*

As the morning progressed, more and more people were coming to pay their respects at the little cottage. The news had spread, and it seemed like everybody wanted to leave a gift for Granny Weatherwax. For the witch who had always been there for them, even if they hadn't actually *liked* her. Esme Weatherwax hadn't done nice. She'd done what was *needed*. She'd been there for them when they called at the cottage, she'd come out at whatever time of day or night when asked (and sometimes when *not*, which hadn't always been comfortable), and somehow she had made them feel . . . safer. They brought hams and cheeses, milk and pickles, jams and beer, bread and fruit . . .

It also seemed that broomsticks were coming through the trees from everywhere, and there was nothing a witch appreciated more than a bit of free food – Tiffany caught one elderly witch trying to stuff an entire chicken up her knickers. And as the witches turned up, the villagers began to melt away. It didn't do to be around that many witches. Why risk it? Nobody wanted to be turned into a frog – after all, who would bring in the harvest then? They started to make their excuses and sidle off, with those who had partaken of Nanny Ogg's famous cocktails sidling in a rather wobbly fashion.

None of the witches had been invited, but it seemed to Tiffany they had been drawn there, just like the Archchancellor. Even Mrs Earwig turned up. She came in a carriage and pair, complete with black plumes, and her arms jingled with bangles and charms – as if the percussion section of an orchestra had suddenly fallen off a cliff – while her hat was festooned in silver stars. Her husband was dragged along beside her. Tiffany felt sorry for the man.

'Hail, sisters, and may the runes protect us on this momentous occasion,' Mrs Earwig pronounced, *just* loud enough to be heard by the remaining villagers – she did like to advertise her witchiness. She gave Tiffany a long stare, which infuriated Nanny Ogg.

Nanny made the briefest possible bow, then turned and said, 'Look, Tiffany, here's Agnes Nitt. Wotcha, Agnes!'

Agnes – a witch with a waistline that suggested

she had a similar attitude to eating as the Feegles' kelda – was out of breath, saying, 'I've been touring in Stackpole's *Much Ado About Everybody*. I was in Quirm when I heard and I came as fast as I could.'

Tiffany hadn't met Agnes before, but from one look at her sensible face and good-natured smile, she thought she would probably get along with her very well indeed. Then she was overcome with delight as a broomstick wobbled down to land and she heard the familiar 'Um' of her friend Petulia.

'Um, Tiffany, I heard you were here. Um, do you want some help with making any sandwiches?' Petulia offered, waving a big side of bacon as she landed. Petulia was married to a pig farmer and was acknowledged to be Lancre's best pig-borer.* She was also one of Tiffany's very best friends. 'Dimity is here too, and, um, Lucy Warbeck,' Petulia continued – the 'um's always got worse when she was in the company of other witches; amazingly, she never used the word when pig-boring, which had to say something about Petulia and pigs.

Tiffany and Nanny Ogg's grandsons had put up some makeshift tables. After all, everybody knows what a funeral is really for and most people like eating and drinking whatever the occasion. There was music, and over it all, Agnes's heavenly voice. She sang the 'Columbine Lament', and as its soft tune wafted over the roof and into the forest beyond, Nanny said to Tiffany, 'That voice could make the trees cry.'

---

* Pig-boring saved a lot of nasty squealing. A pig-borer, like Petulia, would talk to the pigs until they simply died of boredom.

And there was dancing, no doubt helped along by Nanny Ogg's brews. Nanny Ogg could get any party singing and dancing. It was a gift, Tiffany thought. Nanny could jolly up a graveyard if she put her mind to it.

'No long faces for Granny Weatherwax, please,' Nanny proclaimed. 'She's had a good death at home, just as anyone might wish for. Witches know that people die; and if they manages to die after a long time, leavin' the world better than they went an' found it, well then, that's surely a reason to be happy. All the rest of it is just tidyin' up. Now, let's dance! Dancin' makes the world go round. And it goes round even faster with a drop o' my home liquor inside you.'

Up in the roof of Granny's cottage, swinging from the boughs of the little tree that grew out of the thatch, the Nac Mac Feegles – Rob Anybody, Daft Wullie, Big Yan and the gonnagle, Awf'ly Wee Billy Bigchin – were in agreement with the latter part of that statement, though they were keeping the dancing for later, mind. They stayed mostly out of sight, spotted only by one or two of the more observant witches, but now they came down to the scullery where Tiffany was starting on what the elderly, more senior witches always expected the younger girls to do – clearing up. The senior witches were beginning to gather together outside; it was time to discuss the appointment of a new incumbent to Granny Weatherwax's steading, and Tiffany wanted to keep out of the way while she thought about what she might say.

As the haunting tones of Awf'ly Wee Billy Bigchin's

mousepipes played a soft lament for the soul of the hag o' hags, the other Feegles began raiding the tables for any leftovers the witches had missed.

'Alas, poor Granny, I knew her well,' sighed Big Yan, swigging from a bottle of Nanny's home-made hooch.

'No you didn't,' Tiffany snapped. 'Only Granny Weatherwax really knew Granny Weatherwax.' The day was still too raw for her, and the witches outside were making her nervous.

'Ha ha,' laughed Daft Wullie. 'It weren't me, this time, Rob. Nae me what put my foot in it. I sez the hag were upset, Rob, didnae I?'

'I'll put my *boot* inta yer face if ye don't shut up,' Big Yan growled. They'd had the drinkin' and eatin', postponed the dancin', but wasn't it time for a wee fight? He clenched his fists, but then had to suddenly retreat as Tiffany's friends came into the scullery.

'I think it's going to be *you*, Tiffany,' Dimity hissed, poking her in the back. 'Nanny Ogg just stood up and asked for you. You'd better get out there.'

'Go on, Tiff,' Petulia urged. 'Everyone knows, um, what Granny Weatherwax thought of you . . .'

And so, pushed and pulled by her friends, Tiffany left the scullery, but she hovered by the back door of the cottage, unwilling to take that final step. To make a claim. This was *Granny's* cottage, she still felt. Even though the not-Granny-ness was beginning to feel like a huge hole in the air around her. Tiffany looked down at her feet; You was twining around her legs, arching her back and rubbing her hard little head against Tiffany's boot.

Outside, some of the witches were looking at Nanny Ogg, who was saying, 'Yes, ladies, Esme did tell us who her successor was to be.' She turned and gestured to Tiffany to come nearer. 'I wish I'd been there,' she added, 'when Esme Weatherwax was made witch by Nanny Gripes. You think who makes you a witch is the kind of witch you're goin' to become, but we all has to find our own way, as we go along like. Granny Weatherwax was always her own true witch self – never just another Nanny Gripes. And though I think we can all talk for ourselves, people like the Archchancellor, and Lord Vetinari, and indeed someone like the Low Queen of the dwarfs – well, they want to know sometimes that they can talk to somebody who can speak, officially like, for all witches. And I'm pretty certain they looked on Esme as bein' that voice of witchcraft. So we needs to listen to her voice too. And she *tol'* me who her successor should be. Yes, and wrote it on this here card.' Nanny brandished in the air the card Granny Weatherwax had left on her bedside chest.

Someone had clearly raised the idea of Mrs Earwig taking over the steading – or Mrs Earwig had raised the prospect of her latest trainee getting the cottage. Nanny glared at her, and there was no trace of the jolly witch in her now, oh no.

'Letice Earwig just makes shiny things for her would-be witches!' she stated. She ignored the 'Humph' from Mrs Earwig as she continued, 'But Tiffany Aching – yes, sisters, *Tiffany Aching* – we've all seen what *she* can do. It's not about shiny charms. Not about *books*. It's about bein' a witch to the bone in the darkness, an' dealing with the lamentation an' the tears! It's about bein' *real*. Esme Weatherwax knew this, knew this with every bone in her body. And so does Tiffany Aching, and this steadin' is *hers*.'

Tiffany gasped as the other witches turned to look at her. And as the muttering began, she stepped forward hesitantly.

Then You meowed, the cry cutting through the murmuring in the crowd, and the white cat came again to Tiffany's side. Suddenly there was a humming in the air, and the bees were there too. They flowed out of Granny Weatherwax's hive, circling Tiffany like a halo, crowning her, and swarm and girl stood on the threshold of the cottage and Tiffany reached out her arms and the bees settled along them, and welcomed her home.

And after that, on that terrible day when a farewell was said to the witch of witches, there was no more argument as Tiffany Aching became in all eyes the witch to follow.

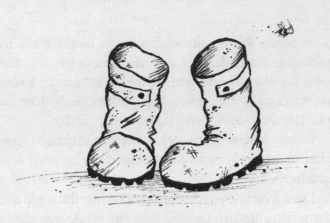

CHAPTER 5

A Changing World

The Queen of the Elves sat in state on a diamond throne in her palace, surrounded by her courtiers, foundlings and lost boys, and creeping creatures with no names – all the detritus of the fairy folk.

She had chosen to sparkle today. The everlasting sunlight shining through the exquisitely carved stone windows had been pitched exactly to strike the tiny gems on her wings so that delicate rainbows of light danced around the audience chamber as she moved. The courtiers lounging about the place in lace-trimmed velvet and feathers were almost, but not quite, as beautifully dressed.

Her eyes slid sideways, ever alert to the actions of her lords and ladies. Was that Lord Lankin over there in the corner with Lord Mustardseed? Whispering . . . And where was Lord Peaseblossom? One day, she thought, she would have *his* head on a pole! She didn't trust him at all, and his glamour had been strong of late, almost as glorious as her own. Or, she reminded herself bitterly, as glorious as her own had been . . . *before*.

Before that young witch – Tiffany Aching – had come into Fairyland and humiliated *her*.

Lately she had felt shivers between their two worlds, understood that things were shifting, the edges becoming more blurred. Softer. A few of the stronger elves had even been slipping through from time to time for a little mischief. Perhaps soon she could lead the elves on a proper raiding party . . . fetch another child to play with. Have her revenge on the Aching witch. The Queen smiled at the thought, licking her lips in anticipation of the fun ahead.

But for now there was other troubling news to deal with. *Goblins!* Mere worms, who should be grateful if an elvish lord or lady even looked their way, but who were now foolishly refusing to do her bidding. She would show them all, she thought. Lords Lankin, Mustardseed, Peaseblossom – they would all see how powerful she was again. They would see her strike down this goblin filth . . .

But where *was* Peaseblossom?

The goblin prisoner was brought into the audience chamber under guard. The whole effect was visually stunning, the goblin thought sourly. Exactly as a fairy court would look in a human child's story book. Until you looked at the faces and realized that there was something not quite right about the eyes and the expressions of the beautiful creatures in the scene.

The Queen considered the goblin for a while, resting her fine-boned chin on the fingers of one exquisitely thin hand. Her alabaster brow furrowed.

'You, goblin, you call yourself Of the Dew the Sunlight, I believe. You and your kind have long enjoyed the protection of this court. Yet I hear talk of rebellion. A refusal to do my bidding. Before I hand you over to my guards for their . . . amusement, tell me why this is.'

Her melodious voice was rich with charm as the words were spoken, but the goblin seemed unmoved. He should have fallen to his knees and begged for her forgiveness, hypnotized by the power of the Queen's glamour, but instead he stood his ground stockily and grinned at her. Grinned at the Queen!

'Well, Queenie, it's like this, you see. Goblins is now treated as upright citizens in human world. Humans say goblins useful. We likes being *useful*. We gets paid for being useful and finding out things and making things.'

The Queen's beautiful visage slipped and she glared at the cheeky creature in front of her.

'That's impossible,' she shouted. 'You goblins are the dregs, everyone knows that!'

'Ah ha!' laughed the goblin. 'Queenie not so clever as she thinks. Goblins riding on hog's back now. Goblins know how to drive the iron horses.'

There was a shiver in the court as the goblin uttered the word 'iron' and the magical glimmer dimmed. The Queen's dress changed colour from silver gossamer to blood-red velvet and her blonde ringlets turned into straight, raven-black locks. Her courtiers followed suit as the pastel silks and lace made way for leather breeches, scarlet sashes and scraps of fur over woad-covered torsos. Elven stone knives were drawn and sharp teeth bared.

The little goblin did not flinch.

'I don't believe you,' said the Queen. 'After all, you are just a goblin.'

'Just a goblin, yess, your queeniness,' he said quietly. 'A goblin what understands iron *and* steel. Steel as goes round and round and chuffs. Takes people to faraway places. And a goblin what is a citizen of Ankh-Morpork, and you know what *that* means, my lady. The dark one there gets upset when his citizens get killed.'

'You are lying,' said the Queen. 'The Lord Vetinari would not care what happens to *you*. You goblins always lie, Of the Dew the Sunlight.'

'Not my name any more. I am now Of the Lathe the Swarf,' said the goblin proudly.

'Swarf,' said the Queen. 'What is that?'

'Itty bits of iron, they is, Queenie,' said the goblin, his eyes hardening. 'Of the Lathe the Swarf no liar. You talks to me like that again, your majisteriousness, I opens my pockets. Then we sees what swarf is!'

The Queen drew back, her eyes fixed on the goblin's hands hovering near the pockets of his dark blue jacket, wooden toggles fastening it over his skinny chest.

'You dare threaten me?' she said. 'Here in my own realm, you worm? When I could shrivel your heart within you with just a word? Or have you dropped where you stand?' She gestured to the guards standing ready with their crossbows aimed at the goblin.

'I is no worm for you, Queenie. I have the swarf. Tiny bits of steel that can float in the air. But I is here to bring news. A warning. Of the Lathe the Swarf still has fancy for the old days. I likes to see humans squirm. Likes to see you fairy folk stirring things up, I does. Some goblins thinks as I does, but not so many now. Some goblins almost not goblins now. Almost human. I don't likes it but they says the times they is a-changing. The money is good, see, Queenie.'

'Money?' sneered the Queen. 'I give you goblins money, you wor—' She paused as she saw the goblin's hand move into his pocket. Could the horrible little creature really be bringing *iron* into her world? Iron – a terrible substance for any of the fairy folk. Painful. Destructive. It blinded, deafened, made an elf feel more alone than any human could ever feel. She finished her sentence with gritted teeth. 'Worthy creature.'

'Gold as melts away as sun rises,' said the goblin. 'They – we – gets real money now. I just wants goblins to remain goblins. Goblins with status. *Respect.* Not pushed around no more by you or anyone else.' He glared at Peaseblossom, who had suddenly stepped to the side of the Queen.

'I don't believe you,' said the Queen.

'Your funeral, Queenie,' said the goblin. 'Don't believe me. Go to gate. Not so much trouble now old witch gone. You sees for yourself. World has changed, Queenie.'

And the Queen thought, Changed, yes. She had felt the tremors, known something momentous was afoot, but not known exactly what. So the old witch was gone. With no hag to stop them, why, she realized, we can ride through in splendour once more. Then her face fell. Except for this . . . swarf. This *iron*.

'Bind this maggot's arms behind him,' she ordered her guards, pointing at the goblin. 'I wish to see if he speaks true. And he will ride with us . . .' She smiled. 'If he speaks false, we will tear out his tongue.'

Next morning, alone in Granny Weatherwax's cottage – *her* cottage, now – Tiffany woke early knowing that her world had changed. You was watching her like a hawk.

She sighed. It was going to be a busy day. She had been in many houses where death had recently visited, and always the lady of the house, if there was one, would be shining anything that shined and cleaning everything that could be cleaned. And so, with rags and polishing cloths, Tiffany Aching cleaned everything that was already spick and span clean: it was a kind of unspoken mantra – the world had gone bad, but at least the grate had been polished and now had a fire ready to light in it.

All the time, like a statue, there was You, staring at

her. Did cats know about death? she wondered. What about the cats of witches? Especially . . . what about *Granny Weatherwax's cat*?

Tiffany tidied that thought away for now, and started on the kitchen, burnishing anything that could be burnished, and yes, it shone. She was cleaning things already clean, but the algebra of mourning required the effort of getting all the death out of the house; and there was no shrinking from it: you cleaned everything, regardless.

She'd finished in the kitchen and the scullery, leaving everything so bright that her eyes watered, and then there was nothing for it but to go upstairs. On her hands and knees, with bucket and brush and rags and grease – that is, elbow grease – Tiffany cleaned and cleaned until her knuckles were red and she was satisfied.

But that wasn't the end of it: there was Granny's small wardrobe, with its few well-worn and serviceable dresses hanging in there, along with a cloak. All black, of course. Tucked away on a shelf was the Zephyr Billow Cloak Tiffany herself had given Granny – unworn, as far as she could see, but kept carefully, like a special possession. She felt her eyes begin to prickle . . .

Beside the bed were Granny Weatherwax's boots. Good, serviceable boots, Tiffany thought. And Granny had hated waste. But . . . to actually wear them? She was going to find it hard enough to follow in Granny's footsteps. She swallowed. She was sure she could find a good home for the boots. In the meantime, well, she poked forward a toe and pushed them out of sight, beneath the bed.

Then of course there was the kitchen garden and, above all, the herbs. Tiffany found a pair of heavy gloves in the scullery – you didn't go into Granny's herbs without heavy gloves until they knew you. Granny had foraged, bartered and been given herbs from just about everywhere, and she had Rotating Spinach, and Doubting Plums, Ginny Come Nether, Twirlabout, Tickle My Fancy Root, Jump in the Basin and Jack-go-to-bed-and-never-get-up, Daisy-upsy-Daisy and Old Man Root. There was a clump of Love Lies Oozing by the Jack by Moonlight and a very active Maiden's Respite. Tiffany did not know what all of them were for; she would have to ask Nanny Ogg. Or Magrat Garlick, who – like her husband Verence, the King of Lancre – was very enthusiastic about herbs.* Though *un*like her husband, Magrat did actually know her Troubling Tony from her Multitude Root.

It was never easy being a witch. Oh, the broomstick was great, but to be a witch you needed to be sensible, so sensible that sometimes it hurt. You dealt with the reality – not what people wanted. The reality right now was suddenly You, meowing and banging her head against Tiffany's legs, demanding food, which she then ignored completely when Tiffany went

---

* Basically, if it had something herbal in it, Magrat and Verence thought it would do you good. With some of the herbs in Granny's garden, this might be doubtful. At least in the short term. And it might not be wise to stray too far from the privy.

back into the kitchen and placed a dish of it down for her on the floor.

Tiffany went outdoors again and fed the chickens, let the goats out to graze, had a word with the bees and then thought, I've done my bit. The place is spotless, the bees are happy, even the lean-to is clean. If Nanny can come in and feed the animals, keep an eye on You, then I can go back home for a few days . . .

Reaching the Chalk after a flight that was long and, sadly, very wet, since the rain was teeming down,* she flew to the house of young Milly Robinson, the Feegles clinging on behind, under and actually *on* her in their usual style.

Milly's two baby boys looked well fed, but the little girl – baby Tiffany – didn't. Unfortunately Witch Tiffany was used to this sort of thing, especially when the mothers weren't very clever or had bossy mothers and thought feeding the boys was the main thing in life. It was why, just after the baby's birth, she had whispered that spell into the baby's ear. A simple tracking magic, so she would know if any harm befell the little girl. Just a precaution, she had told herself at the time.

There was no use getting nasty about all this, so she took the young woman aside and said, 'Milly, listen. Yes, your boys have to be straight and strong when they grow up, but my mother always used to say to me: *Your son's your son until he takes a wife, but*

---

* And contrary to popular belief, no witch Tiffany knew had yet managed to control a broomstick whilst also using an umbrella.

your daughter is your daughter all of your life. And I think that's right enough. You help your mother out still, don't you? And she helps you. So fair shares for the little girl is the right thing to do. Please.' Then, because the carrot – or in this case, the breast milk – sometimes needed to be accompanied by the stick, she added sternly, the pointy hat making her seem older and wiser than she would otherwise appear, 'I shall be watching after her interests.' A little bit of menace often did the trick, she had learned. And, of course, she *would* watch.

Then there was only one person she wanted to talk to; and the rain was getting harder still as her stick drifted down towards the Feegle mound on the hill, Rob and the other Feegles toppling off as she approached. Daft Wullie made a spectacularly bad landing, head first into the gorse, and a rabble of young Feegles rushed up joyously to unscrew him.

There were a couple of Rob's older sons lounging around outside the entrance. They were scrawny, even by Feegle standards, with barely a wisp of beard hair between them and impractically low-slung spogs knocking about their knees, their kilts hung low on their skinny hips. To Tiffany's amazement, she could see the top bands of *coloured pants* riding high above them. *Pants?* On a Feegle? The times were indeed changing.

'Pull yon kilts up, lads!' Rob muttered as they pushed their way past.

The kelda was in her chamber, surrounded by

Feegle babies, all rolling around on a floor covered with the fleeces of sheep gone to another land. And the first words she said were, 'I know . . .' She sighed and added, 'It's grieving I am, but the wheel takes all in time.' Her face crinkled into a huge smile. 'It's happy I am to see you as leader of the witches, Tiffan.'

'Well, thank you,' said Tiffany. How did Jeannie know? she wondered for a moment. But every kelda used the way of the hiddlins to see things past, present and future . . . and it was a secret known only to the keldas, passed down one to the other.

She understood too that although Jeannie was very small, she was someone to whom she could tell every secret, in the assurance that it would never be passed on to anyone. And now she hesitantly said, 'Jeannie, I don't think I could ever fill her boots.'

'Really?' said the kelda sharply. 'Dinna you think Esmerelda Weatherwax may nae have kenned the same thing when the position was gi'n to her? Do ye suppose yon hag then said, Nae me. I'm nae guid enough?' The wise little pictsie was looking at Tiffany as if she was some kind of specimen, a new plant perhaps, and then she lowered her voice and said, 'I ken well enough that ye will be a guid leader.'

'Though only the first amongst equals rather than a leader,' Tiffany added. 'At least, I'm sure that's what the other witches think . . .' Her voice trailed off, her doubts hanging in the air.

'Is that so?' said the kelda. She went quiet for a moment, then said softly, 'Ye who kissed the spirit of winter and sent him packing, aye. Yet I ken that ye have in front of ye something less easy, Tiffan. There is a change coming in the heavens, and ye will need to be there.' Her voice grew even more sombre and her small eyes were fixed on Tiffany now. 'Be aware, Tir-far-thóinn; this is a time of transition,' she said. 'Mistress Weatherwax is nae longer wi' us, and her goin' leaves a . . . hole that others willnae fail to see. We mus' watch the gateways, and ye mus' tak' great care. For them ye don't wish to know might be seeking ye out.'

It was good to be home, Tiffany thought, when at last she arrived there. Back at her parents' farm – it was even *called* Home Farm – back where her mother cooked a hot dinner every night. Back where she could sit at the big wooden kitchen table, which was scarred by generations of Achings, and become a little girl again.

But she wasn't a little girl any more. She was a witch. One with two steadings to look after. And over the next week as she flew back and forth from the Chalk to Lancre, from Lancre to the Chalk, in weather that seemed to be enjoying a competition to be the wettest ever for the time of year, it seemed to her that she was always arriving late, wet and tired. People were nearly always polite – to her face, anyway, and certainly to the pointy hat – but she could tell from what they didn't say that somehow, indefinably, whatever she did, it wasn't quite enough. She got up earlier every day and went to bed later, but it still wasn't enough.

She needed to be a good witch. A strong witch. And in between the carrying and the healing, the helping and the listening, she could feel sudden prickles of alarm run up and down her body. Jeannie had warned her that something dreadful might be coming . . . Would she be up to the job? She didn't even think she was doing very well with all the usual stuff.

She couldn't be Granny Weatherwax for them in Lancre.

And it was getting harder and harder to be Tiffany Aching for the Chalk.

Even at home. Even there. She struggled in wearily one night, longing for food, peace and her bed, and as her mother pulled a huge pot from the big black oven and placed it in the centre of the table, a family row was just starting.

'I met Sid Pigeon outside the Baron's Arms today,' her brother Wentworth, a strapping lad not *quite* old enough for the pub yet, but certainly old enough to hang around outside, was saying.

'Sid Pigeon?' Mrs Aching wondered.

'The younger of the two Pigeon brothers,' her father said.

Younger, thought Tiffany. That counted for a lot in farming country. It meant the older brother got the farm. Though if she remembered correctly, the Pigeon farm was a pretty poor place, not very well run. Wasn't Mr Pigeon a regular at the Baron's Arms? She tried to remember Mrs Pigeon, and failed. But yes, she remembered Sid. She'd seen him only a few weeks back, up near Twoshirts – a small boy who had seemingly grown into his name when someone had given him a peaked cap and a whistle to hang around his neck.

'He was telling me about them railway jobs,' Wentworth went on enthusiastically. 'He's earning good money, is Sid. Says they need more men. It's the future, Dad. Railways, not sheep!'

'Don't get any daft ideas, lad,' his father warned. 'Railways is for them as don't take on land to farm. Not like us Achings. Not like *you*. You know what your future holds for you. It's right here, where it's always been for an Aching lad.'

'But—' Wentworth wasn't happy. Tiffany shot him a look. She knew how he felt. And after all, she herself wasn't doing what had been expected of her, was she? If she had, she'd be getting married about now, like her sisters had, getting ready to produce a few more grandchildren for her mother to fuss over.

Her mother seemed to be thinking of the same thing. 'You always seem to be somewhere else these days,' she said, changing the subject from Wentworth to Tiffany, trying hard not to sound like she was complaining. 'I wish you could be with us more, Tiff,' she added a bit sadly.

'Don't bother the lass. She's some kind of top witch now, you know. She can't be everywhere,' her father said.

Feeling like a little girl, Tiffany said, 'I try to be around here as much as possible but we don't really have enough witches to do the work that's needed.'

Her mother smiled nervously and said, 'I know you work hard, dear. There's lots of people who stop me in the road to say that my girl has helped their kid or their father. Everybody sees that you are running about like nobody's business. And you know what people are saying? They are saying to me, you are growing up like your granny. After all, she used to tell the Baron what to do. And you do the same.'

'Well, Granny Aching wasn't a witch,' said Tiffany.

'That depends,' said her father, turning away from Wentworth, who stomped out and slammed the kitchen door behind him. Joe Aching looked after him for a moment, then sighed and winked at Tiffany. 'There are surely different kinds of witches. You remember how your granny wanted the shepherd's hut burned down once she was dead? "Burn everything," she told me.' He smiled and said, 'I almost did what I was told. But there was a thing she had and it was not for the burning, so I wrapped it up, and now, seeing you, my girl, here's a little memento from Granny Aching.'

To Tiffany's surprise her father was crying, under his smiles, as he gave her a little package wrapped up in crinkled paper and tied with a piece of old wool. She opened it and turned the little ridged object over in her hand.

'It's a shepherd's crown,' she said. 'I've seen them before – they are quite easy to find.'

Joe Aching laughed and said, 'Not this one. Your granny said it was special – the crown of crowns. And if the Shepherd of Shepherds picked it up, it would turn into gold. Look, beneath the grey you can see the hints of gold.'

Tiffany looked at the little object while she ate her stew, made as only her mother could make it, and she thought about the days when Granny Aching would come down to the farm for a meal.

It seemed to some that the old woman had lived on Jolly Sailor tobacco; and there was no doubt about it – when it came to sheep, Granny Aching knew everything. But the mind starts running all by itself and Tiffany thought about all the things Granny had done and the things that Granny had said. Then the memories came as a cavalcade, whether she wanted them or not, settling on her like snow.

Tiffany thought of the times she had walked with her granny. Mostly in silence, sometimes with Thunder and Lightning – Granny Aching's sheepdogs – at their heels. She had learned a lot from the old woman.

She taught me so much, she said to herself. She *built* me as we were walking around after the sheep, and she told me all those things that I needed to know, and the first thing was to look after people. Of course, the other thing had been to look after the sheep.

And all she had ever asked for was her shepherd's hut and some horrible tobacco.

Tiffany dropped her spoon. It was all right to sob in this familiar kitchen like she had when she was a girl.

Immediately, her father was there beside her. 'You can do a lot, jigget, but no one could do it all.'

'Yes,' said her mother. 'And we keep your bed ready every day. And we know you are doing a lot of good and I am proud when I see you flying around. But you can't do everything for everybody. Don't go out again tonight. Please.'

'We like seeing our girl, but it'd be nice to see her properly and not always in a blur,' her father added, putting his arm around her.

They finished their dinner in silence, a warm silence, and as Tiffany prepared to go up the stairs to her childhood bedroom, Mrs Aching stood and pulled out an envelope from where she had tucked it out of the way on the dresser, amongst the blue and white jars that, surprisingly in a working farm kitchen, were simply for show. 'There's a letter here for you. From Preston, I expect.' Her tone was very mother-ish now; she only had to say 'Preston' and there was a question there.

And Tiffany crept up the stairs, feeling the care and love of her parents flowing around her, and into her room, relishing the familiar creak of the boards. She placed the shepherd's crown on the shelf by her few books – a new treasure – and pulled on her night-dress wearily. Tonight, she decided, she would try to forget her fears, allow herself to just be Tiffany Aching for a while. Not Tiffany Aching, the Witch of the Chalk.

Then, while there was still light to see, she read Preston's letter, and the weariness fled for a moment, replaced by a wave of sheer happiness. Preston's letter was wonderful! Filled with new language, new words – today he wrote about taking up a scalpel – 'such a sharp, strong word' – and how he had learned a new way to suture. 'Suture,' Tiffany said quietly to herself.

A soft word, so much smoother than 'scalpel', almost healing. And in a way she needed healing. Healing from the loss of Granny Weatherwax, healing from the strain of too much to do – and healing from the effort of trying to match the expectations of the other witches.

She carefully read every word, twice, then folded the letter up and put it away in a small wooden box in which she kept all his letters, as well as the beautiful golden hare pendant he had once given her. There was no point resealing it: she could keep nothing secret from the Feegles and she preferred not to have the box full of the snail slime they used to restick anything they had opened.

Then she slept in her childhood bedroom. And beside her there was the cat, You.

And Tiffany was a child again. A child with parents who loved her very much.

But also a young girl. A girl with a boy who sends her letters.

And a witch. A witch with a cat that was very . . . special.

While her parents lay in bed, talking about their daughter . . .

'It's right proud of our girl I am,' Joe Aching began.

'And of course she is a really good midwife,' Mrs Aching said, adding rather sadly, 'But I wonder if she might ever have children of her own. She doesn't talk about Preston to me, you know, and I don't much like to ask. Not like with her sisters.' She sighed. 'But so much is changing. Even Wentworth, tonight . . .'

'Oh, don't worry about him,' Mr Aching said. "Tis right for a lad to want to find his own feet, and most likely he'll bluster for a bit and shout and argue, but he'll be here when we've gone, looking after the Aching land, you mark my words. There's nothing to beat land.' He sniffed. 'Certainly not them railways.'

'But Tiffany's different,' his wife continued. 'What she's going to do I really don't know, though I do hope, in time, that she and Preston might settle round here. If he's a doctor and she's a witch, that's no reason why they can't be together, is it? Tiffany could have children too then, like Hannah and Fastidia . . .' They thought of their other daughters, of their grand-children.

Joe sighed. 'She's not like our other daughters, love. I believe Tiffany may even surpass her grand-mother,' he said.

And then he blew out the candles, and they slept, thinking of their Tiffany, a skylark among the sparrows.

CHAPTER 6

Around the Houses

Walking steadily along the road to Lancre with Mephistopheles trotting beside him and his little cart rattling behind, and swallows swooping overhead, Geoffrey realized that his old home seemed a long way away now. It had only been a week or so, but as they climbed higher into the Ramtops he began to understand what 'geography' meant in reality, rather than in the books Mr Wiggall had let him read – Lancre and its surrounding villages had a *lot* of geography.

At the end of a day's long but satisfying walk for both boy and goat, they arrived outside a village pub which proclaimed its name as The Star, the sign promising excellent ales and food. Well, let's see how excellent it is, Geoffrey thought. He unhitched the cart and went into the pub with the goat following close behind.

The pub was full of working men, who were now not working but enjoying a pint or two before dinner. It was rather stuffy inside with the usual rural tint of agricultural armpit. The regulars were used to people bringing a working dog in with them but they were amazed to see a dusty but well-dressed lad bringing a goat into their pub.

The rather skinny barman said, 'We only allow dogs in here, mister.'

All eyes in the pub were by now focused on Mephistopheles and Geoffrey said, 'My goat is cleaner and more knowledgeable than any dog. He can count to twenty, and when the time comes he'll go outside to do his business. In fact, sir, if I can show him your privy now, he will use it when he needs it.'

One worker appeared to take umbrage at this point. 'Do you think that just because we work on the land, we don't know nothing? I have a pint here that says that the goat can't do it.'

Innocently Geoffrey said, 'You have a knowledge-able pint there, sir.' And everyone in the pub laughed. Now every eye was on Geoffrey as he said, 'Mephistopheles, how many people are in this pub?'

The goat looked down his nose – and it was a nose a dowager would have been proud of – at the men around the bar and started his count, delicately hit-ting the floor with his hoof, the noise suddenly being the only sound in the place.

He hit the floor eight times. 'He got it right!' declared the barman.

'I saw something like that afore,' said one of the

men. 'There was a travelling show. You know, clowns and tightrope walkers and folk with no arms and travelling doctors.* They called it a carnival. And they had a horse they said could count. But it was just a trick.'

Geoffrey smiled and said, 'If a couple of you gentlemen would care to step out for a moment, I will ask my goat to do it again, and you will see that there is no trick involved.'

Intrigued now, several of the men stepped out while the others started to take bets amongst themselves.

'Gentlemen, my goat will tell you how many people are still in the room,' said Geoffrey.

Once again, daintily, Mephistopheles tapped out the correct number.

Hearing the cheers, the men who had gone out came back in again, looking curious – and Mephistopheles's hoof registered each one as he entered. The barman laughed. 'This trick deserves a meal for you and your remarkable goat, mister. What does he like?'

'It's no trick, I assure you, but thank you. Mephistopheles will eat almost anything – he's a goat. Some scraps would be most acceptable. And for myself, just some bread would be welcome.'

A bowl of kitchen scraps was produced for Mephistopheles and Geoffrey sat down beside him with his pint and a slab of bread and butter, chatting

---

* There was the usual man-who-puts-weasels-down-his-trousers in action too. Hence the need for a doctor.

to some of the men who were interested in the goat. An interest which only deepened when Mephistopheles went out in the direction of the privy and after a while came back again.

'You actually managed to get him to do that?' said one of them in wonder.

'Yes,' said Geoffrey. 'I trained him from when he was very small. He's quite docile really. Well, if I'm around.'

'What do you mean?'

'It means he does what he's told, but he has a mind of his own as well. I wouldn't lose him for anything.'

Just then, there were raised voices at the other end of the bar as one drinker, filled with the bluster that ale can give to a man, started a fight with someone else who had just come in. The more sensible people moved away as the two began to trade blows, seemingly intent on beating one another to death, while the barman bellowed about the damage to his furniture and threatened to wallop them with his grandfather's knobkerrie, a souvenir from the Klatchian campaign, if they didn't stop.

Mephistopheles was suddenly alert at Geoffrey's side, and every drinker who was sober understood in his soul that this was no time to be unpleasant to the lad. They didn't know *how* they knew, but there was a kind of visceral power there waiting to be unleashed.

'Why are they fighting? What's wrong?' Geoffrey asked his neighbour.

'An old grudge about a young lady,' said the man,

rolling his eyes. 'A bad business. Someone's going to get hurt, you mark my words.'

To everyone's astonishment Geoffrey strolled across the pub, his goat watching his every step, dodged the wildly swinging blows and stood between the two men, saying, 'There's no need to fight, you know.'

The barman's face fell – he knew what happened to people who tried to get between two idiots smelling blood. And then he could hardly believe his eyes, for the two men abruptly stopped fighting and were standing there, looking rather bemused.

'Why don't you two just meet the young lady and see what *she* thinks before you start beating each other to death?' Geoffrey said softly.

The men looked at one another and the bigger of the two said: 'He's right, you know.'

And the pub audience laughed as the two looked around at the wreckage, seemingly amazed that this could have had anything to do with them.

'There, that was easy, wasn't it?' said Geoffrey, returning to the bar.

'Ah,' said the landlord, astonished that he wasn't having to pick a battered Geoffrey off the floor. 'You're not a wizard, are you?'

'No,' said Geoffrey. 'It's a knack. It happens to me all the time, when I need it.' He smiled. 'Mostly with animals and sometimes with people.' But alas, he thought to himself, not with my father, never with him.

'Well, you must be *some* kind of wizard,' said the

barman. 'You've broken up a fight between two of the nastiest bruisers we have around here.' He glared at the two miscreants. 'As for you two,' he said, 'don't come back here until you are sober. Look at the mess you've made.' He grabbed both of them and pushed them out the door.

The rest of the drinkers got back to their pints.

The barman turned back to Geoffrey and looked at him in shrewd appraisal.

'You want a job, lad? No pay, but you get your keep.'

'I can't take a job, but I'd be happy to stay for a few days,' said Geoffrey with alacrity. 'If you can find some vegetables for me – I eat no meat. And can there be a place for Mephistopheles as well? He's not very smelly.'

'Probably no worse than the people we have in here,' said the barman, laughing. 'I tell you what. You and your goat can stay in the barn and I'll give you your dinner and breakfast, and then after that, we'll see.' The man held out a rather dirty hand. 'A deal, then?'

'Oh yes, thank you. My name is Geoffrey.'

The man hesitated. 'My name's Darling. Darling Dove.' He looked at Geoffrey mournfully and said, 'Have a laugh about it, will you? Everyone does. Might as well get it out of the way.'

'Why?' said Geoffrey. 'Darling is a kind word and so is Dove. How can these be anything to worry about?'

That night, Mr Dove told his wife, 'I got us a new

bar boy. Funny cove he is too. But he seems, well, harmless. Sort of easy to talk to.'

'Can we afford it, Darling?' his wife said.

'Oh,' said Darling Dove, 'he just wants feeding – doesn't even want meat – and somewhere to sleep. And he's got a goat. Quite a smart one, really. Does tricks and all. Might bring some more customers in.'

'Well, dear, if you think it's a good idea. What are his clothes like?' asked Mrs Dove.

'Pretty good,' said Mr Dove. 'And he talks like a toff. I wonder if he is running away from something. Best not to ask any questions, I reckon. I tell you what, though: between him and his goat, we won't have any trouble in the bar.'

And indeed Geoffrey stayed at The Star for two days, simply because Mr Dove liked him hanging around the place. And Mrs Dove said she was sad when he told her husband that he had to move on. 'A strange boy, young Geoffrey. He kind of gives me the idea that everything is all right, even if I don't know what it is that *is* right. A sort of rightness, floating in the air. I'm really sorry that he's going,' she said.

'Yes, dear,' said Mr Dove. 'I asked him to stay, I really did, but he said he must go to Lancre.'

'That's where they have the witches,' said his wife. She made a face.

'Well,' Mr Dove said, 'that's where he wants to go.' He paused, and added, 'He said the wind is blowing him there.'

*

Battling into a bitter headwind on her long journey back to her parents' farm, Tiffany felt that there was altogether too much wind in and around Lancre. Still, at least it wasn't raining, she told herself. Yesterday's rain had been awful – the kind of joyous rain where every cloud had decided to join the party once one cloud had cracked open the first deluge.

She had felt proud of having the two steadings at first, flying between Lancre and the Chalk every few days, but broomsticks are not very fast. Or warm.* It was good that she could go back home to where her mother did the cooking, but even back home there was no time to rest, and being away in Lancre for half the week meant she was facing a plethora of demands from the Chalk. People weren't getting nasty about it – after all, she was a witch, and Lancre had more people than the Chalk – but there were these little strains beginning to develop. A few mutters. And she had a horrible feeling that some of the muttering was coming from other witches – witches who were finding queues at their doors, people who had gone to find Granny Weatherwax and just found an empty cottage.

Some of the problem in both steadings was with the old men left behind when their wives had died; a lot of them didn't know how to cook. Occasionally some of the old ladies would help and you would see them carrying a pot of stew round for the old man next door. But the witch part of Tiffany couldn't help

---

* It gets awfully cold up there, and no sensible witch ever took to the skies without several layers of flannelette between her and the stick.

but notice that this happened more often if the old lady was a widow and the old man had a nice cottage and a bit of money put by . . .

There was always *something* that had to be done – and some days it seemed mostly to be about toenails. There was one old man in Lancre – a decent old boy – whose toenails were as sharp as a lethal weapon, and Tiffany had to ask Jason Ogg, a blacksmith, to make her a pair of secateurs tough enough to break through them. She always closed her eyes until she heard the patter of his toenails banging off the ceiling, but the old man called her his lovely lady and tried to give her money. And at least she now knew that the Feegles had a use for the toenail clippings.

Witches liked useful things, Tiffany mused, as she tried to take her mind off the chill wind whipping around her. A witch would never have to ask for anything – oh no, no one wanted to *owe* a witch anything – and a witch didn't take money either. Instead she accepted things she could make use of: food, and old clothing, and bits of cloth for bandages, and spare boots.

Boots. She had tripped over Granny Weatherwax's boots again that very day. She had put them in the corner of the room now, and there they sat, almost staring at her when she was too weary to think. *You're not good enough yet to fill these boots*, they seemed to say. *You'll have to do a lot more first.*

Of course, there always *was* such a lot to do. So many people never seemed to think about the consequences of their everyday actions. And then a witch on her broom would have to set out from her bed in the rain at the dead of night because of 'I only' and its little friends 'I didn't know' and 'It's not my fault'.

I only wanted to see if the copper was hot . . .

I didn't know a boiling pot was dangerous . . .

It's not my fault – no one told me dogs that bark might also bite.

And, her favourite, *I didn't know it would go off bang –* when it said 'goes bang' on the box it came in. *That* had been when little Ted Cooper had put an explosive banger* into the carcass of a chicken after his mum's birthday party and nearly killed everybody around the table. Yes, she had bandaged and treated everybody, even the joker, but she hoped very much his dad had kicked his arse afterwards.

And when the witch wasn't there, well, what harm was there in trying out a few things for yourself? Most people knew about using plants to cure things. They were certain about that. But the thing about plants is that many of them look like all the others, and so Mistress Holland, wife of the miller of the Chalk, had treated her husband's unfortunate skin condition with Love Lies Oozing rather than with Merryday Root and now his skin had turned purple.

Tiffany had treated the man, but then it had been time for her to go back to Lancre, and she was up, up and away again on her stick, hoping that they had both learned their lesson.

She was very thankful that Nanny Ogg was not too far away from Granny's . . . no, *her* cottage. There

---

* Another tiny clue.

were a lot of things that Tiffany was good at, but cookery wasn't one of them, and so just as she relied on her mum and dad for meals in the Chalk, in Lancre she relied on Nanny. Strictly speaking, this meant she was relying on Nanny's army of daughters-in-law, who couldn't do enough for their old Nanny.*

But wherever the pair of them took their meals – either in Tiffany's little cottage in the woods, or at Tir Nani Ogg, the overcrowded but very comfortable home where Nanny Ogg ruled the roost – it seemed that You was there too. No cat could move as fast as her, but you never *saw* her move fast, she just *arrived*. It was baffling. What was also baffling was how Greebo – Nanny's ancient tomcat who treated a bit of eyeball scratching as a friendly hello – slunk away when You appeared.

The white cat had clearly made her decision and was a constant presence in Tiffany's life in Lancre. Now, when Tiffany got ready for an afternoon of going round the houses, You would jump on the broomstick before Tiffany had even looked at it, which made Nanny laugh, saying, 'She's got you down pat, my girl. Maybe she could go round the houses by herself!'

Nanny Ogg was actually rather impressed by Tiffany. But also worried. 'Really,' she said to her one day as they shared a quick meal, '*you* know you're good, Tiff. I know you're good. *Granny*, wherever she

---

* 'Enough' wasn't really a long enough word to describe the numerous little tasks any young woman marrying into the Ogg family found were expected of her.

is now, knew you was good, but you don't have to keep tryin' to do it all on your own, my girl. Let some of them young girls around here – the apprentices – take some of the strain.' She paused as she chewed on a big mouthful of stew, then added, 'That young lumberjack up in the mountains what Esme sewed up just the day afore she died? Well, young Harrieta Bilk's been goin' on up there to see to him, *an'* doin' a good job too. Tiff, you have to do it your own way, I know, but you ain't the only witch in Lancre. Sometimes you needs to put your feet up and let the parade go by.'

Tiffany had barely had time to listen before she was back on her stick and heading down to the Chalk again. No rest for the busy witch with two steadings! But as the ear-numbing wind whistled by, she considered what Nanny had said. It was true that there were other witches in Lancre, but in the Chalk – unless Letitia decided to stop being just a baroness – Tiffany was the only witch. And if her forebodings were right, if Jeannie's words came true, then one witch for the Chalk might not be anywhere near enough.

She shivered. She was looking forward to getting out of the icy wind and into the warmth of her mother's kitchen. But there was one person she needed to see first . . .

It took Tiffany a long time to find Miss Tick, but eventually she landed in a little wood just outside Ham-on-Rye where the travelling witch, the witchfinder, had stopped her caravan for tea. A small mule was tethered nearby enjoying the contents of its feed bag. It looked at Tiffany as she approached and neighed.

'He's called Joseph,' said Miss Tick. 'A real witch's mule.'

It had started to rain again and Miss Tick quickly waved Tiffany up the wooden caravan steps. Tiffany was glad to see that there was a kettle bubbling on a little stove. She perched herself on the edge of a bench seat fitted just inside the door, facing the stove, and gratefully took the offered cup of tea.

Inside the caravan, it was just as Tiffany expected. Miss Tick had everything ship-shape without needing a ship. On the walls were lots of little racks, neatly filled with many things, and all annotated in Miss Tick's careful teacher-y hand. Tiffany looked closer and, *yes*, they were in alphabetical order. Elsewhere were little pots without labels, so you would never know what was inside them, and by the side of her bed there was a chart showing a variety of knots – escapology was a useful hobby for a witch.

'I'll be grateful if you don't touch my little jars,' said Miss Tick. 'Some of those concoctions might not work properly and the results are often unpredictable. But, you know, one should keep on experimenting.'

That's what's in all the pots, thought Tiffany, taking a sip of her tea. Experiments.

'Glad to see you,' Miss Tick continued. 'I am hearing about you all the time. You know, almost every girl I meet wants to be you. They see you whizzing about all over the place on your broomstick and they all want to be *you*, Mistress Aching. Suddenly it's become a career choice to be a witch!'

'Oh yes,' said Tiffany. 'That's how it starts out, and then you tell them exactly what they would spend their life doing, and quite a few of them decide to go to the big city and be a hairdresser or something.'

'Well, I make no bones about it,' said Miss Tick firmly. 'I tell them to think hard; it's not all magic and waving wands and all that silly business. It's dirt and grime.'

Tiffany sighed. 'Being a witch is a man's job: that's why it needs women to do it.'

Miss Tick laughed and continued, 'Well, I remember a little girl who was unsure of herself and I told her that I would give her lessons that she would never forget in a hurry.'

Tiffany smiled. 'I remember. And now I am in a hurry everywhere these days. But Miss Tick' – she paused and her voice went a bit quiet – 'I have a feeling that some of the older witches are beginning to think I might not be able to cope . . .' She swallowed. 'Up in Lancre, mostly. But it means I do have to be there a lot.' She bit her lip – she *hated* asking for help. Was she saying that she wasn't really up to the job? *Letting Granny Weatherwax down*, since Granny had been the one to put her name up for it. She couldn't remember Granny ever asking for help. 'Down here, on the Chalk,' she said, 'I think I maybe need to . . . er . . . train an apprentice. Have some help.'

The heavens didn't open. There was no gasp of horror from the other witch at this request. Miss Tick simply crossed her arms sternly. 'It's Letice Earwig, I suppose, who's put those doubts into people's heads. She thinks things always have to be done the same way, so that means she would take over, I suppose? She's a senior witch who believes she knows every blessed thing, but it's all just tinkly-winkly stuff. The stupid woman who wrote *My Fairy Friends* should be ashamed to call herself a witch, and certainly shouldn't hope to walk in the footsteps of Granny Weatherwax. Hah, Letice Earwig certainly couldn't manage two steadings at once. She can't really even cope with *one*.' She snorted derisively. 'Do not forget, Tiffany, that I am a *teacher*.* And we teachers can be really nasty when it comes to it. *Ten Steps to Witchcraft* and *The Romance of the Broomstick* are not what *I* would call proper books. Oh, I'll certainly look out for a girl or two for you – it's a very good idea. But you don't need to worry about what Mrs Earwig might say, oh no . . .'

---

* Said in a way that made anyone listening know this instantly.

CHAPTER 7

A Force of Nature

Letice Earwig was not someone who would take being balked lying down. Or standing up, come to that. In truth, she was a force of nature and she hated to back down on anything.

It hadn't taken her long to hear that there had been a queue one day outside Nanny Ogg's home. Tiffany Aching, Mrs Earwig decided, was Not Coping. And it needed a witch of senior stature to Do Something about it. In Letice Earwig's opinion – never a small thing – she was in fact the *only* witch who had the stature to act, especially as that old baggage Nanny Ogg wouldn't do a thing.

Mrs Earwig had married an elderly retired wizard many years before. 'Wizards ain't allowed to get married,' Nanny Ogg had told Tiffany scornfully. 'But the silly man got what was comin' to him. Talk about hen-pecked, he was *earwig*-pecked. She got through all his money, so they says!'

Tiffany wisely didn't rise to that; it was quite probable that 'they' were actually Nanny Ogg, who hated Mrs Earwig with an unrelenting determination.

But that was why she was relieved when Nanny Ogg wasn't there when Mrs Earwig arrived at Granny's cottage one morning a week or so later, for what she called 'one of her little chats'. It would have been better, on reflection, if Mrs Earwig hadn't found Tiffany out in the garden up to her elbows in suds in the middle of doing some washing for old Mr Price.

Tiffany's heart sank when she saw the woman coming,* but she wiped her hands on a towel and welcomed her visitor into the cottage with as much politeness as she could muster. Mrs Earwig had a tendency to treat Tiffany like a child, and also she had bad manners, such as sitting down without being asked. Mrs Earwig did, indeed, sit down in Granny's old rocking chair, and she gave Tiffany a smile of blatant insincerity, then made it worse by saying, 'My dear girl!'

'*Woman*,' said Tiffany quietly as Mrs Earwig looked her up and down. She was acutely conscious of the suds still clinging to her apron and her dishevelled hair.

---

* And heard her. For Mrs Earwig's copious amount of jewellery announced the witch with such a cheerful jangle that it was as if it had ambitions to move from being a set of charms and amulets to being a full instrumental fanfare.

'Well, never mind,' said Mrs Earwig, as if it didn't matter. 'Now, I thought I should come, as a friend and as one of the oldest witches in this area, to see how things were going and to offer some constructive advice.' She looked around the kitchen with a superior air, with a *particularly* sharp glare at the dust that was happily playing little games with itself over the stone flagstones, and Tiffany was suddenly very aware of the spiders which had remained in residence in the scullery, with lots of little ones adding to the colony – she hadn't the heart to move them.

'Don't you think you are overstretched trying to look after two steadings, my dear?' Mrs Earwig added with a saccharine smile.

'Yes, my dear Mrs Earwig,' Tiffany said back, rather sharply. 'I *am* stretched because there is a lot to do in both places and not much time.' Which you are taking up, she thought. But two can play at your game. 'If you have some advice,' she added with a smile to match Mrs Earwig's, 'I'll be glad to hear it.'

Mrs Earwig was never one to ignore an invitation. Not that she had needed one, anyway, since she immediately launched into a prepared speech.

'I'm not saying you are a bad person, my dear. It's just that you can't cope, and people are talking about it.'

'Perhaps they do,' said Tiffany. 'And often they thank me, but I am just one woman – that is *woman*, not girl – so I can't do everything at once. It's just a shame that there aren't more elder witches around . . .' Her voice trailed off, the memory of Granny

Weatherwax lying in her willow casket still too fresh in her mind.

'I understand,' said Mrs Earwig. 'It isn't your fault.' Now her voice was silky smooth, but just a shade beyond patronizing and moving towards out and out rudeness. 'You have indeed been flung into areas you can't manage, and you are in fact far too young, dear Tiffany. To take the right steps on the path of Magick, you surely need the counsel of an elder witch.' She sniffed. 'A *serious* elder witch with the right . . . approach. No . . . family ties.' And it was clear that she did not consider Nanny Ogg to be a candidate for this task.

Tiffany bridled. If there was one thing she hated more than 'my dear girl', it was 'dear Tiffany'. And she well remembered the 'counsel' Mrs Earwig had given to her protégée Annagramma Hawkin, who had taken over a witch's cottage knowing everything possible about runes and tinkly spells but nothing at all useful. *She* had needed *Tiffany's* help. As for implying that Nanny Ogg would not be a good mentor . . .

'Well, my dear,' Mrs Earwig continued, 'as one of the most senior witches in this area, I therefore feel I should take the place of Granny Weatherwax. It's the way it has always been done, and for a good reason – people need a senior witch to be a person whom they can respect, someone they can look up to. After all, my dear girl, a witch of high standing would never be seen doing the washing.'

'Really?' said Tiffany, gritting her teeth. A *second* 'my dear girl'? One more and she would want not only to thrust Mrs Earwig into the suds but also to hold her head under for quite some time. 'Granny Weatherwax always said, "You do the good that is in front of you," and I don't care *who* sees me doing an old man's washing. There's lots to do and a lot of it is *dirty*, Mrs Earwig.'

Mrs Earwig flamed at that and said, '*Ah-wij*, my dear girl.'

'Not my dear girl,' Tiffany snapped. 'Mrs *Earwig*' – not a trace of *Ah-wij* – 'your last book was called *To Ride a Golden Broomstick*. Can you tell me, Mrs Earwig, how does it fly? Gold is rather heavy. You might say, in fact, that it is extremely heavy.'

Mrs Earwig growled. Tiffany had never heard her growl before but this one was a heavy-duty growl. 'It's a metaphor,' she said sharply.

'Really?' said Tiffany. Now she was angry. 'What's it a metaphor *for*, Mrs Earwig? I'm on the sharp end of witchcraft, which means doing what should be done as best you can. It's all about the people, Mrs Earwig, not about the books. Have you ever gone round the houses, Mrs Earwig? Helped a kid with his arse halfway out of his trousers? Do you even *see* the little children with no shoes? The cupboards with no food in them? The wives with a baby every year and a man down the pub? You have been kind enough to offer some advice. If I may offer you some advice in return, you will impress me if you too go round the houses – and not before. I am the acknowledged successor of Granny Weatherwax, who was brought up as a witch by Nanny Gripes, who learned it from witches going all the way back to Black Aliss, and that doesn't change, whatever you might think.' She stood up and opened the front door. 'Thank you for taking the time to come and see me. Now, as you have pointed out, I have lots to do. In my own way. And clearly you *haven't*.'

One thing about Mrs Earwig, Tiffany thought, was that she could flounce. She flounced so much that it almost hurt. Things jingled a merry farewell around her, and one charm even made a spirited attempt to stay by hooking itself around the doorknob as Mrs Earwig turned at the threshold.

The last thing she said to Tiffany as she untangled the little pendant was, 'I tried, I really tried. I invited you to take advantage of all I know about witchcraft. But no. You flung my good will right in my face. You know, we could really have been friends, if you weren't so stubborn. Farewell, *my dear girl*.' Having got the last word in, Mrs Earwig slammed the door behind her as she left.

Tiffany looked at it and said to herself, I do what is needful, Mrs Earwig, not what I want to do.

But the banging of the door as punctuation caused Tiffany to think and she thought suddenly, I want to do it my way. Not how the other witches think it should be done. I can't be Granny Weatherwax for them. I can only be me, Tiffany Aching. But she realized something else too. 'Mrs Earwig was right about at least one thing,' she said aloud. 'I *am* trying to do too much. And if Jeannie is right and there is something awful coming' – she shuddered – 'which I will have to deal with, well, I really hope Miss Tick can find me a girl who might be some use. I do need some help.'

'Aye, would seem so,' said the voice of Rob Anybody.

Tiffany almost exploded. 'Are you always looking after me, Rob Anybody?'

'Och aye. Remember, there's a geas upon us tae look after ye day and nicht and it's a greet geas.'

A geas. Backed up by tradition and magic, Tiffany knew that a geas was an obligation no Feegle would ever fail to meet. Except Daft Wullie, of course, who often mixed up his 'geas' with a flock of big burdies. She understood all this, but it still rankled. 'You watch me all the time? Even when I'm bathing?' she said wearily. It was a familiar argument. Tiffany – for no reason Rob could understand – seemed to take exception to the Feegles being around her *everywhere*. They had already come to an agreement about the privy.*

'Och aye, that we do. Not lookin', ye ken.'

'Well,' said Tiffany, 'could you do me a favour?'

'Och aye,' said Rob. 'Would you like yon Earwig wifie dropped in a pond or something?'

Tiffany sighed. 'Alas, no. I'm not that kind of person.'

'Ah, but we is,' said Rob Anybody cheerfully. 'And anyway, 'tis traditional, ye ken. And we are guid at

---

* Though a Feegle will cheerfully lie about almost anything, so Tiffany still went into any privy with her eyes peeled for flashes of Feegle; she had even once had a nightmare about a Feegle popping up out of the other hole of her parents' two-holer.

tradition, bein' as we are part of *folklore* . . .' He smiled hopefully.

'A very nice thought,' said Tiffany. 'But no, once again, no. Mrs Earwig is not really a bad soul.' That is true, she thought. Stupid, sometimes overbearing, unfeeling, and not really, if you get down to it, a very good witch. But there is a steel there at the core.

Tiffany knew Nanny Ogg rarely did any washing – what were daughters-in-law for? – but she realized suddenly that she had never seen Granny Weatherwax doing any laundry for the old gentlemen either, and that thought stopped her for a moment. I need time to work this out, she thought, looking at the Big Man of the Nac Mac Feegles standing in front of her, ready for anything. This would be a tough task for them, she knew.

'I've a wee geas tae lay on ye,' she said.

'Och aye?'

'Rob, have you heard of washing clothes?'

'Och aye, we ken it happens,' said Rob Anybody. He scratched at his spog and a mixture of dead insects, half-gnawed chicken's foot bones and the like showered out.

'Well then,' said Tiffany, 'I would deem it a favour if you could spend some time in my scullery whilst I am about my business. You would be helping an old man, indeed you would. He likes to be clean, and to have clean clothes.' She glared down at him. 'A circumstance, Rob, which would be well considered by yourself.'

*

She approached the scullery door in trepidation when she got back from her visits. Everything was shining clean, and draped among the trees outside were old Mr Price's unmentionables, as white as white could be. Only then did Tiffany draw breath.

'Excellent,' she said to Rob Anybody.

He smiled and said, 'Aye, we kenned this would be a tricky job.'

'Good job I wuz with ye this time,' came a voice. It was Wee Mad Arthur, a Feegle who didn't mind washing, due to his having been raised by a bunch of cobblers, and then being a polisman in the big city. Wee Mad Arthur, Tiffany often thought, had a battle raging inside him between his Feegle half and the city half, but since every Feegle liked a good punch-up, well, a fight inside yourself was just an extra treat.

Big Yan pushed Wee Mad Arthur aside and said, 'We dinnae mind helping old bigjobs and getting them squeaky clean, but we are the Feegles and we treasure our dirt. Washing makes a Feegle wither awa'. We cannae abide the soap, ye ken.'

'Nae me, Rob. Nae me,' came a happy voice and Daft Wullie fell off the wall of the goat paddock. Bubbles floated away on the air as he rolled across the grass.

'I've told ye about that, Wullie,' Rob snapped. 'It just makes bubbles come out of your ears.'

Tiffany laughed. 'Well, you could make your own soap, Wullie. Make some for Jeannie. Take a wee present home to your kelda. It's easy to make – you just need some fat and some lye.'

'Och aye, we're good liars, we are,' Rob put in proudly. 'Famed for it, ye ken.'

Well, I tried, thought Tiffany. And anyway, their spirits are pure, if not particularly clean.

Down on the Chalk, at the edge of a dark forest on the top of a hill overlooking Twoshirts, a small town with growing aspirations of being a bit more than one store, a coaching inn and a blacksmith's shop, the Queen of the Elves smiled in satisfaction.

It was a warm night and the air smelled as it always did, and the sky looked as it always did. There appeared to be a new road or stream into the town which glimmered in the moonlight, but otherwise things seemed just as they had been on her last visit.

She turned to look at her goblin prisoner, who was perched with his hands bound on the saddle behind one of her guards. She smiled, and it was not a pleasant smile. She would hand him over to Lord Lankin, she thought. The elf would enjoy tearing the wretched goblin limb from limb – after he had had his pleasure playing with his prey, of course.

But first, this goblin filth had led them here – to this hillside. The Queen and her raiding party looked down at the sleeping valley ahead. Her warriors wore scraps of fur and leather, feathers tucked into headbands and dangling around their necks – and they carried bows with the arrows already nocked.

The gate between the worlds had given them very little trouble in the end. It had not taken much effort for the stronger elves to push through – the barrier was, indeed, very weak just now. Before, the old witch would surely have kept it strong, kept them out. For she had been always on the watch for the fairy folk.

Animals noticed them too. At the very moment the Queen stepped onto the Chalk, the hares on the downs had turned and frozen, whilst the owls out hunting had soared higher, sensing the unwelcome presence of another predator.

Humans, however, were usually the last to notice anything. Which made them so much more fun . . .

Apart from a glow above a mound on the hillside and a distant noise of roistering that the Queen recognized as being the usual sounds of the Nac Mac Feegle, there had been nothing so far to trouble the first elf incursion into the Discworld for many years, and the elves had begun to enjoy themselves. They had caroused through a couple of villages, letting out cows, upturning carts, turning the milk in the churns sour, spoiling a cask of ale and generally amusing themselves with such trifles. But the growing little town below promised all sorts of entertainment for elves who had been denied the pleasures of a raid for far too long.

Apart from the delicate tinkling of myriad bells attached to the harnesses of the raiding party's black horses, there was silence as the elves waited for their Queen to give the signal.

She raised her arm.

But before she could do anything, suddenly, screaming through the air, there came a noise as though someone was killing a gigantic pig.

It was a sound which enveloped the whole of the Chalk. A screaming whistle which screeched around the hills, setting everyone's teeth on edge. Down in the valley, the air now seemed to be full of fire as a huge iron monster tore along the silvery trail towards the town, clouds of steam marking its path.

The elves reeled, panic spreading rapidly from elf to elf as they shrank from the noise. From the sound. From the very *scent* of iron in the air.

Nonchalantly Of the Lathe the Swarf jumped down from the saddle, used his teeth to steal a stone knife from the guard, whose hands were now covering his pointy ears in an effort to block out the sound, and swiftly sliced through his bonds.

'Told you. Iron Horse, that is,' he said importantly. 'Last train into Twoshirts is that. That's where goblins work. With steel and iron.'

The Queen hadn't flinched. She knew that. Some of the others had, but she could deal with them later – no elf should show fear in front of his queen. But in her mind, she thought: *Train?* It's big. It's iron, and we don't know about it. And what we don't know about it could get us killed. 'How can we tame it?' she demanded. 'More importantly, can we make it ours? What grief we could make with something like that!'

Peaseblossom – a calm Peaseblossom, seemingly impervious to the general sense of terror among the elves – was at her elbow and smiled; a smile the Queen didn't like. It cut through the dramatic style of the face he had chosen to wear, his eyes cold and merciless. He said, 'We can torment the goblins until they tell us how to control it. Then they can do it for us.'

'They won't,' said Of the Lathe the Swarf, giving Peaseblossom a dirty look. 'Why should they?'

Peaseblossom reached down to grab the goblin, and Of the Lathe the Swarf reacted quickly, thrusting his small hands into his pockets and throwing a shower of silvery scraps over the elf. Peaseblossom screamed in pain as he fell from his horse.

The goblin laughed as the other elves hastily backed away. 'Forgot what's in my pockets, Mr Pee-pee flower? Told you about swarf, I did. Part of my name. Hurts, does it? Touch clever goblin these days, nasty things happens. Especially to elves.' He pointed down at Peaseblossom, whose glamour had completely deserted him under the onslaught of the shower of iron filings.

The elf lay writhing on the grass, a small, weak, pathetic creature, crying from the pain.

'Funny, no?' said the goblin. 'In this new world, little things like swarf – and goblins – *do* matter.'

CHAPTER 8
The Baron's Arms

The Baron's Arms was the kind of pub where John Parsley, hereditary landlord and bartender, was happy for the locals to mind the pumps when there was a rush or he needed to answer the call of nature. The kind of pub where men would arrive proudly carrying a huge cucumber or any other humorously shaped or suggestive vegetable from the garden just to show it off to all their friends.

Quite often there would be arguments, but arguments for the truth and not for a fight. Occasionally someone would try to wager money but this was frowned on by John Parsley. Although smoking was allowed – lots and lots of smoking – spitting was not tolerated. And, of course, there was swearing, with language as ripe as the humorous vegetables. After all, there were no women there except for Mrs Parsley, who turned a blind ear and would certainly put up with language such as 'bugger', it being considered nothing more than a colourful expression, used plentifully in this context as 'How are you, you old bugger?' and, more carefully, 'Bugger me!'

The Barons, knowing the value of a thriving pub and not being above dropping in from time to time, had over the generations added improvements for the entertainment of their tenants. Soon after his marriage, for instance, the new young Baron had given the pub everything needful for playing darts. This hadn't been a total success – in one enthusiastic match Shake Gently, widely acknowledged as the best ploughman on the Chalk, but not known for his intellectual acumen, had almost lost an eye. The darts were therefore now looked upon as deadly by all the locals, and the shove ha'penny board had been carefully put back into favour.

After a long day's slog in the fields or sheds, the pub was a welcome refuge to many. Joe Aching, tenant farmer of Home Farm, had been promising himself a quiet pint throughout a day which had been beset by obstreperous animals and broken equipment. A pint, he had told himself, would put him in a better frame of mind for the discussion which he knew awaited him over supper about his wedding anniversary, which to his dark dismay he had forgotten. From long experience, he knew that this meant at least a week of cold dinners and cold shoulders, even the risk of a cold bed.

It was Saturday, a warm late summer evening,

a clear night. The pub was full, though not as full as John Parsley would like. Joe took a seat at the long oak table outside the pub with his dog Jester curled around his ankles.

Coming from a long line of Achings who had farmed on the Chalk, Joe Aching knew every man who lived in the area and their families; he knew who worked and who didn't work much, and he knew who was silly and who was smart. Joe himself wasn't smart, but he was clever and a good farmer and, above all things, every Saturday night, wherever he actually sat, he held *the* chair in the pub. Here he was the fount of all knowledge.

At a smaller table just outside the door, he could hear two of the local men arguing about the difference between the paw prints of the cat and of the fox. One of them moved his hands in a slow pavane and said, 'Look, I tell you this again, the cat, she walk like this, you old bugger, but Reynard, he do walk like this.' Once again fox and cat were demonstrated by the other man. I wonder, Joe thought, if we might be one of the last generations to think of a fox as Reynard.

It had been a long day for all the men, working as they were with horses, pigs and sheep, not to mention the scores of chores that faced any countryman. They had a dialect that creaked, and they knew the names of all the songbirds throughout the valleys, and every snake and every fox and where it could be found, and all the places where the Baron's men generally didn't go. In short, they knew a large number of things unknown to scholars in universities. Usually, when one of them spoke, it was done after some cogitation and very slowly, and in this interlude they would put the world to rights until a boy was sent to tell the men their dinners were going cold if they didn't hurry.

Then Dick Handly – a fat man with a wispy fluff of a beard that should be ashamed to call itself a beard in this company – quite abruptly said, 'This ale is as weak as maiden's water!'

'What are you calling my beer?' said John Parsley, clearing the empties from the table. 'It's as clean as anything. I opened the cask only this morning.'

Dick Handly said, 'I'm not saying maiden's water is all that bad.' That got a laugh, albeit a small one. For they all remembered the time when curmudgeonly old Mr Tidder, putting his faith in a traditional cure, had asked his daughter to save some of her widdle to pour over his sore leg, and young Maisie – a sweet girl, but somewhat lacking in the brains department – had misunderstood the request and poured her father out a drink with a very unusual flavour. Amazingly, his leg had still got better.

But another pint was pulled, from a new cask, and Dick Handly pronounced it satisfactory. And John Parsley wondered. But not much. For what was a pint among friends?

The landlord sat down with his customers now, and said to Joe, 'How do you think the young Baron is settling in?'

The relationship between the Baron and Mr Aching, his tenant, was not that unusual in the countryside. The Baron owned the land. Everyone knew that. He also owned all the farms in the neighbourhood, and the farmers, his tenants, farmed the land for him, paying rent every quarter day. He could, if he chose, take a farm back and throw a farmer and his family out. In the past, there had been barons who had occasionally indulged in displays of authority such as burning down cottages and throwing out whole families, sometimes just on a whim, but mostly as a daft way of showing who had the real power. They soon learned. Power means nothing without a decent harvest in the barn, and a flock of Sunday dinners grazing on the hills.

Roland, the young Baron, had made a bit of a rocky start – made worse, it has to be said, by his new mother-in-law, a duchess who made sure that everyone knew it too. But he soon learned. Knowing that he wasn't yet experienced at farming the land, he had followed his father's general practice of wisely leaving his farmers to run their farms and their workers as they saw fit. Now everyone was happy.

Also wisely, Roland would from time to time talk to Joe Aching, as had his father before him, and Joe, a kindly man, would offer to speak about the things the Baron's land agent and rent collectors might not see, such as a widow who had fallen on bad times or a mother struggling to cope after her husband had been trampled by a bad-tempered young bull. Joe Aching would point out that a certain amount of charity would be a good thing and, to give the young Baron his due, he would do what he was told in a strange sort of way, and the widow would find that somehow she had managed to pay her rent in advance, so owed nothing for the time being, and a helpful young lad from the estate who needed to learn farming might turn up at the young mother's little holding.

'I don't like to judge too soon,' said Joe, leaning back on the bench and looking solemn in a way only a man who had the right to *the* chair on a Saturday had the right to look. 'But to tell you the truth, he's doing rather well. Picking it up as he goes along, you might say.'

'That's good then,' said Thomas Greengrass. 'Looks like he's going to follow in the footsteps of his old man.'

'We'll be lucky then. The old Baron was a good man – tough on the outside, but he knew what was what.'

Parsley smiled. 'His young lady, the Baroness, has learned a lot of lessons without being taught them – have you noticed that? She's always around the place talking to people, not putting on airs. The wife likes her,' he added with a sage nod. If the wife approved, well, that was good. It meant peace at home, and every countryman wanted *that* after a day's hard work. 'I heard tell she'd been round to say well done whenever a man's wife was having kids.'

On that subject, Robert Thick said, 'My Josephine will be having another one shortly.'

Somebody laughed and said, 'That's pints all round, you know.'

'Be sure to have a word with Joe's Tiffany then,'

said Thomas Greengrass. 'When it comes to birthing a child, I've never seen better.'

Over his pint, Thomas added, 'I saw her whizzing past yesterday. It made me right proud, it really did, a girl of the Chalk. I'm sure you must be just as proud, Joe.'

Everyone knew Tiffany Aching, of course; had done ever since she was very small and played with their own children. They didn't much like witches up on the Chalk, but Tiffany was *their* witch. And a good witch to boot. Most importantly, she was a girl of the Chalk. She knew the worth of sheep, and they'd seen her running around in her pants when she was growing up. So that was all right then.

Tiffany's father tried to smile as he reached down and gave his dog a pork scratching. 'A present for you, Jester.' He looked up. 'Of course, Tiffany's mother would like to see her here more often, though she's made up about our Tiff; can't stop telling people about what she does, and neither can I.' He looked over at the landlord. 'Another pint for me when you've time please, John.'

'Of course, Joe,' said John Parsley, heading into the bar and returning with the foaming tankard in his hand.

As the pint was passed down to its destination, Joe said, 'It's strange, you know, when I think about how much time our Tiffany spends over in Lancre these days.'

'Be a shame if she moved up there,' Dick Handly commented. And the thought was there, floating in the air, though nobody said anything further. Not to Joe Aching, not on a Saturday.

'Well, she's always very busy,' Joe said slowly, tucking Dick's comment away in his head to think about later. 'Lot of babies round here, lads!' This brought a smile.

'And it's not just birthing. She came to my old mother when she was going,' said Jim Twister. 'Was with her all night. And she took the pain away! She does that, you know?'

'Yes,' said Joe. 'It's not just for barons, but that's how the old boy went, you know – he had a nurse, but it was Tiffany who sorted him out. Made sure he had no pain.'

There was a sudden silence at the table as the the drinkers reflected on the many times Tiffany Aching had crossed their paths. Then Noddy Saunters said, almost breathlessly, 'Well, Joe, we are all hoping as your Tiffany stays round here, you know. You have got a good one there and no mistake. Mind you tell her that when you sees her.'

'I don't need telling, Noddy,' said Joe. 'Tiffany's mother would like her to settle down, o' course, on the Chalk with her young man – you know, young Preston, who's gone off to learn to be a proper doctor in the big city. But I reckon she won't, not for a while anyway. As I see it, there's lots of Achings around here but our Tiff is following in the footsteps of her granny, only more modern thinking, if you get me? I reckon she's out to change the world, and if not the world, then this little bit called the Chalk.'

'She's a right good witch for us shepherds,' Thomas Greengrass added, and there was a murmur of agreement.

'Do you remember, lads, when shepherds would all turn up here and fight in the Challenge?' said Dick Handly after a pause to empty his glass. 'We didn't have witches then.'

'Aye,' said Joe Aching. 'Those old shepherds didn't fight with their sticks, mind you. They arm-wrestled. And the winner would be named head shepherd.'

They all laughed at that. And most of them thought of Granny Aching, for Granny Aching had really been the last head shepherd. A nod from Granny Aching and a shepherd would walk like a king for the day, Challenge or no Challenge.

'Well, we don't have no head shepherd nowadays. We got a witch instead. Your Tiffany,' said Robert Thick after another long silence in which more beer was drunk and pipes were lit.

'So if we have a witch instead of a head shepherd ... do you think any of you ought to arm-wrestle her?' asked John Parsley with a big grin – and a sideways look at Tiffany's father.

Robert Thick said, 'A witch? No fear. I would mend my manners.'

Joe chuckled as the others nodded in agreement.

Then they looked up as a shadow passed over them and the girl on her broomstick shouted down, 'Evening, Dad! Evening, all. Can't stop. This one's having twins.'

*

Roland de Chumsfanleigh,* the young Baron on the Chalk, *did* want to be like his father in many ways. He knew the old man had been popular – what was known as an 'old school baron', which meant that everyone knew what to expect and the guards polished up their armour and saluted, and did what was expected of *them*, while the Baron did what was expected of him, and pretty much left them alone.

But his father had also been a bit of a bad-tempered bully at times. And *that* bit Roland wanted to forget about. He particularly wanted to sound the right note when he called round to see Tiffany Aching at Home Farm. For they had once been good friends, and, to Roland's alarm, Tiffany was thought of as a good friend by his wife Letitia. Any man with sense was wise to be fearful of a wife's best friends. For who knew what . . . little secrets might be shared. Roland, having been educated at home and with limited knowledge of the world outside the Chalk, feared that 'little' might be *exactly* the kind of comment Letitia might share with Tiffany.

He chose his moment when he saw her broomstick descend early that Saturday evening, at a time when he knew Joe Aching would be at the pub.

'Hello, Roland,' Tiffany said, not even turning

---

* Pronounced 'Chuffley' under that strange rule that the more gentrified a family is, the more peculiar the pronunciation of their name becomes. Tiffany had once heard a highborn visitor named Ponsonby-Macklewright (*Pwt*) refer to Roland as *Chf*. She wondered how they managed at dinner when *Pwt* introduced *Chf* to *Wm* or *Hmpfh*. Surely it could lead to misunderstandings?

round as he rode into the farmyard and dismounted from his horse.

Roland quivered. He was the Baron. Her father's farm was his. And as he thought this, he realized how stupid a thought it was. As Baron, he had the bits of paper that proved his ownership. But this farm was the Achings'. It always had been, and it always would be. And he knew that Tiffany knew exactly what he'd just thought, so he went a bit pink when she turned round.

'Er, Tiffany,' he began, 'I just wanted to see you and . . . er . . . well, it's like this . . .'

'Oh, come on, Roland,' she urged. 'Just get on with what you've come to say; it's been a busy day and I need to get back to Lancre tonight too.'

It was the opening he needed. 'Well, that's what I came about, Tiffany. There have been . . . *complaints*.' It wasn't the right word, and he knew it.

Tiffany reeled at the word. 'What?' she said sharply.

'Well, you're never *here*, Tiffany. You're supposed to be our witch, be here for *us*. But you're off to the Ramtops almost every other day.' He straightened up, a metaphorical broomstick up his spine. He needed to sound official, not wheedle. 'I am your baron,' he said, 'and I ask that you look to your responsibilities, do your duty.'

'Do my duty?' Tiffany echoed weakly. What did he *think* she had been doing over the past few weeks, bandaging legs and treating sores, birthing babies and taking pain away from those nearing the end of their days, and visiting the old folk and keeping an eye on the babies, and . . . yes, *cutting toenails*! What had *Roland* been doing? Hosting dinner parties? Admiring Letitia's attempts at watercolours? It would be far better if he could have offered Letitia's help. For Roland knew, just as Tiffany did, that Letitia had the natural abilities of a witch. She could be *useful* on the Chalk.

And then she thought, that was mean. For she knew that Letitia visited every new baby. Talked to the women.

But she was angry with Roland.

'I shall think on what you say,' she said with an exaggerated politeness that made him blush even more.

With the imaginary broomstick still rigidly attached to his back, Roland strode over to his horse, remounted and rode off.

Well, I did try, he told himself. But he couldn't help but feel that he had made a bit of a mess of it.

There had been pandemonium when the Queen and her followers got back through the stone circle.

The glittering Fairyland palace was gone and the council was taking place in a clearing in the depths of what might have been a magical wood if the Queen had bothered to put in the requisite details such as butterflies, daisies and toadstools. Even now, trees were frantically scribbling in branches and twigs as she passed, and parts of the ground seemed to be having a little race to create blades of grass on either side of her.

She was furious. A goblin – a piece of filth – had dared to attack one of her lords. And he had *fallen* in front of that goblin, a goblin so fleet of mucky foot as he had run from her anger. But although it had been Peaseblossom who had fallen – and secretly the Queen was pleased that it had been him and not another of her lords – she knew that her elves blamed *her* for the shame. The failure. For she had led the raiding party, taken the goblin with them.

Despite her orders, Peaseblossom was still with them. He'd been pale and staggering at first, but his glamour was almost back to its normal strength now the terrible iron had been cleansed from his body. Behind him were ranked her guards and she could feel defiance flowing from them.

She glared at Peaseblossom with disdain, and said to one of the guards, 'Take that weakling away. Get him out of my sight!'

But the guard did not move. Instead, he smiled insolently, and fingered the crossbow in his hands, casually nocking a feathered arrow and daring to point it in her direction.

'My lady,' Peaseblossom said with thinly veiled scorn, 'we are getting lost. Our hold on the human world is weak. Even the *goblins* are laughing at us now. Why do we only learn from one of *them* that the humans have been encircling their world with iron? Why haven't you done anything to stop this? Why haven't we been out on the hunts? Why have you not allowed us to be true elves? It's not like the old times.'

His glamour was nearly powerful enough again to

match hers, but his will was even stronger. *How did I not fully see this?* the Queen thought, though her face showed nothing of what she was feeling. Is he daring to *challenge* me? I am the Queen. The King may be in another world, lolling in his barrow, luxuriating in his pleasures, but I am still his queen. There is always a queen to rule. Never a *lord*. She pulled herself up to her full height and glared at her treacherous lord, willing her glamour to its full power.

But there was a chorus of agreement with Peaseblossom from several elves. It was indeed a rare day when an elf agreed with another elf – *disagreement* was a far more normal state of being – but the mass of warriors seemed to be drawing closer together right now, their cold eyes examining their queen. Pitiless. Dangerous. *Nasty.*

The Queen looked at each one before turning back to Peaseblossom. 'You little squib,' she hissed. 'I could put out your eyes in a moment.'

'Oh yes, madam,' Peaseblossom continued as the pressure built. 'And who lets the Feegles run amok? Now that the old crone is gone, the witches are weak. As is the gateway between our worlds. But you, despite all this, you seem still afraid of the Aching girl. She nearly killed you before by all accounts.'

'She did not,' said the Queen.

But the other elves were looking at her now, looking at her like a cat looks at its prey . . . And he spoke true. Tiffany Aching *had* defeated her. The Queen felt her glamour flickering, fading.

'You are weak, madam,' said Peaseblossom.

The Queen *felt* weak. And small, and tired. The trees were closing in. The light seemed to fade. She looked at the faces around her, then rallied and summoned up what power she had left. She was still the Queen. Their queen. They *must* listen to her.

'The times are a-changing,' she said, pulling herself to her full height. 'Iron or not, goblins or not, that world is no longer the same.'

'So we hide away, at your bidding,' said Peaseblossom, his voice full of contempt. 'If the world is changing, it is we who must change it. *We* who must decide how it will be. That is how it has *always* been. And how it *must* be again.'

The elves around him sparkled their approval, their finery dazzling, their cold narrow faces surrounded by the glow of their glamour.

The Queen felt lost. 'You don't understand,' she tried. 'We have that world there, for our pleasure. But if we try to act as it has always been, well, we will be rolled over by time. Just . . . fairies. This is what the iron in that world tells us. There is no future for us there.'

Peaseblossom sneered and said, 'This is rubbish. This talk of no future? We make our own futures. We don't care about humans or goblins. But *you* – you seem to be rather soft on them. Could the great Queen be afraid? You are not certain of yourself, lady. That makes *us* uncertain of *you*.'

The allegiance of elves is spider-web thin and the currency of Fairyland is glamour. The Queen could feel her glamour draining away more and more as her adversary talked.

And then he struck.

'You have become *too* soft, madam,' he roared. 'It began with that . . . girl. And it will end with . . . *me*!' And now his glamour was growing in intensity and his eyes were glowing and the power was building around him, making the other elves wary and obedient. Peaseblossom pointed at the Queen, watching myriad faces and visages flicker across her features – golden hair, dark hair, long hair, short hair, wispy hair . . . balding, baby's hair. Tall, strong . . . weak, childlike. Upright, curled over . . . whimpering. 'The goblins no longer come at your beck and call these days,' he hissed. 'And Fairyland cannot survive without a strong leader. We elves need somebody to prevail – over goblins, over humans and everybody else. What we need now, what our king in the barrow needs, is a *warrior*.'

Peaseblossom was like a snake now, his gaze piercing his victim, even as she shrivelled further and wept from the loss of her glamour.

'We can't be governed by such as *this*,' he concluded contemptuously. He turned to the other elves and said, 'What do you say?'

And in the blankness of their eyes, the Queen saw her future drop away.

'What should we do with her, Lord Peaseblossom?' It was Mustardseed, striding forward to support his new leader.

'She must quit the throne!' another elf called out.

Peaseblossom looked down at his former queen with disdain. 'Take her away, toy with her as you will

– and then *tear off her wings*,' he commanded. 'That will be the penalty for those who fail. Now,' he continued, 'where are my musicians? Let us dance on the shame of her who was once our queen. Kick her memory, if you will, out of Fairyland with her, and may she never come back.'

'Where should she go?' Mustardseed called, grabbing the Queen by one of her tiny, stick-like arms.

But Peaseblossom had gone, weaving amongst the throng of courtiers who now danced in his footsteps.

As the helpless little elf who had once been a queen was dragged from his sight, Mustardseed heard her whisper a few words in her desperation: 'Thunder . . . and Lightning . . . may you feel the force of Thunder and Lightning, Peaseblossom, and then the wrath of Tiffany Aching. It stings to the bone . . .'

And the rain started and became hail.

CHAPTER 9

Good with Goats

The boy standing in the rain looking at Tiffany at the back door of the cottage that was now hers – no longer Granny's – was not like her usual visitor. He was grubby, yes, but it was the grubbiness of the road rather than that of poverty, and he had a goat with him, which wasn't usual. But he didn't look *in need*. She looked closer. His clothing had once been expensive, high-class stuff. *Needy*, though, she thought. A few years younger than her too.

'Are you Mistress Aching, the witch?' he asked nervously as she opened the door.

'Yes,' said Tiffany, thinking to herself, Well, at least he has done *some* homework and he's not come knocking asking for Granny Weatherwax, and he's knocked at the back door just as he should; and I've just made myself some pottage and it will be going cold. 'What can I do for you? I'm sure you need something?' she continued, because a witch turned nobody away.

'No, mistress, by your leave, but I heard people talking about you as I was walking along the road. They say you are the best witch.'

'Well, folks can say anything,' said Tiffany, 'but it's what the other witches think that matters. How can I help you?'

'I want to be a witch!' The last word resonated in the air as if it was alive, but the boy looked serious and unhappy, and he ploughed on doggedly, saying, 'Mr Wiggall – my tutor – told me of one witch who became a wizard, so surely, mistress, the concept must go both ways? They say what's good for the goose is good for the gander, don't they?'

'Well, yes,' said Tiffany, uncertain of herself. 'But many ladies do not like to deal with an unknown man, as it were, in private circumstances. A lot of our work involves being midwives, you know, with the accent on *wives*.'

The boy's Adam's apple was shaking, but he managed to say, 'I know that in the big city the Lady Sybil Free Hospital helps women and men alike. There is no doubt about it, mistress, that when it comes to surgery, there are ladies who are sometimes glad to see the surgeon.' The boy seemed to brighten up for a moment and said, 'I really feel I can be a witch. I know a lot about country things, and I have very little fingers which were of great use some while ago on the road, when I had to deal with a goat in labour, and it was in trouble. I had to roll up my sleeves and fiddle about with care to get the kid lined up to leave his mother. It was messy, of course, but the kid was alive, and the old man who owned the goat was in tears of gratitude.'

'Really,' said Tiffany stonily, wondering when 'good with goats' had become a qualification for being a witch. But the boy looked like a lost soul – so she relented and invited him in for a cup of tea. The goat was shown an overgrown patch of Creepalong Minnie under the apple tree, out of the rain, and seemed content to be left outside, although Tiffany could not help noticing – as any witch would notice – that it gave her an odd look of a kind not often seen in a goat's slotted eyes. The type of look that makes you wary of turning your back, definitely, but something . . . more than that too.

As she beckoned the boy in, she saw You stroll past the apple tree and suddenly stop, her back arching and her tail fluffing out to a remarkable size as she spotted the goat. There was a pregnant pause as the two eyed each other up – and Tiffany could have sworn she saw a quick flash of fluorescent light, greenish-yellow-purple – and then all was suddenly calm, as if there had been an agreement signed and sealed. The goat returned to its nibbling, and You subsided to her normal size and strolled past, almost brushing against the goat's legs. Tiffany was amazed. She had seen Nanny Ogg's cat Greebo run from You! What kind of goat *was* this? Perhaps, she thought with interest, this boy is also more than he seems.

As they sat at the little kitchen table, she learned that the boy's name was Geoffrey and that he was a long way from home. She noticed that he didn't seem to want to talk about his family, so she tried another tack.

'I am intrigued, Geoffrey,' she said. 'Why do you want to be a witch instead of a wizard, which is something traditionally thought of as a man's job?'

'I've never thought of myself as a man, Mistress Tiffany. I don't think I'm anything. I'm just me,' he said quietly.

Good answer! Tiffany said to herself. Then she wondered, not for the first time, about the differences between wizards and witches. The main difference, she thought, was that wizards used books and staffs to create spells, *big* spells about big stuff, and they were men. While witches – always women – dealt with everyday stuff. *Big* stuff too, she reminded herself firmly. What could be bigger than births and deaths? But why shouldn't this boy want to be a witch? She had chosen to be a witch, so why couldn't he make the same choice? With a start, she realized it was her choice that counted here too. If she was going to be a sort of head witch, she should be able to decide this. She didn't have to ask any other witches. It could be her decision. Her responsibility. Perhaps a first step towards doing things differently?

She looked at Geoffrey. There's something about this lad and I don't know what it is, she decided. But he seems harmless and looks quite down-trodden, so I will decide, and I choose to give him a try. As for the goat . . .

'Well,' she said, 'I can give you some bedding in the lean-to, and some food and drink for today. Your goat is your responsibility. But it's getting late now, so we will talk again tomorrow.'

Next morning, whilst waiting for Nanny to drop by, Tiffany went to the lean-to with some food. The boy was asleep. She coughed carefully and the boy jumped at the sound.

'Very well, Geoffrey, now tell me the truth. Are you running away from somebody? Parents, perhaps?'

'No, I'm not,' said Geoffrey, taking a mouthful of the bread Tiffany had brought but pushing the slice of ham to one side.

You little fibber, thought Tiffany, like any witch good at spotting a lie.* She sighed. 'Are you just running away from home then?'

'Well, you could say that, mistress, but I am sixteen and I just wanted to leave.'

'Don't get on with your father, do you?' said Tiffany, and she saw the boy metaphorically jump, as if she'd hit a nerve.

'How could you see that, mistress!'

Tiffany sighed. 'It does say *witch* on the door, doesn't it? I might not be much older than you, but you aren't the first runaway I've dealt with, and I'm absolutely certain there will be many more. Although,' she added, 'never one as highborn as you are, Mister

* Spotting the *truth* was much harder.

Geoffrey. Good coat, you see. Well now, of what use can you be to me and my steading, Geoffrey?'

'Oh, quite a lot, mistress,' he said, trying to sound definite but just seeming hopeful.

And at that moment Nanny Ogg came round the corner of the cottage, not there one minute and then suddenly there, which was, Tiffany knew, Nanny's way. She looked at Geoffrey, made an instant judgement, then winked at Tiffany and said, 'Anythin' going on, Tiff?' Tiffany saw a suggestive grin on Nanny's wrinkled face, as if an apple was suddenly leering at her. Geoffrey looked as if he was going to flee.

'It's all right, Nanny. Meet Geoffrey here,' Tiffany said sharply. 'He wants to be a witch.'

'Really?' Nanny chortled. 'You mean he wants to do magic. Send 'im to the wizards!'

Now Geoffrey looked like a little fawn about to dash away. Nanny Ogg could affect people like that.

'No, he wants to be a *witch*, Nanny. Do you understand?'

Tiffany saw a naughty little gleam in Nanny's eyes as she said, 'So, he wants to be a witch, does he? Perhaps he should learn what us witches has to put up with before he decides proper like. I mean, he might still want to give them wizards a go if he's got any magic in 'im. I know, make him a backhouse boy.' A backhouse boy was like a male scullery maid, doing all the odd, and usually dirty, jobs around the homestead. Things like killing chickens and stringing pheasants, cleaning shoes, peeling potatoes and any

other task that was messy, and occasionally dangerous. There was usually one on Home Farm, gradually
learning what farming was all about. 'I tells you what,'
Nanny continued, looking at the trembling boy, 'let's
try him out with Mr Nimlet. You knows what his toenails is like.'

Yes, like all old men's toenails, Tiffany thought.
She looked at the boy who was so terribly anxious to
be helpful and took pity on him and said, 'There's
more to being a witch than you think, Geoffrey, but if
you'd like to be my backhouse boy, we'll see how you
go. And first of all, I'd like you to do something about
an old man's horrible toenails.'

'You may need a shield,' said Nanny Ogg.

The boy looked at Tiffany questioningly.

'Oh dear,' said Tiffany. 'Mr Nimlet's toenails tend
to be thick and strong and very, very difficult to deal
with. You need really sharp secateurs, and even then
the blessed things go pinging off around the room.
You have to be careful about your eyes too.' She stud-
ied the boy's face; he looked determined to meet any
obstacle, even flyaway toenails. Nanny was grinning,
so Tiffany said, 'I've got a birth to see to. Nanny, would
you be kind enough to take Geoffrey to Mr Nimlet
and see how he does. Oh, and tell him to remember to
collect the clippings – Rob Anybody has a use for
them, so he does.'

'Can I take Mephistopheles with me?' Geoffrey
asked.

Nanny spun on her heels. 'Mephis*what*?' she said
slowly.

'My goat,' Geoffrey said, pointing towards the paddock where Mephistopheles was investigating the remains of the dandelion patch. 'Or rather, he is his *own* goat, but we travel together. He is a very clever companion.'

Nanny snorted.

'See,' Geoffrey added proudly as they watched Mephistopheles daintily cross the paddock and nose open the door of the little shed by the beech tree. 'He has even learned to use the privy.'

And Nanny – for once in her life – was speechless.

CHAPTER 10

Treasure

Deep in the heart of Fairyland, the triumphant Peaseblossom surveyed his court.

Lord Lankin – tall, elegant, a tunic of moss and gorse slung casually over his darkened skin – lounged by his side, toying with a bronze dagger.

'I am your king now,' Peaseblossom declared.

There was silence in the great hall as the elves considered this development and their chances. And one bold elf said, 'What about the King himself? Down in the barrow? What do you think he will say?'

'Something like *this*,' said Peaseblossom, hurling a feathered arrow at the elf, striking him down. Injured, but not dead. Good, Peaseblossom thought. More fun for me later. He gestured to his warriors and the stricken elf was dragged away. 'To hell with the King!' he said, and this time there was no argument.

Every elf knew that Peaseblossom wanted a showdown with the world of humans, of dwarfs and goblins and all the other peoples, wanted elves to run free and fierce through that world once again.

'We have been elves since the dawn of time,' Peaseblossom thundered. 'Too long have humans had the upper hand. Upstart goblins will feel our wrath! The hootings of mechanical rubbish will be swept away! We will take back the world we have been denied!' He smiled, and added softly, 'Those who are not with us will suffer.'

In the world of the train and the swarf, iron could kill elves. But no elf wanted to be the one to feel the dreadful temper of Peaseblossom by gainsaying him. And they were very aware that he knew *exactly* how to make a short word like 'suffer' turn into a very long experience.

And as their new king's glamour built and he stood tall and strong above them, they felt a sense of their world waking up once more.

'What fools these mortals be!' Peaseblossom roared. 'They think they can stop us? They *need* us. They *call* to us. And we will come. We will make them want what they can't have and we will give them nothing but our laughter. We will take everything!'

And the elves cheered.

Becky Pardon and Nancy Upright, dressed in their best, stood in trepidation in front of Miss Tick, who said, 'It's not all spells and broomsticks. It's heavy work, sometimes. Sometimes quite nasty. Yes, Becky?'

'I was there as my granddad died,' said Becky, 'and I watched all the things that had to be done. My dad said I shouldn't, but my mother said, "Let the girl see. She'll find out sooner or later how things are in the world."'

'What I want to know, girls, is that you can deal with magic. Both of you ought to have some basic magic, like blowing out a candle just by thought. What do you think we do with magic?'

Becky said, 'You can cure warts. I know that one. My granny could do that. Magic can make you *beautiful*.' Her tone was wistful, and Miss Tick looked a little more closely at her. Oh, a rather nasty birthmark on one cheek.

'You can magic someone to be your best friend,' Nancy added. 'Or' – with a bit of a blush – 'make a boy like you.'

Miss Tick laughed. 'Girls, I can tell you this, magic won't make you beautiful if you are not. And it certainly won't make you popular. It is not a toy.'

Her face even redder, Nancy said, 'But about boys . . .'

Miss Tick's face did not move a muscle, and then she said, 'What about them?' Nancy's blush was now impressive – if she went any redder, Miss Tick thought, she would look like a lobster. Miss Tick continued, 'You don't have to use spells to get boys, Nancy, and if you wish to know more about that, I daresay Mistress Tiffany will point you towards Nanny Ogg, or possibly your grandmother.'

'Do you have a beau, mistress?' asked Nancy.

'No,' said Miss Tick. 'They get in the way. Now, let's see if you can make a shamble. If you can't do that you are very unlikely to be a witch. A shamble will give you *focus*.' She flung her hand into the air and something was there. The very air seemed to be boiling. Dancing, fluttering . . . alive. And Miss Tick said, 'See how the air moves, how it waits – it's the place where my shamble could be. Where it could advise me.' Suddenly, she had produced an egg in her hand, with some thread, twigs, a small nut. 'These items I had about me could make that shamble,' she said. She looked at the serious little faces, sighed and said, 'But now it's time for each of you to make *your* shamble, and it must have something living in it. Look, just shut your eyes and make a shamble out of anything you have with you.'

She watched them, their faces as solemn as a dirge as they pulled things out of their pockets. Miss Tick knew her witches, knew these girls had the innate magical talent, but to decide to train to be a witch was the kind of decision that took more than just a bit of talent. Hard work would have to come into it too. A lot of hard work. Even then it would not be easy, she knew. Apart from anything else, they had to have parents who would support their choice. A girl might be useful at home, helping with the younger children or working in a family business, for instance. That was *before* the question of grandchildren cropped up. And it always did, oh yes, always.

Miss Tick knew too that you can find out a lot about somebody from what's in their pockets, and sometimes a lot about them from what they *don't* have. She herself generally had a small cheese in one of her pockets – you couldn't do good magic without a snack. Out loud, she said, 'Even a worm is alive, so keeping one in a little box with some wet leaves will help.'

Nancy pulled off one of her boots, saying, 'I've got a caterpillar in there.'

'Well done,' said Miss Tick. 'You have been lucky, but being lucky is only part of being a witch.'

Becky looked rather glum. 'I've got a hairpin – am I allowed to use that?'

Miss Tick sighed. 'In your shamble? Of course, but you must still have something living. Butterflies or ants or things like that, but remember – you shouldn't kill them. Let them fly free.'

'Oh, all right,' said Becky. She rummaged around in the bushes behind them for a moment, then held up a large green hairy caterpillar.

'Copycat!' said Nancy.

Miss Tick laughed. 'Part of being a witch is being clever. Using your eyes and learning from what you see. Well done, Becky.' For Becky now had the caterpillar neatly trussed in a bit of old string, which also seemed to be knotted somehow around one of her fingers. Her other fingers were struggling to push the hairpin into the shamble.

Nancy pouted and held up *her* caterpillar, which appeared to be trying to burrow into a tuft of sheep's wool.

There was a rumble of thunder and a strike of

lightning and both girls said, 'That was me, with my little shamble.'

Miss Tick smiled again. Why were people so keen to look at a sunrise, a rainbow, a flash of lightning or a dark cloud and feel *responsible* for it? She knew that if either girl really believed they could control a storm in the skies, they would be running home, screaming in terror – and their mothers would probably have to wash out the girls' underclothing. Still, a bit of self-belief in a witch was a good start.

'Miss, miss!' said Becky and pointed. There was a hairpin now floating in the air alongside her caterpillar.

'Well done,' said Miss Tick. 'Very well done indeed.'

'Well, what about this, then?' said Nancy, as her own shamble collapsed and the sheep's wool floated to the ground, the little caterpillar perched on top like a witch on a broomstick. She raised her finger, and fire appeared to come out of the tip.

'Excellent,' said Miss Tick. 'Both of you have got the hang of it. After that, it's just a matter of learning, learning every day,' she said sternly.

But what she thought was, Well, Mistress Tiffany will want to see you two and no mistake.

The music was playing in Fairyland – a harmonious melody, notes spiralling into the empty air, where a lazing elf perched on a slender branch near the top of a blossoming tree allowed himself the pleasure of turning each note into a colour, so that they danced above their heads, delighting the court. It doesn't take much to delight an elf. Hurting something is usually top of their list, but music comes a close second.

The musician was a human, lured into the woods by the glamour of an elf's harp, then snatched through to play, play, play for the Lord Peaseblossom. Elves were skilled at keeping their playthings alive, sometimes for weeks, and the man with the flute was a delightful new toy. Peaseblossom wondered idly how long the man would last.

But he was pleased. His warriors were making little sorties into the human world, bringing him back presents such as this. And he knew that with each successful incursion their confidence was growing. Soon they would be ready to make their move . . .

He frowned. He had to speak to Mustardseed. He needed to know that the elf had indeed thrown the wretched remains of the Queen out of Fairyland. He wanted no . . . complications.

Just as he loved to watch wildlife, so Geoffrey observed people. He found them fascinating, and he watched closely all the time, learning more and more from what he saw.

One thing he saw was that the old men seemed somehow *in the way* in their homes. It was so different from Geoffrey's own home, where his father had decidedly ruled the roost. Here, where there were women in the old men's lives, the women held all the power indoors – as they had for the years their men had been out working – and they had no intention of giving any of it away.

This thought was in his mind when he went to tidy up the nostril hairs of Sailor Makepeace, an errand which even Nanny Ogg disliked. Now Mrs Sally Makepeace – too short-sighted to be trusted with a pair of scissors near her husband's nose, as an earlier attempt had proved – appeared to be a good woman, but Geoffrey had noticed that she treated her husband almost as part of the furniture, and that made Geoffrey sad – sad that a seafaring man who had seen so many interesting things now spent much of his time in the pub because his wife was always washing, cleaning, polishing and, when no alternative was around, dusting. She only *just* managed to avoid washing, cleaning and dusting her husband if he sat still for long enough.

Gradually it dawned on Geoffrey that the pub was both an entertainment and a refuge for the old boys. He joined them there one day and bought them all a pint, which got their attention. Then he had Mephistopheles do his counting trick. By the second pint the old boys had become quite avuncular and Geoffrey broached a subject which had been on his mind for a few days.

'So, may I ask what you do, gentlemen?'

As it happened, he got laughter, and Reservoir Slump – a man whose grin, unlike his name, never slipped – said, 'Bless you, sir, you could call us gentlemen of leisure.'

'We are as kings,' said Laughing Boy Sideways.

'Though without the castles,' Reservoir Slump added. ''Less'n I had one once and lost it somewhere.'

'And do you like your leisure, gentlemen?' said Geoffrey.

'Not really,' said Smack Tremble. 'In fact, I hate it. Ever since my Judy died. We never had kids, neither.' There was a tear in his eye and a break in his voice, which he covered up by taking another swig from his tankard.

'She had a tortoise though, didn't she?' Wrinkled Joe, who had been built to a size big enough to pick up cows, put in.

'Right enough,' Smack said. 'She said she liked it because it walked no faster 'n her. Still got the tortoise, but it ain't the same. Not much good at conversation. My Judy would rattle on all day about this 'n' that. The tortoise listens well enough, mind you, which is more'n I could say for Judy sometimes.' This got a laugh.

'It's a petticoat government, when you get old,' said Stinky Jim Jones.

Geoffrey, now pleased to have got the ball rolling, said, 'What do you mean by that?'

And then there was a kind of grumble from every man.

'It's like this, backhouse boy,' said Wrinkled Joe. 'My Betsy tells me what I am to eat and when and where, and if we are together, she fusses around me like an old hen. It's like being a kid.'

'Oh, I know,' said Captain Makepeace. 'My Sally is wonderful and I knows I would be lost without her but, well, put it like this: I was a man once in charge of many other men, and when the weather was fearsomely bad, I would be up there making sure that we didn't founder because it was my job and I was the captain.' He looked around, seeing nods from the others, and then said directly to Geoffrey, 'And best of all, young man, I was a *man*. And now? My job is to lift my feet while she sweeps around me. It's our home and I love her, but somehow I'm always in the way.'

'I know what you mean,' said Stinky Jim. 'You know me, I'm still a good carpenter, well known in the Guild, but my Milly frets about me handling all the tools and so on; and I tell you, when she's got her eyes on me, my hands shake.'

'Would you like them to stop shaking?' asked Geoffrey, though he had in fact seen Stinky Jim lift a tankard to his lips with a hand as steady as a rock. 'Because you gentlemen have given me an idea.' He paused, hoping they would listen. 'My maternal uncle came from Uberwald and his name was Heimlich Sheddenhausen – he was the first man known to have a "shed".'

Stinky Jim said, 'I've got a shed.'

'No offence, you may *think* you have,' said Geoffrey, 'but what is in it? There are goat sheds and chicken sheds and cow sheds, but these sheds I'm proposing are for *men*. I reckon what we need around here is sheds for men. A *man* shed.'

And now he did have their attention. Especially when he hailed the landlord with a 'Let's drink to that, gentlemen! Another pint all round, please!'

The ladies in the villages had taken Geoffrey to their hearts, too. It was astonishing. There was something about his willingness to stop and talk, his gentle smile and pleasant manner, that made them immediately warm to him.

'Mister Geoffrey is so calm, all the time. He never gets in a tizz, oh no, and he speaks wonderful! A real educated man,' old Betsy Hopper said to Tiffany one day.

'And that goat of his!' Mrs Whistler added, folding her impressive arms under her even more impressive chest. 'Looks a testy animal to me, but that Geoffrey has him trotting along all peaceful like.'

'Wish he could do the same to my Joe!' Betsy cackled, and she and Mrs Whistler chortled together as they headed off down the street.

Tiffany watched them go, and began thinking about her backhouse boy, wondering how he made things settle down so well, and she thought, I've seen those people before – the ones who seem to know everybody. They hold the ring, stop the fighting. I think I shall let him go round the houses with me now, and see what he does.

And so Geoffrey went out the next day with Tiffany, hanging on behind her on the broomstick, his face lighting up with sheer joy as Tiffany awkwardly steered the much heavier stick into the mountains; and the houses lit up as soon as he came in, so cheerfully alive. He could be funny, he could sing songs, and somehow he made everything . . . a bit better. Crying babies began to gurgle instead of howl, grown-ups stopped arguing, and the mothers became more peaceful and took his advice.

He was good with animals too. A young heifer would stand for him, rather than skitter off in fright at a stranger, while cats would stroll in and immediately decide that Geoffrey's lap was the place to be. Tiffany once saw him leaning up against a woodland cottage wall with a family of rabbits resting at his feet – *at the same time as* the farm dog was by his side.

Nanny Ogg, after seeing Geoffrey with Tiffany one day, said, 'His heart's in the right place, I c'n smell it. I knows men, you know.' She laughed. 'I've seen a great many in my time in all kinds of circumstances, believe you me. I won't say as he's rich material right now, and some of the other witches might not like a boy comin' into the business, but, Tiff, never let no one tell you as Granny Weatherwax wouldn't like it. Remember, she chose you to be her successor, not none of them. An' you got to do it your way too. Not hers. So if'n you wants to train up this lad, well, you go 'n' do it.'

Tiffany herself was becoming fascinated by Geoffrey's goat. Mephistopheles came and went, but unless she and Geoffrey were off on the broomstick he would usually be somewhere near Geoffrey and it seemed to Tiffany that the goat watched over the boy. They had a code. It was as if the goat could talk just by tapping a hoof, and occasionally there would be a staccato of complicated hoof taps. If Mephistopheles had been a dog, he would have been a pointer, she thought. His master was his friend, and woe betide anyone who took advantage of Geoffrey's good nature – the hooves of Mephistopheles were exceedingly sharp.

When Geoffrey was away, the goat often took himself off. He had soon got the goats at Granny's cottage doing his bidding, and Nanny Ogg said once that she had seen what she called 'that devil goat' sitting in the middle of a circle of feral goats up in the hills. She named him 'The Mince of Darkness' because of his small and twinkling hooves, and added, 'Not that I don't like him, stinky as he is. I've always been one for the horns, as you might say. Goats is clever. Sheep ain't. No offence, my dear.'

The triumph of Mephistopheles – proving Nanny right on both counts – happened at the edge of the woods surrounding the cottage, near the foothills of the nearest mountain, when Geoffrey had taken the cart over to look at a small boy who needed medicine.

On this homestead, on this particular day, the mother was watching Geoffrey. In the flurry of worry about her son she had left the gate to the sheep pen open. And the sheep, like all sheep, got hysterical and were getting out and running away before she looked out of the window and noticed.

'My husband isn't going to like this. It takes ages to get them settled down,' the young mother wailed. 'Look at them, running everywhere!'

Geoffrey put his head out of the window and made a clicking sound to Mephistopheles, whom he had unhitched from the cart and allowed to graze. The goat stopped eating the herbage – and then what happened next went all round Lancre. To hear it, the goat Mephistopheles rounded up those sheep like the best of shepherds. The sheep outnumbered him, of course, but carefully – one after the other – he herded them neatly back through the gate.

When the mother told her husband later that the goat had not only got the sheep into the pen but had also *shut the gate* after them, he thought that was a bit far-fetched, but it still made a good story down the pub, and the legend of Mephistopheles spread rapidly.

Geoffrey and Nanny Ogg told Tiffany the tale. Along with Geoffrey's work for the little boy, that made it a day well done. But Tiffany couldn't help looking at the slot-eyed Mephistopheles. She knew goats. But this goat had a purpose, she was sure. And it was watching her, she noticed, and watching You, who was watching the goat whilst, of course, pretending to look anywhere else. Everybody was watching everybody else, it seemed. She smiled.

And made a decision.

The following morning she took Geoffrey to one side, and told him that she had something special to say to him.

'There's something else,' she said. 'Some . . . little friends I want to introduce you to.' She paused. 'Rob,' she called. 'I know ye is there, and I ask ye to come out now.' She paused. 'There's a wee drop o' scumble here for ye.' She placed a cup with a few drops of the liquor in it on the floor.

There was a movement in the air, a flash of red hair, and Rob Anybody was there, a shiny claymore in his hand.

'Rob, I want you to meet . . . Geoffrey,' Tiffany said slowly, carefully, turning to see how Geoffrey was taking the sight of his first Feegle, but Rob took her by surprise.

'Ach, the wee laddie, we kens him already,' he announced.

Geoffrey coloured up. 'Well, I have been sleeping in the old lean-to,' he said. 'These gentlemen were kind enough to allow me to share their sleeping space.'

Tiffany was astounded. Geoffrey had met the Feegles already! How had she not known! She was the witch. She should have *known*.

'But—' she began, as other Feegles began to appear, one swinging down on string from the ceiling beams, another sidling out from behind a handy bucket, a group edging over to form a semicircle around the scumble on the floor.

'Nae trouble,' said Rob, waving a hand in the air. 'We has had the most interrresting discussions, ye ken, when ye are in your nightie and asleep.'

'But we still watch over ye— *mmpfh, mmpfh*.' Rob had his hand clamped over Daft Wullie's mouth.

'In my *nightie*?' Tiffany began, but then gave up. Oh, what was the use. The Feegles would always be watching over her, and if she had to choose between having Feegles or no Feegles in her life, well, it was an easy decision.

'Ye don't mind, mistress?' Rob added, shuffling his feet as he always did when he found himself having to do the Explainin'. 'Jeannie sez as ye ha' this yon laddie here, and he is a treasure. And ye knows how we Feegles are with treasure – we just ha' to pick it up.'

As one, the Nac Mac Feegles sighed in happiness.

And Tiffany pushed the cup towards them, saying, 'Well, you aren't goin' to steal *this* treasure. But I ken – I *think* – it may be time for me to take Geoffrey along to meet the kelda.'

It was raining hard and they dried off sitting in front of the great fire in the mound. Geoffrey was elated after the trip, and seemed completely unfazed by having to squeeze through the bushes and wriggle down into the Feegle mound.

Involuntarily he squirmed a little,* for every Feegle eye was upon him. Especially that of Maggie, Jeannie's eldest daughter, who had just bravely squeezed in to see the big wee hag and her friend. She ran her hands through her fiery hair now, and put on her best pout.

Jeannie sighed. It would soon be time for her daughter to leave. There could only be one kelda.

Just as she thought this, Rob held out his arms and Maggie scrambled across the chamber to sit by his side. 'My daughter, Maggie,' Rob said proudly to Geoffrey. 'Soon to be off to her ain clan, ye ken, now she is a big grown-up lassie.'

Maggie bridled. 'But can't I stay here?' she wheedled, putting on her best little-lassie voice for her father. 'I like it here, ye ken, and I dinnae want to ha' a husband' – she said the word like it was an abomina-

---

* It was a brave man indeed who could look upon a clan of Feegles and not want to tie the bottoms of his trousers tight around his ankles.

tion to her – 'and babbies. I want to be a *warrior*.'

Rob laughed. 'But ye is a lassie, Maggie,' he said, with a worried look at Jeannie. Had she not taught the hiddlins to Maggie? Taught her what she needed to know to be kelda herself in her own clan?

'But I kens how to fight,' Maggie said sulkily. 'Ask Wee Duggie Bignose – I gave him such a kickin' when we las' had a wee brawl, ye ken.'

Wee Duggie Bignose – one of Rob's scrawnier teenage sons – scuffled his feet awkwardly in the corner and hung his head so that only his nose was visible as the beads in his plaits smacked him on the chin.

'An' I talked to the Toad,'* Maggie went on. '*He* said I dinna ha' to follow tradition, ye ken. He says it's my Yuman Rites.'

'Well, ye ain't a human,' Jeannie snapped. 'An' we'll ha' nae more o' that nonsense. Gae and fetch oor guest a nice bit of mutton now, with some of oor special relish.'

Tiffany knew of the Feegles' relish. Snail was one of the key ingredients.

'Snails,' she murmured to Geoffrey under her breath as Maggie flounced off. To Tiffany's amazement, the young Feegle lassie flounced in *exactly* the same way Mrs Earwig flounced. Except, of course, for the obvious fact that Maggie was only five inches tall, whilst Mrs Earwig was as tall as Tiffany's father.

Jeannie had sharp ears for a little woman. 'Aye, it's

---

* The Toad was the Feegles' lawyer, his toad body the result of a misunderstanding with a fairy godmother.

amazin' what my boys can do with snails, ye ken,' she said. 'They can even make snail whisky.'

Geoffrey smiled politely. 'I thank you kindly, Kelda,' he said softly, 'but I do not eat anything that has been running, swimming or crawling around. And that includes snails. I prefer to let them live.'

'Actually the Feegles cultivate snails,' said Tiffany. 'Everyone has to have a living, Geoffrey, there's no getting away from that.'

'Indeed,' said Geoffrey. 'But not at the expense of others.'

Jeannie leaned forward, her eyes bright, and laid a small nut-brown hand on his arm. The air stilled, and now Geoffrey and Jeannie were looking into each other's eyes.

'There were many like you once,' Jeannie said quietly at last. 'I was right. I sees ye in my cauldron and I sees that ye are one of those who can stop a fight, bring peace . . .' She turned to Tiffany. 'Treasure him, Tir-far-thóinn.'

As they left to head back to the farm for tea, Tiffany pondered on the kelda's words. *Stop a fight. Bring peace.* She might have need of just those very skills. And as she thought this, a shiver ran down her spine, one of those nasty little shivers that are like a message that something dreadful might be about to happen, hard to ignore. On the other hand, she thought, perhaps it was just her body telling her that if it was all right by her, next time perhaps she should say no to the snail relish . . . She did her best to shake the unsettling feeling off, focusing instead on Geoffrey. *Treasure him.* Jeannie is right about him, she decided. There might just be some things that a boy like this can do best.

And right there and then, she made a decision. She would go to Ankh-Morpork – and take Geoffrey with her. It was time anyway, as a sort of head witch, to make a trip to the city. What if all the city witches had heard of her and were talking about her like she was some little upstart? She ought to *know*. And, a little voice whispered in her head, I can maybe see Preston too. She tried to push the thought away. This trip was not about her. It was about being a witch, about doing what she ought to do, and *that* was what she would inform Nanny Ogg when she told her she'd be away for a few days. But the thought of seeing Preston again still crept back into her mind and made her feel a bit . . . tingly.

Geoffrey had got some way ahead down the path, but when Tiffany called him, he came back with a question in his eyes.

'Geoffrey,' she said, 'tomorrow we will go to get you your first broomstick.'

CHAPTER 11

The Big City

It was a long journey to Ankh-Morpork. Tiffany and Geoffrey had to stay over on the way, one night at a local witch's cottage and the other in a barn where the farmer had been delighted at Geoffrey's ability to help him with a troublesome goat. But now they were there – at the great city – and Tiffany watched Geoffrey's mouth drop open as they flew carefully along the route of the river Ankh and into the heart of the capital. Well, she thought to herself, Geoffrey had said he wanted to see the world. Ankh-Morpork would be a very good start.

But she herself was amazed too when she went to the site of the old broomstick workshop, and they were directed to a new site. The railway was still in its infancy – and already there were these arches.

There's a kind of magic in the cavernous spaces

under railway arches and a mystery known only to those who work there. There are always puddles, even if it hasn't rained for weeks, and the puddles are glossy and slimy, the air above filled with the taint of oil and working man's armpit.

It is easy to recognize a habitué of the railway arch. He (it is rarely a woman) is the kind of man who keeps useful nails in old jam jars, and he might spend a considerable time talking about the merits of different kinds of grease or sprocket, and occasionally an onlooker might hear a proprietor saying quietly, 'I can get them for you next week.' Sometimes accompanied with a knowing look and a finger tap to the side of his nose.

If anyone comes and asks for something, well, there will always be someone, often a dwarf, who knows where everything is, and almost always it's *right at the back* of the arch in a darkness of stygian proportions. And when the right piece is found and brought out, well, some people would call it a piece of junk, but in the arch the junk has somehow metamorphosed into *exactly* the item that the buyer really, really wants – no one knows why. It is as if that piece had just been waiting for the right person to wander in.

The dwarfs Shrucker and Dave had relocated their established broomstick business to the second arch in the row, just after an arch where a passer-by's ears were assaulted by the weird noises of musical instruments, and before one where the tang of a harness-maker's fresh leather made its own happy raid on the nose.

It was Dave who rushed towards Tiffany when she came in with Geoffrey in tow. He recognized her immediately – he had had a bad moment when she'd called in a year or two back and let slip she knew the Feegles.* Once a dwarf workshop gets the Feegles, well, they might as well just pack up and go back to the mountains. Taking a big axe with them.

Tiffany noticed how Dave's eyes were everywhere. 'Don't worry, I haven't got any Nac Mac Feegles with me,' she said, though she knew that this might not be quite accurate, for although she had told Rob Anybody that this was hag's business and he and the Feegles had a geas to stay behind, there was no knowing if one hadn't crept into the bristles of her stick somehow and would suddenly pop up waving a big stick and shouting 'Crivens!' But when she said they weren't with her, she heard a sigh, and the dwarf almost grinned. Tiffany dodged a drip that fell merrily from the top of the arch, and added, 'This is Geoffrey, and we've come to get him a stick.' She looked along the row of arches. 'Took a bit of finding you, actually. Your new workshop.'

Dave was eyeing Geoffrey up and down. 'Good for us here,' he said. 'We gets our supplies quicker. And it's easier to go see my old mum. Long journey though.' A belch of smoke from a train steaming over the arches almost enveloped both the dwarf and Geoffrey, and when Tiffany could see them again, Dave – who now had bits of smut sticking to his face –

---

* The Feegles had, in fact, accidentally set fire to Tiffany's broomstick, creating a need for new bristles.

had decided *exactly* what the lad would need. 'A number three, I think,' he said. 'Reckon we've got just the one in stock. Top-of-the-range, you know. Wood all the way from the Ramtops. Special *wizard* wood.' He stroked his beard, flicked the cinders off his nose, and walked around Geoffrey. 'Training to be a wizard then, lad?'

Geoffrey didn't quite know what to say. He looked over at Tiffany. Should he tell these men that he wanted to be a witch?

'No,' said Tiffany, the witch in her making her answer for Geoffrey. 'My friend here is a calm-weaver.'

The dwarf scratched his iron helmet, stared at Geoffrey and said, 'Oh, and what do *they* do, miss?'

Tiffany thought, then said, 'At the moment, Geoffrey just helps me. And for that, gentlemen, he needs a broomstick.' She had been holding two broomsticks, her own and one other, and now she held out the spare. 'But we don't want a new stick,' she said. 'You know how we witches hand our sticks down one to the other. Well, I've got this one, and I think it would do my friend very well with a bit of repair work on it.'

At the word 'repair' Shrucker loomed out of the workshop. He looked almost affronted. '*Repair?*' he groaned, as though anyone choosing to reject the new sticks on offer was missing out on the opportunity of a lifetime. 'You want the lad to begin his career on a used broomstick?' And then he saw the stick, and reeled back on his heels, grimacing and clutching at his back. 'That's . . . Granny Weatherwax's stick,' he said. 'That's famous, that is.'

'A challenge, then,' said Tiffany smartly. 'Or aren't you gentlemen up to the task? I expect I can find someone else . . .'

'Oh, there's no need to be hasty,' said Shrucker, taking off his helmet and wiping his forehead with a woolly cloth. He lit his pipe, giving himself time to think, and examined the stick in front of him.

'I would be much obliged,' said Tiffany.

Shrucker made the usual sucking noise through his teeth. 'Well,' he said slowly at last, 'I could take the shell off. Perhaps a new staff?'

'One of our gentlemen's staffs,' Dave added. He tapped his nose. 'You know, with the . . . special indentation for the . . . delicate parts. A much smoother ride for the lad.'

'Always wanted to get my hands on this stick,' Shrucker said. 'Do some proper work on it. But the dwarfs up there in the mountains said as Mistress Weatherwax always wanted, well . . .'

'A *bodge*,' Dave put in, his forehead creasing as if the word caused him actual pain.

'Well,' said Tiffany, 'I am not that witch, but it's always useful to be friends with any witch.' She smiled sweetly and added, 'I'm feeling friendly at the moment . . . but I might not later.'

This fell into a very handy pause as an almighty roar announced another train shooting overhead, smoke and smut billowing in the air.

'Mistress Weatherwax was a powerful lady indeed,' Shrucker said carefully once the noise had died down.

'And I heard that she never paid her bills,' Dave added grumpily.

'I've got the money,' said Geoffrey. He had been silent so far, allowing Tiffany to speak up for him, but after all, it was going to be his broomstick.

Tiffany saw the dwarfs look up with a smile, Shrucker only just managing to stop himself rubbing his hands together.

'*Some* money,' she said sharply, 'but I don't want my friend to have to use it – I promised him I would arrange this for him. Now, I will tell you what I will do. I will pay in obs.' Obs were the unspoken currency of the dwarfs. Why waste gold? Humans would call it favours, and the currency was negotiable. The obligation of a witch was particularly valuable, and Tiffany knew that. 'Look,' she added, 'the stick isn't *that* bad.'

Shrucker sat down heavily on a chest brimming with bristles.* 'It's funny you should suggest obs,' he said slowly. 'My lumbago is giving me gyp. Comes with the job, you know. Can you do something about that?'

'All right, then,' said Tiffany. 'Just stay there.' And she walked behind him. He shifted around a bit, then sat up straight with a look of amazement on his face.

'Oh my, how did you do that?'

'I've taken away your pain,' Tiffany explained. 'So now it's my pain. And I have to congratulate you for

---

* There are *some* advantages to wearing layers needing double figures to count. Dwarfs like lots of layers of chainmail, jackets and – of course – the traditional woolly vest which actually makes the chainmail unnecessary.

dealing with it, for it is, I must say, very bad. And now I've got it hovering in the air, like a dog on a leash.' The dwarfs automatically looked over her head, just in case there was some kind of big bubble up there marked 'pain', but all that happened was that a big drop of some oily substance fell right into Dave's beard.

'Is there a stonemason in these arches?' Tiffany asked, watching the dwarf whip off his helmet and rummage through the beard. 'If he needs some rocks split, I can use this pain to break them up!' She looked appreciatively at the helmet. 'But that would do,' she added, and as Dave put it down on the ground, she shot the pain into the iron, which to the dwarf's horror actually buckled, steam shooting up to mingle with the steam from the railways above.

The obs were paid. So, his pain gone, Shrucker – a new, upright, lively Shrucker – was now whipping out his measures. He eyed up both Geoffrey and the old stick as he worked his own form of magic.

'How do you dress, sir?' he asked at one point.

Geoffrey was puzzled. 'I usually dress looking out of the window,' he said.

There was a little hiatus as the dwarfs told Geoffrey what 'dressing' meant in the circumstances.

'Ah yes,' he said. 'I never thought about it before.'

Shrucker laughed and said, 'Well, that's about it. All down to me now, but I daresay that if you come back sometime tomorrow, I will have it working a treat.'

*

They left the dwarfs and Tiffany told Geoffrey they would now be visiting Mrs Proust, a witch who loved living in the city. She headed for the elderly witch's shop, Boffo's Novelty and Joke Emporium on Tenth Egg Street. It would be an education for Geoffrey anyway, Tiffany thought. If he decided to follow the witching path, well, he might also need Boffo's at some point – a lot of the younger witches liked Mrs Proust's artificial skulls, cauldrons and warts to give them the right *image* for the job. To someone in need, someone punched so far down that it might seem there was no getting up again, well, a witch with the right look could make all the difference. It helped them to *believe*.

Mrs Proust – a witch who had no need to add nasty witch accessories to her everyday look, given that she had been naturally blessed with the right kind of hooked nose, messy hair and blackened teeth – heard the novelty graveyard groan of the door opening and came over to greet them.

Tiffany laughed. 'That's a new one,' she said.

'Oh yes,' said Mrs Proust. 'Can't keep them on the shelves. Nice to see you, Mistress Aching, and who's this young man, may I ask?'

'This is Geoffrey, Mrs Proust, and we're in the city to fit him up for a witch's broomstick.'

'Are you indeed? A boy? A witch? On a broomstick?'

'Well,' said Tiffany, 'the Archchancellor uses a broomstick sometimes.'

'I know,' said Mrs Proust, 'but there might be trouble.'

'Well, if there is,' said Tiffany, 'the trouble will come to me. I am the chosen successor to Granny Weatherwax, and I think it could be time for a few little changes.'

'Well done,' said Mrs Proust. 'That's the spirit!' She looked at Geoffrey, who was engrossed in the display of naughty doggy-dos. And then and there she loomed close to him, put a clawed hand on his shoulder, and said to him, 'So you want to be a witch, do you?'

Geoffrey stood his ground well, and Tiffany was impressed. So was Mrs Proust.

'Well, mistress,' he said, 'I think I can help witches anyway.'

'Do you?' said Mrs Proust with a glint in her eye. 'We shall see, young man, won't we?' She turned back to Tiffany. 'I am sure there will be some witches who will hate the idea,' she said, 'but it is your way, Tiffany, your time. And Esme Weatherwax was no fool. She could see the future coming.'

'We're staying in Ankh-Morpork until the dwarfs have finished with Geoffrey's stick,' Tiffany said. 'Can we stop here? We might need to stay overnight.'

Mrs Proust grinned. 'Well, there is plenty of space in my spare room, and it would be good to have a chinwag while you are here.' She looked at Geoffrey. 'Have you been to the city before, young man?'

'No, Mrs Proust,' he replied quietly. 'We lived in the Shires, and my father was the only one to travel.'

'Well then, my son Derek will show you around,' Mrs Proust said, sounding satisfied. She followed this up with a shout for the lad, and Derek – the sort of lad you wouldn't notice in a crowd of two, meaning that he shared very little in common with his mother's looks – came stumbling up the stairs from the workshop below.

Ankh-Morpork, Tiffany thought, would *definitely* be an education.

As the two lads left, Mrs Proust said, 'So how are things going with your young man then, Tiffany?'

Tiffany sighed. Why were elderly witches so *nosy*? But then she thought: Actually, *all* witches are nosy. It's part of what being a witch *is*. And she relaxed. At least Mrs Proust wasn't trying to push her Derek at her again.

'Well,' she said, 'I do like Preston and he likes me – he's my best friend – but I'm not sure either of us are ready for, well . . . anything *more*. You see, he does a lot of wonderful work at the hospital and we write to each other and even meet up sometimes.' She paused. 'I think we are married to our jobs.' She swallowed, a lump suddenly appearing in her throat. 'It's not that we don't want to be together . . . I mean, I . . . but . . .' The words trailed off and Tiffany just looked totally miserable now.

Mrs Proust did her best to look sympathetic. 'You're not the first witch to have that problem, my dear,' she said. 'Nor will you be the last.'

Tiffany could feel the tears beginning. She said, 'But why do I feel like this? I know a part of me does want to be with Preston – and it would make my family so happy! – but I also want to be a witch. And

I'm *good* at it – I know it's a terrible thing to say, but I measure myself against the other witches and I know I'm better than most of them when it comes to witch-craft. I can't *not* do it.' A tear threatened to trickle down her cheek. 'Just like Preston can't not be a doctor,' she finished sadly.

'Oh, I understand all that,' Mrs Proust said. 'But this is today. It's soon going to be tomorrow and things can change. Things are changing, especially for you young people, when you both want to do different things. Just do the work you find in front of you and enjoy yourself. After all, you are both still young, so you still have options for the future. Just like my Derek.'

'But that's the difficulty,' said Tiffany. 'I don't really *want* options. I know what I want to do. I enjoy my work, I really do.' This last word came out as a squeal. 'I just wish Preston could be with me,' she added quietly. 'Not here in the city.'

'But you tell me he is training to be a doctor,' said Mrs Proust. 'And he loves his work. You wouldn't want him to give that up for you, now would you? So don't worry so much. Think yourself lucky and don't run ahead of the world. There is a saying, Don't push the river. Although, of course, in *Ankh-Morpork* you can push very hard,' she added with a cackle.* More encouragingly, she continued, 'Maybe in a year or two your young man can be a doctor in the same place

* 'River' as a term doesn't quite describe the sludge of the river Ankh in its course through the city, though it is of course a decent torrent up in Lancre.

where you are a witch. I had my Mr Proust. You can have your Preston. Just not yet.'

'When I go around the houses,' Tiffany said quietly, 'I also see how some of the marriages, well, they're not really . . .' That hung in the air.

'There *are* happy marriages,' Mrs Proust said. 'Think of your parents, maybe? Isn't that a happy marriage? Now, let your Auntie Eunice give you some help. Go and see your boy and have a chat to him.' She paused and added shrewdly, 'He's not interested in anyone *else*, is he?'

'Oh no,' said Tiffany. 'He's working with the Igors* and he said that he didn't fancy the Igor girls because he likes a girl who stays the same shape every day. The Igorinas like to experiment.'

Geoffrey came back late with Derek, singing a song worthy of Nanny Ogg, but Tiffany got a good night's sleep – a rare treat! – and then a breakfast of ham and eggs courtesy of Mrs Proust. While Geoffrey and Derek still slept, Tiffany decided to go and visit Preston. Mrs Proust's words had got her thinking.

She headed for the Lady Sybil Hospital over in Goose Gate, but paused at the door, strangely uncertain. She hadn't told Preston she would be in the city. Would her visit be a good one, or . . . ?

---

* Uberwald servants, usually working as doctors, or assistants to mad scientists, who believe a stitch in time saves a lot of bother later. They like to swap body parts from an early age, often within the same family, such that an Igor saying 'He's got his uncle's nose' really *means* something.

It was a free hospital, so there was a queue of people waiting, all hoping for the happy result of seeing a doctor *before* old Boney turned up with his scythe. It looked like nobody would be moving for some time, so Tiffany did something she knew she shouldn't.

She stepped outside her body, leaving it standing demurely by the gates. It was an easy trick for a witch, but still dangerous, and she had no real reason to take the risk. Except . . . the Igor girls? They were beautiful . . . once you looked past the discreet stitches, anyway.

She slid silently through the crowd, doing her best to ignore her First Thoughts, Second Thoughts and even her Third Thoughts, and drifted into the hospital itself, floating along the corridors until she found Preston.

He was in his element, his gaze focused on a patient with a rather unsettling hole in the stomach – and when Preston looked at anything, it *knew* it was being looked at and was liable to stand up and salute. This was especially true of some of the spare parts the Igors used – a most unsettling experience – and Preston was indeed surrounded by Igors. And yes, that included girls. But, happy sight, he was paying them *no attention.*

Tiffany sighed with relief, and then – allowing herself to listen to her Second Thoughts, which were telling her off in a style uncomfortably like the voice of Granny Weatherwax – whisked herself back into her body, which wobbled slightly as she took control again.

The queue had moved a few inches. But the pointy hat took her to its head and the porter let her through immediately. She waved away his offer of directions and marched confidently off down the corridor, leaving the porter to mutter, 'I didn't even need to tell her where he was. That's a proper witch, that is.' For at the hospital it was all too easy to set off confidently for one place but find yourself in the basement – which these days was home to goblins, who maintained the huge boilers and had set up a workshop manufacturing the very finest surgical instruments. Still, most people eventually made it out of the hospital and the record seemed to be improving.

Preston was very glad to see Tiffany, saying, 'I heard about Granny Weatherwax. Well done for being the top witch, it couldn't happen to a better person; are you allowed to tell all the other witches what to do now?'

'What!' Tiffany laughed. 'It's like herding goblins. No! Goblins are easier. Anyway, it works like this: I don't tell them what to do, and they allow me to work hard – just as I like it.'

'Just like me and the Igors,' said Preston. 'But I've got good news too. Doctor Lawn is getting on now and he has promoted me to be a surgeon; usually only Igors can be surgeons, so that's a real feather in my hat.'

Tiffany kissed him, and said, 'That is good news; I am so proud of you! But I do wish he would give you more time off – and you could come and see me. Letters can only say so much . . .' Her voice faltered. 'Though I do so love the way you write.'

'And I like your letters too,' Preston said, 'and I wish I could visit home more. But I do enjoy the work here, Tiffany. And people need me. Every day. I've got a talent and it would be criminal not to use it.'

'Yes, I know,' said Tiffany. 'That's the story of my life as well. Our skills, you will find, could be our gaolers.' And it struck her that just as Preston was looking into people in one way – he knew the names of all the bones now, and could even say hello to a few of them – she was learning to look into people another way: into their heads, their minds. 'But I couldn't do anything else,' she finished, a touch wistfully.

Preston said, 'No. Me neither.'

Then the time for talking was over, and it was just Tiffany and Preston, together, snatching the moment and saying more with their eyes than any words could convey.

And it was magic; a different kind of magic.

Mrs Proust went with them to pick up Geoffrey's broomstick – Granny Weatherwax's stick had been a *legend*, and she was curious to see if the dwarfs had managed to make it work.

Dave greeted them and said, 'Well, here it is. It's a good stick, it really is. I reckon Mistress Weatherwax never took any care of it at all, no matter what we dwarfs did to fix it up.'

'All she did was curse it,' Shrucker put in a bit sourly. It was clear that, to him, a broomstick was almost like a living creature.

The stick gleamed. It shone. It looked almost alive, and the bristles were sleek. It was *almost* Granny Weatherwax's old stick, if you discounted the new shell for the staff and new bristles.* Tiffany and Geoffrey stared at it in amazement while the two dwarfs looked on, smiling.

'It's the best we ever made – I mean, mended,' Shrucker added. 'But please, use it gently and keep it oiled. Nothing but the best for Mistress Aching.' He straightened up proudly, a dwarf who could stand tall to his full four foot once again.

Mrs Proust ran her fingers against the stick and nodded. 'This is an excellent stick,' she said. 'Look, it's even got a little cup to hold your drink.'

Shrucker gave her a funny look. 'And special today, for our good customers,' he said instead, 'those who *don't* bring . . . trouble' – with a sideways glance at Tiffany – 'we have a bonus little gift.' He proudly presented Geoffrey with two furry white cubes covered in assorted spots. 'You can tie them on the strap,' he said. 'Very popular with the lads for their carriages, these. Some lads also keep birds in a little cage to sing as they go along. They call it in-carriage entertainment.'

Geoffrey shuddered at the thought. A bird, in a cage? His heart felt sorrow for them. But the broomstick, well, he could barely wait to have a go on it.

Dave sniffed and said, 'There you go, young man. So, do you want to give it a test drive then?' He

---

* So a new stick, really. As new as the famous nine-hundred-year-old family mining axe owned by the King of the Dwarfs was anyway.

handed him the stick, and said, 'Go on. Go to the end of the arches and give it a whirl.'

Tiffany was about to speak, but already Geoffrey was sparkling with excitement. She looked at his glowing eyes and said, 'Well, all right, Geoffrey. You've been on my stick with me, and watched the broomsticks going past overhead. Go up slowly, just a bit at a time.'

She might as well have talked to the wall. Geoffrey straddled his broomstick, ran past the neighbouring arch, jumped – and went skywards very fast. A series of nightmares flashed through Tiffany's mind. There was a distant *boom!* Then a little dot in the sky got bigger, and there was Geoffrey, coming back down, grinning from ear to ear.

Tiffany almost squealed. 'Look, Mrs Proust. He's picked it up already. It took me *ages* to learn how to fly.'

'But of course,' said Mrs Proust. 'That's this here technology.'

And Shrucker said, 'Wow! He's a natural. Not even the goblins can do that.' For Geoffrey had just looped the loop, then got off his stick, leaving it hovering a few feet above the cobbles.

'How did you do *that*?' asked Tiffany, genuinely impressed.

'I don't know,' said Geoffrey. 'Just a knack, I suppose.'

And Tiffany thought: When Geoffrey's not anxious, he radiates calmness, which probably means he sees more things and finds more things than other people do. It makes him open to new things too. Yes, it's a knack all right.

Waving a goodbye to the dwarfs and Mrs Proust, Tiffany and Geoffrey took off together and floated back towards Lancre and the distant mountains, Geoffrey getting the feel of his stick immediately and disappearing into the sky ahead of Tiffany.

She caught him up just outside the outskirts of Ankh-Morpork – he was soaring and swooping at a ferocious speed. 'You do know your trousers are smouldering, don't you?' she said with a laugh.

Geoffrey patted the smoke away with a sudden anxiety that made the stick wobble, saying, 'Please don't tell Nanny about this when we get back! She'll laugh at me!'

But after they had travelled back to Lancre – quite a bit faster than on the outward journey – and before she set off back to the Chalk, Tiffany did of course tell Nanny Ogg. And the older witch did indeed laugh.

'It was amazing, though,' Tiffany said. 'Flying seemed so natural to him.'

'Ha!' said Nanny. 'Every man has a broomstick in the house, but they just don't often know how to use 'em!'

CHAPTER 12

An Elf among the Feegles

There was thunder and there was lightning. It was raining and there was water everywhere, running down the chalk hills.

The Queen screamed as she was thrown out of Fairyland, her wings torn from her body, her blood staining her shoulders. A scream with a life of its own, which ended in a dew pond on the Chalk, surprising a stoat on the prowl.

And Tiffany Aching woke up.

Her heart was thumping, a sudden chill making her shiver in the dark of the night. She looked over at the window. What had made her wake? Where was she needed?

She sat up and reached wearily for her clothes . . .

Up on the downs, the Feegle mound was still its usual

hive of activity and song, a Feegle mound being very like a beehive but without the honey, and to be sure a Feegle could sting much worse than a bee. But when something was being celebrated – and they didn't need much to pick a reason for a celebration – the Nac Mac Feegles always made sure that it went on happily for a long time.

A short time past midnight, however, the revels that night were interrupted by Big Yan, the Feegle nightwatchman, as he ran in from the storm raging outside.*

He kicked the helmet of his chief, the Big Man of the clan, and shouted, 'There's elves here! I can smell it, ye ken!'

And from every hole in turn, the clan of the Nac Mac Feegle poured out in their hundreds to deal with the ancient enemy, waving claymores and swords, yodelling their war cries:

'Ach, stickit yer trakkans!'

'Nac Mac Feegle wha hae!'

'Gae awa' wi' ye, yer bogle!'

'Gi'e you sich a guid kickin'!'

'Nae king! Nae quin! We willnae be fooled agin!'

There is a concept known as a hustle and bustle, and the Feegles were very good at it, cheerfully getting in one another's way in the drive to be the first into battle, and it seemed as if each small warrior had

---

* The Baron had given the Feegles their own land and the promise that no sharp metal beyond a knife would go near them, but the Feegles lied all the time themselves, so liked to be ready with boot and heid and fist should any other liar come calling.

a battle cry of his own – and he was very ready to fight anyone who tried to take it away from him.

'How many elves?' asked Rob Anybody, trying to adjust his spog.

There was a pause.

'One,' said Big Yan sheepishly.

'Are ye sure?' said Rob Anybody, as his sons and brothers flowed around him and hurried past to the mouth of the mound. Ach, the embarrassment. The whole Feegle colony bristling with weaponry, full of alcohol and bravado and apparently nothing to do with it. Of course, they were always itching for a fight but most Feegles itched all the time, especially in the spog.

They rushed about on the sodden hilltop looking for the enemy, while Big Yan led Rob to the dew pond on the top of the hill. The storm had passed and the water gleamed under the stars. There, half in, half out of the pond, the battered body of an elf lay groaning.

And indeed it was, apparently, a solitary elf. You could almost hear the Feegles thinking: One elf? Feegles loved a spat with the elves, but . . . just one? How did that happen?

'Ach crivens, it's a long time since we had a reely good fight.' Rob sighed, and for a moment he was, for a Feegle, quite sombre.

'Aye, but where there's the one, there's sure to be a plague o' them,' Big Yan muttered.

Rob sniffed at the air. The elf just lay there and it was doing nothing. 'There are nae ither elves aboot. We'd smell them if they were,' he pronounced. He reached a decision. 'Big Yan, ye and Wee Dangerous Spike, grab a-hold of that scunner. Ye know what to dae if it gets feisty. Awf'ly Wee Billy Bigchin' – he looked for the clan gonnagle, who was the least likely to mangle the facts – 'hie ye awa' tae the kelda and tell her what's abroad. What we are bringin' back to the mound.' Then he shouted so that the rest of the clan could hear him, 'This elf is oor prisoner. A hostage, ye ken. That means ye are nae tae kill it until ye are told.' He ignored the grumbles from the clan. 'As tae the rest o' ye, tak guard around yon stones. And if they come in force show them what the Feegles can dae!'

Daft Wullie said, 'I can play the harmonica.'

Rob Anybody sighed, 'Aye, weel, I suppose that puts the willies up me, so wud likely keep them awa'.'

Back at the mound – *outside*, mind, for no elf would find itself a place for long inside a Nac Mac Feegle mound – the kelda looked at the stricken elf and then back at Rob Anybody.

'Just one?' she asked. 'Weel, one elf alone is nae challenge tae a young Feegle even. And this elf has been beaten, aye, its wings torn from its back. Did oor boys dae that?'

'No' us, Jeannie,' said Rob. 'Big Yan said it drappit oot o' the sky intae the auld dew pond up by the stones, ye ken. It were battered like that afore it got there.' He looked anxiously at his wife, who had a frown on her face. 'We be warriors, no' butchers, Jeannie. The lads are raring tae gae, o' course, and if yon elf was facin' me in a fight, my claymore would ring aloud, but whin it looks like a wee slunkit mowpie there's nae honour in killin' it.'

'Brawly spoken, Rob,' said the kelda as she considered the unconscious creature. 'But why just one? Are ye sure?'

There was a groan from the elf and it stirred. Rob's claymore leaped into his hand but the kelda gently held him back. The bedraggled elf groaned again and whispered something, its voice weak and faltering. The kelda pricked up her ears and listened carefully before turning to her husband with some surprise.

'It said, "Thunder and Lightning"!' she said.

The elf whispered again and this time Rob could hear the words too: *Thunder and Lightning.*

Everyone on the Chalk knew about Granny Aching's famous dogs, Thunder and Lightning, long gone but, as all the local farmers believed, still roaming the hills in spirit. Several years before, young Tiffany Aching had summoned them to help rid the Chalk of the Queen of Fairyland. Now here was an elf, at the very entrance to a Feegle mound, invoking their names.

'There's somethin' I dinnae like aboot this,' said the kelda. 'But I cannae decide what it means withoot oor hag. Can ye send for her, Rob?'

'Aye, Hamish can gae. I mun get back to the stones and the clan.' He looked at his wife anxiously. 'Will ye be all richt here wi' that scunner?'

'Aye, I'll take it inside, ye ken, to dry by the fire. It's too weak tae dae anything tae me. And the boys kin look after me.' Jeannie nodded over at a happy bundle of young Feegles, who were tumbling out of the mound, waving their crescent-shaped clubs in the air.

'Aye, it will be good practice for them,' Rob said, looking at them proudly. And then ducked as one of the Feegles let loose his club and it shot through the air and nearly smacked him on the ear.

To his amazement, the weapon swung round in the air and shot back to the young Feegle who had hurled it, giving him a bang on the head, saving Rob the trouble.

'Ach, boys,' Rob shouted. 'It fights ye back! Now that's a weapon fit for any Feegle. Double the fun, ye ken.'

Tiffany had just begun to dress when there was a whistling sound outside, followed by the thump of something falling past, merrily breaking branches, and then a tapping on the window.

She opened the window and she could see a tangle of cotton and cloth down below, which after a good kickin' fell away to reveal Hamish, the Feegle aviator.*

With the window open, it was suddenly very cold in the bedroom, and Tiffany sighed and said, 'Yes, Hamish, now tell me what you need me for.'

Hamish, adjusting his goggles, jumped up onto the sill and into the room. 'Oor kelda hae sent for ye, hag o' the hills. I mun get ye tae the mound as soon as ye can.'

---

* Hamish's trained buzzard Morag did the actual flying, of course. Mastering the art of flying wasn't a problem for Hamish. Landings were another matter.

It had been a long day, but Tiffany knew that if the kelda wanted her, even after midnight, then that was where she needed to be. So she put on her heavy-duty travelling pants, left a saucer of milk on the hearth and cranked up the broomstick.

And once again You was staring at her, the white cat who seemed now to be everywhere.

The fire inside the mound was like a furnace.

The young Feegles who had been left to guard their kelda were all scowling at the hated adversary. When Rob Anybody returned, each Feegle wanted to look like he had been the one to keep the scunner from causing any trouble. Especially now she was *inside* the mound.

But the elf appeared to have been crying.

The kelda shifted her bulk and said softly, 'So now, elf, you come to me. For what purpose? Why do we nae kill ye right noo?'

This caused a susurration of expectation among the Feegles, each of whom was hoping to kill an elf before too long, and trepidation on the part of the elf.

The kelda turned away, then said softly, 'I ha' the secrets of the hiddlins, and what I see is that everything we do today was ordained afore the seas were made. There is nae turning back. But there is a mist in what is afore me. I cannae see for sure beyond this day, ye ken.'

There was a shiver from the elf.

'Haed yer tongue richt noo, elf,' Jeannie mused.

'For I wonder what my position were tae be if things were otherwise. Yoor people are sae . . . inventive.'

That caused the young Feegles to brandish their weapons playfully, and the kelda turned back to the elf and went on, 'Ye are sent tae me by the calling of Thunder and Lightning. I ken those twa spirit dogs, aye, and also their owner, will be with us soon enough. Right now, shivering elf, tell me what is the geas you are under? Why are ye here? Who are ye? What is your name? And dinnae lie tae me, elf. Because I ha' a way of kenning.' The kelda looked at the elf – tiny, shrivelled, rags and drying blood – something that could have been kicked about for days before being left to end its life in a dew pond.

'I can't ask for anything, Kelda. I am empty to your pleasure or your wrath.' The Queen's voice was very small. 'But I was – until just now – the Queen of the Elves.'

The young Feegles stopped rattling their weapons and began to crowd nearer. Could this wee little mowpie be the fearsome Quin they had heard about from the Big Man? Wee Duggie Bignose leaned over and bravely poked the elf with his finger, the effect slightly spoiled by his rabbit-skull helmet falling over his eyes and making him reel forwards as it stuck on his nose.

'Get awa' wi' ye, lads,' the kelda said sharply, rapping Duggie's helmet with her fist and spinning him away from the elf. She turned back to the Queen. Drily she said, 'Then it appears ye ha' had a misfortune, your majesty. And I've a mind to mention that there appear to be many queens of the elves. I ask myself, which one do we have here? What I want is your *name*, madam. Be careful: if ye should gi' me a name which is nae yours, your majesty will find me somewhat acerbic.'

The elf said, 'My name, Kelda, is *Nightshade*.'

The kelda sent a sideways look to Rob Anybody that said, What have we here? The real Quin? For she knew that although there were many leaders among the elves of Fairyland, there had always been only the one King and Queen. The King, of course, had gone away some years ago, creating a separate world just for himself and his pleasures, leaving the Queen behind. And although it was rarely used, the Queen did have a name of her own. A name known to the Feegles from their time in Fairyland. A name now to be passed from each kelda to her successor. The name of *Nightshade*.

Quietly she said, 'We are the Nac Mac Feegle, and we dinnae bow down to queens.'

Rob Anybody was silent, but the sound of him whetting his claymore against the stone was a song, an invitation to death. Then he looked up and his gaze was fearsome. 'We are the Nac Mac Feegle! The Wee Free Men! Nae king! Nae quin! Nae laird! Nae master! *We willna' be fooled again!*' he thundered. 'Your life, elf, is on the edge o' my blade.'

There was a scuffling noise behind them and Tiffany crawled in, followed by Hamish, with more Feegles pushing around after them.

'It's happy I am tae see ye, hag o' the hills,' Jeannie

said. 'We have ourselves . . . an *elf*. Tell us, what shall we dae with it?' And at that word 'elf' every weapon sang.

Tiffany looked at the elf. It was in terrible shape and she said, 'We aren't the kind of people who kill those who are unarmed.'

Rob Anybody put up his hand. 'Excuse me, mistress, but some of us do, or are.'

Nonplussed, Tiffany thought, Well, I'm their big wee hag, and the kelda has asked for my help. And then, despite its bedraggled state, she recognized the Feegles' captive. After all, how could she have forgotten?

'I know you, elf, and I told you never to come here again,' she said. She frowned. 'You remember? You were a great elvish queen and I was a little girl. I drove you away with Thunder and Lightning.'

She watched the elf's face when she said that. It had gone white.

'Yes,' said the elf faintly. 'We came raiding into your world, but this was before the time of . . . iron.'

Her face twisted with fear and Tiffany sensed a change in the world, a feeling that she stood between two courses of action, and what she did next would *matter*. This, she realized, was what she had suspected was coming her way, what Jeannie had warned her about. A witch is always on the edge, between the light and the dark, good and bad, making choices every day, judging all the time. It was what made her human. But what was it that made an elf? she wondered.

'I hear that the goblins believe that the railway engines have a soul, elf,' she said softly. 'Tell me, what kind of soul have you? Do you run along your own elvish rails? With no time or place for turning?' She looked at the kelda and said, 'Granny Aching told me to feed them that was starving and clothe them as is naked and help the pitiful. Well, this elf has come to my turf – starving, naked, pitiful – do you see?'

The kelda's eyebrows rose. 'Yon creature is an elf! It has nae care for ye! It has nae care for anyone – it disnae even care for other elves!'

'You think then there is no such animal as a good elf?'

'Ye think there *is* such a thing as a guid elf?'

'No, but I am suggesting that there is a possibility that there *might* be one.' Tiffany turned to the cowering elf. 'You are no queen now. Do you have a name?'

'Nightshade, my lady.'

'Aye,' said the kelda. 'A poison.'

'A word,' said Tiffany sharply.

'Well, yon *word* has been kicked out as if life was nae more than a game o' chess; and now it turns to the lassie she tried to destroy years ago,' the kelda said. 'She ha' been beaten verra severely, but here she comes, to your steading, asking ye for sanctuary.' There was a gleam in her eye as she said, 'What now, Tiffan? It's up to ye. Only ye can decide. This elf nearly killed ye afore, and yet ye want to help her . . .' The kelda's face looked grave. 'Fairies are nae to be trusted, we Nac Mac Feegle ken that! But ye are the girl who made the Wintersmith mind his manners. Don't fret for the Quin, but through her footsteps there may be a war . . .'

Tiffany bent down to the shrunken, quivering elf. Face to face with her she quietly said, 'Last time we met, Nightshade, I was a small girl, hardly capable of any magic whatsoever.' She pushed her face closer. 'How much better at magic am I now! I am the successor of Granny Weatherwax, aye, and you elves were right to fear *her* name. And now you might say that the life of elves is hanging on you. And if you let me down, I'll send you back to the Feegles. They have no love for elves.' The kelda caught her eye and Tiffany said, 'Does that sit well with you, Kelda?'

'Och, weel,' said the kelda, 'somebody had to taste the first snail.'

'Yes,' said Tiffany. 'And goblins were treated as nobodies until somebody gave a thought to them. Give the Lady Nightshade no reason to hate you, but if she breaks the rules then I promise you – and, ye ken well, a promise from the hag o' the hills is a serious business indeed – that will be the end of it.'

Feegle eyes were still watching Nightshade with unabashed loathing. It seemed to Tiffany that the air between them and the elf was humming with hatred, in both directions.

Rob Anybody said, 'You, elf, ye know that your kind will nae trick us agin. And so it is for the sake o' Mistress Aching that we are lettin' ye live. But be told. The hag o' the hills gets a bit restive when she sees us killin' people, and if she wasnae here, ye would be bleeding again.'

There was a chorus of threats from the Feegles – it was clear that if they had their preference, Nightshade would be a damp little piece of flesh on the floor by now.

Rob Anybody smashed his claymore against the ground. 'Listen to the big wee hag, ye scunners. Aye, ye, Wee Clonker and Wee Slogum, Wee Fungus and Wee Gimmie Jimmie. She's made a truce with the auld Quin, believin' yon schemie might have a wee passel o' goodness in her.'

Big Yan coughed and said, 'I dinnae want to gainsay the hag but the only guid elf is a deid elf.'

'I suggest ye dinnae tak that road, brother. As a gonnagle, I say to leave a space for goodness tae get in, as it was in the Lay of Barking Johnnie,' said the gonnagle, Awf'ly Wee Billy Bigchin, an *educated* Feegle.

'Is that the mannie who balanced a thimble on his neb for a week and afterwards had a wonderful singing voice?' asked Daft Wullie.

'Nae, ye daftie.'

'Why are you getting all het up about this? Dinnae fash yersel'. The first time yon elf touches a body, it will be a *deid* elf, an' that's the way to find out,' said Wee Dangerous Spike.

'Weel now,' said Rob Anybody, 'this is what the hag wants and I tell ye, that's the end of it.'

'And I tell you one more thing, Rob Anybody,' Tiffany said. 'I will take this elf away with me. I know that you will come with me, but I will need a Feegle or two to bide by her side and watch her for me. Wee Mad Arthur? You were in the Watch – I pick you for one.' She looked around. 'And ye, Big Yan. Don't let this little elf get the better of *ye*. I want to say to you both, this elf is a *captive*. And captives have to be looked after. As a constable, you – Wee Mad Arthur – know that people don't fall down wells unless they've been pushed. I suggest you think about this. And generally speaking, they don't often fall downstairs either unless they've been pushed. There are to be no little things like, "Ach, weel, we let her out for a walk and she ran away and was knocked over by a rampaging stoat," or, "She died resisting arrest by fifteen Feegles." No great swarm of bees to sting her a lot. No great big bird dropping her in a pond. No great big wind which comes out of nowhere and blows everything away. No "She fell down a rabbit hole and no one ever saw her again."' She looked around sternly. 'I am the hag o' the hills and I will *know* how it happened. And then there would be a . . . reckoning. *Do you understand me?*'

'Oh, waily, waily, there's to be a reckoning,' Daft Wullie moaned, and there was an embarrassed shuffling of feet as the Feegles reconsidered their plans. Big Yan absent-mindedly poked his finger up his nose and closely examined what he found there before stuffing it into his spog for later inspection.

'Right, well, that's settled then,' said Tiffany. 'But I will not abide troublesome elves coming onto my turf, gentlemen.'

CHAPTER 13

Mischief . . . and Worse

The elves liked being troublesome. When elves come, they hunt with stealth. There are little changes in the world, at first just mischief.

As in the cellar in the Baron's Arms, where something had happened to the beer. No matter how often or how thoroughly John Parsley cleaned and changed spigots and barrels, the beer was suddenly full of floaties, barrel gushies, skunkies and the like, and the publican was tearing out his hair – of which he had little enough to start with.

And then, in the bar, someone said, 'It's the elves again. It's their sort of joke.'

'Well, it doesn't make *me* laugh,' said Thomas Greengrass, while John Parsley was almost crying. And as happens in a pub, everyone else joined in, and there was talk of elves, but no one believed it – though later, at home, more than one new horseshoe was suddenly nailed up on the doorframe.

People laughed and said, 'Anyway, we've got our own witch here.'

'Well,' said Jack Tumble, 'no offence, but she's never here these days. It seems she's spending more of her time over in Lancre.'

'Oh, come on,' said Joe. 'My Tiffany is doing a man's work every day.' He thought for a moment (especially since he knew that what he said might easily get back to his wife via Mrs Parsley). 'Better than that, she's doing a woman's work,' he added.

'Well, how do you explain the beer?'

'Bad management?' said Jack Tumble. 'No offence meant, John. It's difficult stuff, beer.'

'What? My pipes are as clean as the rain and I wash my hands when I change a barrel.'

'What is it, then?'

Someone had to say it again, voice their conclusion, and it was said: 'Then it *can* only be the fairies.'

'Oh, come on,' said Joe. 'My Tiffany would have dealt with *them* in a brace of shakes.'

But the beer was still sour . . .

While over in Lancre, high up in the forests of the Ramtop mountains, Martin Snack and Frank Sawyer were anxious. They had trudged for days from the last town, Hot Dang, to get this far and had left the main cart track hours before. Their empty stomachs and the late afternoon shadows were hurrying them up but it was hard going along the faint tracks on the steep hillside. If they didn't find the logging camp soon, this was likely to be their second night without shelter. They had heard wolves howling in the distance the night before. And now, as the temperature dropped, it began to snow.

'I reckon as we are lost, Frank,' said Martin anxiously.

But Frank was listening carefully, and now he heard a roaring sound in the distance. 'This way,' he said confidently.

And indeed, within no more than another five minutes they were close enough to hear the sound of people talking, and soon after, the aroma of something cooking, which seemed a good sign. Then, in a break between trees, they could see the camp. There were a number of large hairy men moving about, while others sat on tree stumps and one was stirring something bubbling over on an almost red-hot portable stove.

As the boys emerged from the trees, the men looked up. One or two laid a hand on their large and serviceable axes which were never far from their sides, and then relaxed when they saw how young the boys were. An elderly lumberjack in a big checked jacket with a fur-lined hood – the kind of man that you wouldn't talk to unless you heard him talk first – walked over to meet them.

'What are you lads doing here? What do you want?' He eyed them up – Frank, small and wiry but strong-looking, and Martin, more muscular but shuffling his feet awkwardly behind his friend, as is often the way of a lad with muscles but not much else who might feel uncomfortable when asked something more demanding than his name.

Frank said, 'We need a job, sir. I'm Frank, and this is Martin, and we want to work on the flumes.'

The old boy gave them an assessing look, then held out an enormous calloused hand. 'My name's Slack – Mr Slack to you two. So, the flumes, is it? What do you know about flume-herding then?'

'Not a lot,' said Frank, 'but my grandfather was on the flumes and he said it was a good life.' He paused. 'We hear there's good money to be had,' he added optimistically.

The problem for lumberjacks working this high up in the mountains was the distance from the remote camps to the main cart track. It was just not practical to have the huge, heavy logs dragged out of the forest by horse, and the solution was to send the logs down the mountain on a fast-running flume of water to the depot on the downs below. From there the logs could be transported to the towns and cities by mule cart.

It was a wonderful idea, and once the first flume got going, the idea spread. The men who became flume-herders lived in little sheds perched precariously on ledges dangerously close to turning points in the flumes, and they needed strength to be able to deal with blockages as several tons of wood came hurtling down the surging water towards them. There was no shortage of young men who would head to the mountains, determined to ride the flumes, if only to say they had done it! Some, of course, never got the chance to say anything to anyone ever again after an early mistake on the logs, but every camp had an Igor, so some parts of them might very well get a second chance. And occasionally you might meet a really old flume-herder who had been doing it for a long time, and might indeed be sporting a young man's arms on his wiry old body.

'The flumes don't like babies,' Mr Slack said. 'It's a man's job and no mistake. I see you've got muscles, both of you, but I don't care about that. There are lots of boys like you with muscles. What we need is boys with muscles in their heads. You never know what the flumes will do to you on a renegade turn.' He frowned at them. 'Do you know young Jack Abbott? Young lumberjack who lives down the mountain with his good mother and young sister? Near as anything chopped his own foot off just a week or so ago. Only just getting better, and *that* thanks to some lass with a squint who the witches sent on up to help. Think on *that*, lads, if you think you can take risks up here. Flume-herding is a lot more dangerous than lumber-jacking.'

The boys looked downcast.

'And it's magic wood, some of this up here,' Slack continued. 'For the wizards. That's why they need us, lads – can't take it on trains, even once it's down in the depot. You all right with that? Magic can do funny stuff to some of the men up here.' He pointed at the snowy trees surrounding them and said, 'These aren't your ordinary pines, these are Predictive Pines. They know the future. Although dang me if I know why or how. What good is knowing the future for a pine tree? It can predict *when* it is going to be cut down – but you still *do* cut them down. Not like it can get away now, ha! But if you touch one, and it likes you, you'll see what is about to happen. So, lads, you still interested?'

Martin wasn't the kind to talk too much, but he said very simply, 'I just need the money, boss. And the grub, of course.'

'Oh, it's good money. And you can buy all sorts and get it sent up here,' said Mr Slack. He dug into a pocket of his checked jacket and pulled out a well-thumbed book. 'Biggerwoods catalogue. We all swear by it. You can get anything you want.'

Frank peered at the catalogue, at its cover. 'Says 'ere you can get a *bride*,' he said in wonder. 'Comes by *train*.'

'Well, there ain't no train gets up here – no iron near *this* wood. Nearest railhead's down at Hot Dang. Near enough. And that there brides is a new offer. Just in time for you lads. It says that you can get a young lady – lots of fancy girls looking for men. Find yourself one, and on what you can make up here she can have a proper indoor privy and no messing and all the clothes she wants. *That's* how good the money is.' He paused and stuffed the catalogue back into his pocket, then added, 'Women's clothes are wonderful, don't you think? Only the other day I met a man who said he travelled in ladies' lingerie . . .'

'Are you sure he was all right?' Martin asked Mr Slack a bit dubiously. He had heard talk of one very remote camp where the tough, strong lumberjacks apparently chose to dress in women's clothing as they sang songs about their big choppers, but he hadn't believed it. Until now, anyway.

The lumberjack ignored his question. 'Well, Martin, you are a fine boy, aren't you?' he said, then turned to Frank. 'You, lad, why do you want to take your chances up here?'

'Well, Mr Slack, I was going out with this girl, but there was this other lad, you know . . .' He hesitated.

Mr Slack held a hand in front of his face. 'Don't tell me anything more, kid. These hills are full of people who really wanted to be somewhere else, and it sounds like you might fancy taking a look at Biggerwoods then, once you've got some money in your pocket. Well, you two seem strong enough. Just sign up and we'll say no more. You can start in the morning, and then we'll see. If you ain't stupid, you'll come away with good wages. And if you go messing about around the flumes, I'll give your dear old mothers your wages, so she'll have enough to bury you with.'

He spat on his thumb, and man and boys made the thumb bargain so common amongst men of the world.

'And I'll tell you what's going to happen to you in the next thirty minutes,' Mr Slack said with a wide grin. 'You'll be over where the logs go into the flumes, watching and learning. And I don't need no Predictive Pine to tell me that!' He laughed, and patted the nearest pine.

But as his fingers touched the bark, his jaw

dropped open and his hood fell back from a face frozen with fear.

'Lads,' he stammered – and that in itself was terrifying, that a man so grizzled should have such a thing as a stammer in his voice – 'get out of here. *Now!* Get down the mountain. We've got a fight coming our way – in about five minutes! – and I need only men who know what to do with an axe up here.' And he turned and ran into the camp, shouting to the lumberjacks.

Martin and Frank looked at each other, shocked, and then Frank reached out tentatively and poked a finger onto the tree. A sudden flash of images shot into his mind – gloriously colourful creatures in velvet and feathers, their bodies painted with woad, came tumbling down out of the trees. But there was nothing glorious about the pain and death they were bringing with them. Then he saw a fur-lined hood bobbing in the waters of a flume, a hood that framed the head of Mr Slack. A Mr Slack who seemed to have somehow been slack enough to lose his body . . .

The two boys stumbled through the lumberjacks, heading for the trees, for the snowy ground that offered a chance of escape.

Not quickly enough. For with a sudden whistle, a storm of elves came dancing from the trees – large, nasty elves, the feathers and velvets of their tunics making them seem like predatory birds swooping from the shadowy heights. The two boys shrank back, frozen to the spot.

And for a few minutes it was lumberjack versus

elf, helped by the camp Igor, who said, 'Keep touching the pineth, it troubleth them and they won't know what day it is. And while they are finding out, you can give them a real rollocking.'

The lumberjacks were not men who would run away from a fight, and the terrible metal of their axes destroyed more than one elf. But more and more elves were pouring into the camp, tipping over the little sheds, kicking at the logs so that they tumbled into the flumes any which way, the elves swinging into the heights of the trees and laughing down at the camp. And there was something enchanting about them . . . something that crept behind the hard exteriors of the lumberjacks and made them fall to their knees, sobbing for their mothers, dropping their axes, easy prey for the victorious fairy folk . . .

'I told you. Get yourselves *away*, get to the flumes, boys,' Mr Slack shouted, chopping with his axe at an elf creeping up behind him. 'Them flumes are faster than elves. I'll be OK.'

Martin took him at his word – though Frank had seen the future and knew that 'OK' wasn't really going to happen for Mr Slack – and leaped into the first bucket, Frank close on his heels, and Mr Slack pushed a lever – and the bucket was off! Down the flume snaking its way down the steep mountainside, round corners so terrible that they had to lean from one side to the other to avoid falling. Soaked to the skin, a jumble of logs in front of them, behind them, alongside them, they tore along deep gorges, dodging arrows from arriving elves who were heading up the mountain like a deadly swarm of insects.

It was wild, it was exhilarating, it was *almost* getting killed – and the *almost* bit is what made it something they would feel able to talk about later, though clearly getting killed would shut up most people.

It was also terrifying – the most terrifying thing that had ever happened to either boy. Even over the roar of the water, they could hear the screams of the lumberjacks from behind them. And there were . . . things coming down with them in the water that no one would want to look at too closely.

The journey ended in a pile of logs. And the depot had many men, big strong men with metal in their hands, angry at the damage to the timber, and as they gathered to march up the mountain, there were laughs and shrieks from above – and then silence. The elves had gone.

The miller of Stank* was a pious man, and the mill itself was complicated, with wheels turning all the time in various directions; his nightmare, which he hoped never to see, would be a day when the mill broke down and all those complicated wheels spun off

---

* You might think that a name like Stank would put people off. But in fact the mountain village of Stank had once been a very popular place for tourists. They liked to send messages home saying, 'We're stinking in Stank.' And go home with presents for their loved ones like tunics with 'I've been to Stank and all I've brought home is this stinking tunic' written on them. Alas for them, with the coming of the railways – or in the case of Stank, the *not* coming of the railways – tourists began to go elsewhere, and Stank was now gradually disappearing into the mud, surviving mostly by taking in washing.

everywhere. But while they kept on turning, well, the miller was a happy man, for after all everybody needed bread.

Then one night the elves came, and oh, they started to interfere with his flour, making holes in the sacks and dropping an anthill into the grain, laughing at him.

But they had made a big mistake.

The miller prayed to Om, but as he got no answer – or, rather, he got the answer in his head that he wanted Om to give him – he let the elves have it, and as the complicated wheels roared into action, they were surrounded by metal – wonderful metal, cold metal, all turning like clockwork.

And the miller locked all the doors so they couldn't get out. He could hear the screams all night, and when his friends then asked him how he could have done that, he just said, 'Well, the mills of Stank grind slow, yet they grind 'em exceeding small.'

Down in the village of Slippery Hollow, Old Mother Griggs woke up with her hair in a terrible tangle – and a bed full of thistles, tearing into her aged skin . . . while an elf laughed in glee as its mount – a young heifer – collapsed to her knees, exhausted from the night-time revels . . .

And an old, crabbed trader in Slice pushed his cart – his only means of survival – into the market square, singing, 'A cabbage a day keeps the goblins away. And an onion a day makes the elv— Aargh!'

*

And at the foot of the Ramtops, a young maiden by the name of Elsie was tickled under the chin by a flower, and suddenly loosed the hand of her little sister, letting the little girl wander into the river, while Elsie gazed lovingly into the eyes of her father's donkey . . . as an unwary traveller skipped deeper and deeper into the woods, dancing to elven music that would never stop, the elves gambolling along beside him, laughing at his distress . . .

And Herne the Hunted – god of the small and furry, those destined to be eaten – crawled under a bush and hid as three elves discovered the gory fun they could have with a family of young rabbits . . .

CHAPTER 14

A Tale of Two Queens

Tiffany took Nightshade – a very small, pathetic creature right now – back to her father's farm with her, tucking her under her cloak for the journey, and then settling her and the Feegles into one of the old-fashioned hay barns.

'It's clean and warm here,' she said, 'with no metal. And I will bring you some food.' She looked sternly at the Feegles. They had a hungry look to them. There was an elf, all by itself. What could they do with it? 'Rob, Wee Mad Arthur, Big Yan,' she said, 'I'm just going to get a lotion for Nightshade, to help heal her wounds, and I do not want you to touch her while I am gone. *Is that clear?*'

'Oh aye, mistress,' said Rob cheerfully. 'Get yeself offski and leave yon scunner wi' us.' He glared at Nightshade. 'If yon elf gi' us any trouble, ye ken, we have oor weapons.' He shook his claymore in a fashion that clearly showed that he was itching to take it out to play.

Tiffany turned back to Nightshade. 'I am the hag o' the hills,' she said, 'and these Feegles will do my bidding. But they do not like you and your kind, so I suggest you mend your manners, madam, and play the game. Or there will be a reckoning.'

And then, indeed, she was offski. But it was a very rapid offski, as she trusted the elf very little and the Feegles even less.

When Tiffany got back, Nightshade took the healing ointment, and it seemed as if with each smooth stroke the little elf blossomed, becoming more and more beautiful. There was a sparkle about her and it was like a syrup that covered everything. It shouted, 'Am I not beautiful? Am I not clever? I am the Queen of Queens!'

Then it seemed to Tiffany that her sense of self was being changed; but she had been waiting for it, and she thought, I'm not having that, my friend. She said, 'You will not try your elvish wiles on *me*, madam!'

But still she felt the elf's magic reaching out for her, like the creep of a sunrise . . .

She screamed, 'You will *not* put your glamour on *me*, elf!' And the words of the shepherd's count that Granny Aching had used were in her mind. '*Yan tan tethera*,' she chanted, over and over, the singing of the words helping her mind become her own again.

It worked. Nightshade began to tone herself down,

and now she looked like a farm girl, a dairymaid. She had conjured up a dairymaid's dress for herself, though one that no real dairymaid would ever wear, given that it was adorned with little ribbons and bows, a dainty little slipper-clad foot peeking out from beneath the hem. As a pretty straw bonnet took shape, Tiffany recoiled – the elf had summoned up an echo of the costume she knew very well, one worn by a china shepherdess she had once given to her granny. And as she remembered Granny Aching she became incredibly angry. How *dare* this elf try this on her, here, on her very turf!

'I demand—' Nightshade tried, and then she saw Tiffany's expression. 'I would hope . . .'

A country girl! The elvish has begun to leave the building, Tiffany thought with delight. But she still folded her arms and glared at the elf. 'I've helped you,' she said, 'but I am also busy helping other people – people who would have a better life if you weren't here.' She narrowed her eyes. 'Especially if your people cause mischief, do things like spoiling our beer. Yes, I know about that, and I know you, elf, and I know what you want. You want your kingdom back, don't you, Nightshade?'

There was a growl from the assembled Feegles, and Big Yan said hopefully, 'Can we nae throw it back there, mistress?'

'Aye,' said Rob. 'Be rid o' yon pest.'

'Well, Rob,' said Tiffany, 'I am sorry to tell ye, there are some folks who think *Feegles* are a pest.'

Big Yan went silent, then said slowly, 'Weel, we

may be pests, ye ken, but a puir bairn has nae reason tae dread Feegles.' He rose to his full height of seven inches – Big Yan was very tall for a Feegle, with the scars on his forehead typical of the taller-than-average, who can find doorways somewhat challenging – and loomed over the elf from the rafters.

Tiffany ignored him, turning back to Nightshade. 'Am I right?' she demanded. 'You want to return to Fairyland? What do you say?'

Cunning flickered across Nightshade's sharp little face. 'We are like bees,' she said at last. 'The Queen has all the power . . . until she gets older, and then a new queen kills her to take the hive.' A wave of anger was suddenly visible. 'Peaseblossom,' she hissed. 'He does not believe that the world has changed. It was *he* who threw me from my people.' A contemptuous sneer crossed her lips. 'He, who is so powerful he can spoil *beer*. When we could once destroy *worlds* . . .'

'I could give you some help with your little friend Peaseblossom,' Tiffany said slowly. 'I would settle for you as Queen of the Elves again if you could make all the elves go back once more to their own land and stay there. But if you and your race should come here for the purpose of making humans your slaves, well, you may think you have seen me angry, but *then* you will know the real meaning of the word rage.'

As she said that everything about her flickered in fire. And she remembered facing the Queen before. Land under wave. Knowing where she had come from, where she was going. And that she could no longer be fooled. Knowing that no matter how many people dreamed, invited the elves to come into the world, *she* would be there, awake, holding firm.

'If you break your vow, the last things you will see are Thunder and Lightning,' she threatened. 'Thunder and Lightning in your head and you will die of the thunder. That is a *promise*, elf.'

From the look of terror that flickered across Nightshade's face, Tiffany knew that the elf understood.

She brought Nightshade some porridge in the morning.

The elf looked up at Tiffany as she took the bowl, and said, 'You could have killed me yesterday . . . *I'd* have killed me. Why didn't you? You know I am an elf, and *we* are merciless.'

'Yes,' said Tiffany, 'but we are human, and we do know mercy. I also know I'm a witch, and I'm doing my job.'

'You are clever, Tiffany Aching, the little girl I almost killed on the hill when the thunder and lightning became solid and hurtful, all teeth and bite.' Nightshade was puzzled. 'What am I now but a ragged pauper? Friendless, but you, one girl, you took me in when you had no reason to.'

'I did have a reason,' said Tiffany. 'I'm a witch, and I thought it possible.' She sat down on a milk churn, and said, 'You must understand that elves are seen as vindictive, callous, spiteful, untrustworthy, self-centred, undeserving, unwelcome nuisances – and that's being *nice*. I've heard much worse language used about them, especially from people whose children have been taken away, I can tell you. But nothing stays the same – our world, our *iron*, your court, your glamour. Did you know, Nightshade, that in Ankh-Morpork goblins have jobs, and are considered to be useful members of the community?'

'What?' said the Queen. 'Goblins? But you humans hate goblins – and their stink! I thought the one we captured was lying!'

'Well, maybe they do stink a bit, but so do their masters, because for some of them a stink is money,' said Tiffany, 'and a goblin who can repair a locomotive can stink as much as he likes. What do you elves have to offer us? You are just . . . folklore now. You've missed the train, in fact, and you have only mischief left, and silly tricks.'

'I could kill you with a thought,' said Nightshade with a sly look.

'Oh dear,' said Tiffany, holding up a hand to halt the Feegles, each of whom wanted to be the one to get the first fist in. 'I hope you don't do so. It would be your last.' She looked at the elf, whose sharp little face was quivering with upset as she found herself surrounded by those she did not understand. 'Oh, please don't cry. An elf who has been a queen – an elf who wants to be a queen again – surely shouldn't cry.'

'A queen shouldn't, but I am a remnant of a queen, lost in the wilderness.'

'No, you are in a hay barn. Do you understand the meaning of manual labour, lady?'

Nightshade looked puzzled. 'No. What does it mean?'

'It means earning a living by working. How are you with a shovel?'

'I don't know. What is a shovel?'

'Oh dear,' said Tiffany again. 'Look, you can stay here until you are better, but you must work hard at something. You could try.'

A boot bounced off the ground beside her, one of her father's, a hole at the toe, and another trying out of sympathy to join in at the heel. 'I cannae abide boots on my feet, ye ken,' said Wee Mad Arthur, 'but if ye recall I wuz raised by shoemakers, and they tol' me a tale o' the elves. Yon scunner ye ha' there might ha' a talent for it, ye ken.'

Nightshade turned the boot gingerly over in her hands. 'What is this?' she said.

'A boot,' said Tiffany.

'An' ye'll get one reet noo up yer backside if I ha' anythin' tae dae wi' it,' Big Yan growled.

Tiffany took the boot from the elf and put it down. 'We'll talk later, Nightshade,' she said. 'Thank you for your suggestion, Wee Mad Arthur, and yes, I do know the story* but I think it is just that, a story.'

'Weel, I tol' ye, Wee Mad Arthur, you shouldnae have listened to that load o' old cobblers,' said Rob.

It was a day of old sheets and old boots and 'make do and mend'. And oh dear, Tiffany thought, she had to

---

* It had been in *The Goode Childe's Booke of Faerie Tales* and told how two little elves secretly helped a poor shoemaker, but sadly experience had taught Tiffany that a lot of what was in that book bore no relation whatsoever to the real Fairyland.

check on baby Tiffany, and drop in on Becky Pardon and Nancy Upright – Miss Tick felt that both girls might be of use if she wanted to take on a trainee in the Chalk. But she couldn't ask the girls to move in while she had Nightshade at the farm, not unless she gave them each a horseshoe necklace so they would be protected by the iron. It would have to wait . . .

She was back and forth to the farm all day, in between visits. Her last call of the afternoon was to Mr Holland the miller. There were only a few purple blotches on his skin now, and she left Mistress Holland with a second pot of the Merryday Root lotion, biting her tongue at the good lady's clear message of 'If only you had been here, I wouldn't have used the wrong herb.'

When she got back, she found Nightshade perched in the corner of the barn, her merciless eyes pinned on You, who had stalked in and was arching her back and hissing at the elf. The Feegles were egging You on, with cries of 'Ach, see you, pussycat, gi' the scunner a wee giftie for the Nac Mac Feegle', interrupted by a sudden, 'Crivens, lads, the big wee hag is back!'

Tiffany stood in the doorway tapping her foot, and Rob shrank back.

'Ach no,' he wailed. 'Nae the Tappin' of the Feets, mistress.'

Tiffany folded her arms.

'Ach, mistress, 'tis a heavy thing to be under a geas,' Rob moaned.

And Tiffany laughed.

But Nightshade had questions for her. She had

seen people coming to the farm during the day, coming for medicines, for advice, for an ear to listen and, sadly, sometimes for an eye to see the bruises.

'Why do you help these strangers?' she asked Tiffany now. 'They are not of your clan. You owe them nothing.'

'Well,' said Tiffany, 'although they are strangers, I simply think of them as people. All of them. And you help other people – that's how we do it.'

'Does every person do it?' said Nightshade.

'No,' said Tiffany. 'Sadly, that is true. But many people will help other people, just because, well, because they *are* other people. That's how it goes. Do you elves not understand this?'

'Shall we say that I am trying to learn?' said Nightshade.

'And what do you find?' said Tiffany, smiling.

'You become a kind of servant.' Nightshade sniffed, her delicate nose wrinkling.

'Well, yes,' said Tiffany. 'But it doesn't matter, because one day I might need that person, and then they will very probably help me. It works for us; it always has.'

'But you have battles,' said Nightshade. 'I know that.'

'Yes, but not always. And we are getting better at the *not*.'

'You are powerful, though. *You* could rule the world,' said Nightshade.

'Really?' said Tiffany. 'Why should I want to do that? I am a witch, I like being a witch, and I like people too. For every nasty person, there's a nice one, mostly. There is a saying, "What goes around comes around," and it means that sooner or later you will find yourself on top, at least for a while. And another time, the wheel turns and you will *not* be on top but you have to put up with it.'

She tried to look into Nightshade's eyes, see what the elf was thinking, but she might as well have looked at a wall. The elf's eyes were emotionless.

'And I remember the darkness and the rain and the thunder and lightning,' she added, 'and what good has it done you? You, elf, found in a ditch?'

For once Nightshade seemed at a loss and looked carefully at Tiffany before saying, 'Your way . . . would not work for elves. Every other elf is a challenge. We kill our queens – every other queen is a rival, and we fight over the hive.' She paused as a new thought struck her. 'Yet you have your queens of wisdom – and thus there was Granny Aching, and Granny Weatherwax, and yes indeed, Tiffany Aching. You grow older, wisdom flourishes and is passed on.'

'And you never prosper, you live in a cycle of decay,' Tiffany said softly. 'And you are not bees. They are productive but they die young and never, ever have a thought . . .'

There was a strange look on the elf's face. She was having to think. Really think. Tiffany could see it. Nightshade had the face of someone who had already begun to think about a world that had changed, a world with iron that was less welcoming for the fairy folk, a world that liked them well enough in *stories* but had no real *belief* in them, gave them no way in; now she was looking closer and she was finding a new world she had never thought about before, and she was trying to reconcile it with everything else she knew.

And Tiffany could see the battle in her face.

Over in Lancre, Queen Magrat had heard about the trouble up in the Ramtops – the attack on the lumber-jacks, the deaths and the lost timber.

Elves, she thought. They'd seen them off last time, but it hadn't been easy, and it had been a long time since she'd posted guards – well, Shawn Ogg, anyway – up by the circle of stones known as the Dancers, or made sure the castle had plenty of horseshoes to hand.

She knew how the memory plays tricks, and the old stories had power, and everyone forgot how 'ter-rific' really meant 'brings terror'. Her people would only remember that the elves sang beautifully. They would have forgotten what their song was about.

Magrat was not only a queen, but also a witch, of course. And although she was mostly a queen these days, the witch part of her knew that the balance was off, that Granny Weatherwax had left a void behind her, and no matter how hard Tiffany Aching was working to fill it – and that nice backhouse boy she now had – Granny Weatherwax was a hard act to follow; she had held the barrier, held it firm.

And if the barrier was no longer strong . . . Magrat shivered. Anyone who had ever met elvenkind knew that 'terror' was absolutely the right response – the *only* response. For the elves were a *plague* that could spread rapidly, destroying and harming and hurting and poisoning all they touched. She wanted no elves in Lancre.

That evening, Queen Magrat went to her garderobe and took out her beloved broomstick, sat on it and very carefully tried a lift and, slightly against her expectations, it took off gently, rising slowly over the castle. She flew around happily for some minutes and told herself, It's true – once a witch, always a witch.

Being a dutiful wife, when she wanted to be, she mentioned her intentions to her husband late that evening, and to her surprise King Verence said, 'Back on the old broomstick, my love? Very glad to hear it. I've seen your face when a witch flies by, and no man can keep a bird in chains.'

Magrat smiled and said, 'I don't feel like a bird in a cage, my dear, but now we don't have Granny, I feel I must help.'

'Well done,' said Verence. 'We are all coming to terms with what's happened, but I am sure Mistress Aching will follow in Granny's footsteps.'

'It isn't like that,' said Queen Magrat. 'I think she is walking in her own footsteps.' She sighed. 'But there are elves afoot,' she said. 'And I believe Tiffany will be at Granny's cottage – no, *her* cottage – later today, so I must go and see her, offer my support.' Her husband shivered at the mention of elves. 'Of course,' Magrat continued firmly, 'I also intend to be a good role model for our children. Young Esme is growing up fast and I want her to see that there's more to being a queen than waving hellos – we don't want her to start kissing frogs, now, do we? We all know how *that* can turn out!'* She turned at the door, and tossed her husband a baby sling. 'I am *quite* sure,' she said sweetly, 'that you can look after our children very well indeed on your own for a little while.'

Verence smiled weakly.

Magrat made a face that only a witch would see. He holds them upside down sometimes, she thought to herself. He is a very clever man, but give him a baby and he doesn't really know what to do. She smiled. He could learn. And when she asked him to change a nappy, when Millie was off helping in the kitchen, he pulled a face but he did try anyway.

'I want to help,' Magrat said firmly to Tiffany, landing her broomstick outside what they both still thought of as Granny's cottage, less than an hour after Tiffany had arrived herself, the news quickly flashing up to the castle since Magrat had made it known she wanted to be informed. 'I am the Queen, but I am also a pretty good witch.'

Tiffany looked into Magrat's eyes and saw her longing to be a witch once more, just for a little while, and then Magrat said, 'We have had elves here, Tiffany. *Elves!*' And Tiffany remembered Granny Weatherwax telling her how Magrat had fought the elves before – shot one right through the eye with a crossbow indeed!

'I have *experience*, Tiffany,' Magrat continued.

---

* Most princesses never tried to kiss toads, however, which had been a source of sadness to the Feegles' toad lawyer for many years.

'And you are going to need everyone you can get if the elves start coming through.' She paused to think. 'Even novices. Have you spoken to Miss Tick?'

'Yes,' said Tiffany. 'She says she has found one or two likely girls, but not everyone can be a witch, even if they want to be. And at the moment it's not . . . possible to take a girl on in my steading on the Chalk.'

'Why not? And what about your friend Petulia, her with the piggery?'

'Well, she has the skills,' said Tiffany, ignoring the first of Magrat's questions. 'But Petulia helps her husband to run the farm – says she spends all her time among creatures who go "grunt", and that sometimes includes the old pig farmers! And you have to admit that pig-boring is good for everybody, even the pigs. It's terrible to hear the squealing if she's not there.'

'Well, we may still need her up here, pigs or not. And heavy waterproof boots can take an arrow,' said Magrat. 'So, any sign of elves down on the Chalk?'

Tiffany coloured, uncertain how Magrat would take her news about Nightshade, but thinking a little guiltily that at least it would save her having to tell Nanny Ogg herself. She told her about the beer first, then about Nightshade. How the elf was staying at her parents' farm, watched over by Feegles. Making it impossible to take on any other help.

Magrat knew the Feegles would keep the elf from causing any trouble, but she was surprised by what Tiffany told her. 'Are you telling me you think you can *trust* an elf?' she said. Her face had paled. 'No elf is trustworthy,' she added. 'They wouldn't even know the *meaning* of the word. Yet you trust this elf? Why?'

'No,' said Tiffany. 'I don't trust her. But I think this elf wants to live. Nightshade has already seen for herself that our world is changing. The iron, you know. And now she has encountered ideas unknown to her. We might just be making some progress, and I think it's worth a try. Perhaps she might then go back to Fairyland and . . . persuade other elves to think like her? To leave us alone.' She paused. 'The kelda of the Feegles warned me, Magrat. She said that Granny's going would leave a . . . hole. That we needed to take great care. It's the elves! It has to be. So if this elf can help, well, I must try . . .'

'Hmm, but if those others do start coming, you're going to need help, Tiffany,' said Magrat. She thought for a moment. 'I understand the Baron on the Chalk has a wife who is a witch . . . ?'

'Yes,' said Tiffany. 'Letitia Keepsake. But she's not trained and her husband is a bit – how should I say it? – snobby.'

Magrat said, 'Well, my dear, if you want, I'll fly down there and drop in for tea one day. And hint, in a subtle way, that the idea of being a witch for the people at large might be a good idea. My Verence, you know, likes to be thought of as a king of the people, and in fact, I feel sure he thinks I am being a good example to the population by working as a witch now. He talks like that, sometimes, but I love him nevertheless. The idea of this Letitia being friends with a queen might stop her husband interfering.'

Tiffany said, 'I am amazed. Just like that?'

'Trust me,' said Queen Magrat. 'Crowns are important, you know.'

Tiffany flew back to the Chalk feeling a bit happier. Magrat would be a useful ally, and perhaps Letitia would be able to help too. But we are still short of witches, so we must take pains to get more, she thought. *Furious* pains. That means pulling in every witch and likely witch to learn at least some of the craft and how to deal with the glamour of elves.

Elves! Nastiness for the sake of being nasty. As Granny Aching had told her, they would take away the stick of a man with no legs. Nasty, unpleasant, stupid, annoying – trouble and discord just for the pleasure of it. Worse. They brought actual horror, and terror, and *pain* . . . And they laughed, which was bad enough because their laughter was actually musical and you could wonder why such wonderful music could come from such unpleasant creatures. They cared for nobody except themselves and possibly not even that.

But Nightshade . . . Perhaps there *was* one elf for whom the wheel was turning. Especially the *iron* wheels . . .

CHAPTER 15

The God in the Barrow

In the dark of the night, down in the Chalk, the wheel was definitely stuck in the old ways – just the way three elves dancing through the gloom of the woods liked it. This world was here for their pleasure, to entertain them, delight them. And the creatures within it were no more than toys; toys that sometimes squealed and ran and shrieked as the elves laughed and sang.

Now they spotted a small home, a poor-looking dwelling with a window slightly ajar. From within came the sound of babies, gurgling happily in their sleep, their bellies full of their mother's milk, their limbs curled beneath the covers of their cots.

The elves grinned at each other and licked their lips in anticipation. *Babies!*

Faces now at the window. Predatory faces, with the eyes of hunters.

Then a hand reached in and tickled the nearest infant under the chin, the little girl waking and gazing in delight at the glorious creature leaning over her, his glamour shining radiantly in the dark room. Her little fingers stretched to touch a beautiful feather . . .

Tiffany's happiness lasted until just after she had gone to bed, when there was a sudden tickling in her head, and in her inner eye she saw young Tiffany Robinson – the baby she had not had time to see yet this week, the little girl on whom she had placed a tracking spell.

But this was not just neglect by baby Tiffany's mum and dad.

The *elves* had taken her!

Tiffany's broomstick could not go fast enough. In a piece of woodland she found a group of three elves toying with the little girl, and what was inside her was not anger. It was something more forensic than that, and as the stick went onwards, Tiffany let her feelings flame up . . . and *release*.

The elves were laughing, but as Tiffany swooped down, she sent fire blazing from her fingertips and into them and watched them burn. She was shuddering with her fury, a fury so intense it was threatening to overcome her. If she met any more elves that night, they too would be dead.

And she had to stop herself there, suddenly appalled at what she had done. *Only a witch gone to the dark would kill*, she screamed at herself inside her head.

And another voice said, *But they were just* elves. *And they were hurting the baby.*

The first voice came sneakily back with, *But Nightshade is also* just *an elf...*

And Tiffany knew that if a witch started thinking of anyone as '*just*' anything, that would be the first step on a well-worn path that could lead to, oh, to poisoned apples, spinning wheels and a too-small stove ... and to pain, and terror, and horror and the darkness.

But it was done. And a witch had to be practical, so Tiffany wrapped her shawl around the baby and slowly flew to the Robinsons' house – 'shack' being, in fact, a better word for the little dwelling. Young Mister Robinson opened the door to her knocking. He looked surprised, especially when Tiffany showed him his baby daughter, swaddled in her witch's shawl.

She walked past him and confronted his wife, thinking, They are young, yes, but that doesn't mean you have to be stupid. Leaving the windows open at this time of year? Surely everybody knows about elves ...

My mother said I never should ...
Play with the fairies in the wood ...

'Well,' said Milly, 'I checked the boys. They seemed to be all right.' She blushed as Tiffany handed her the baby, and Tiffany caught it.

'Let me tell you something, Milly. Your girl has a great future before her. I'm a witch, so I know it. Because you've let me name her, I will see to it that my namesake has what she needs – and mind, it is your *girl* I am talking about. In some way, she's partly mine. Those great big boys of yours will look after themselves. Now don't leave your windows open on nights like this! There are always watchers. You know it! Let no harm attend her.'

Tiffany almost shouted the last bit. This family needed a little prod every so often, and she would see to it. Oh yes, she would. And if they neglected their duty, well, there would be a reckoning. Maybe just a little reckoning, to make them understand.

But right now, as she headed home, she knew she needed to talk to another witch.

She grabbed a warm cloak from her bedroom, then saw the gleam of the shepherd's crown on the shelf and, on a sudden impulse, tucked it into her pocket. Her fingers curled around the odd-shaped little stone, tracing its five ridges, and somehow she felt a strength flow into her, the hardness of the flint at its heart reminding her who she was. I need to keep a piece of the Chalk with me, she realized. My land gives me strength, supports me. It reminds me who I am. I am not a killer. I am Tiffany Aching, witch of the Chalk. And I need my land with me.

She sped through the night sky, back to Lancre, the cool of the air rushing past, the eyes of the owls watching her in the moonlight.

It was almost dawn when she arrived at Nanny Ogg's home. Nanny was already up, or rather she hadn't yet got down, since she had spent the night at a deathbed. She opened her door and blanched a little when she saw Tiffany's face.

'Elves?' she asked grimly. 'Magrat told me, you know. You got trouble over in the Chalk?'

Tiffany nodded, any calm deserting her as tears suddenly choked her voice. And over the requisite cup of tea in Nanny's warm kitchen, she told her what had happened.

Then she came to the bit of the story which she struggled to get out. All she could say was, 'The elves. With little Tiffany. They were going to . . .' She choked a little, then, 'I killed all three of them,' she wailed. She looked despairingly at Nanny.

'Good,' said Nanny. 'Well done. Don't trouble yourself, Tiff. If they was hurtin' that baby, well, what else could you do? You didn't . . . *enjoy* it?' she asked carefully, eyes shrewd in her wrinkled face.

'Of course not!' Tiffany cried. 'But, Nanny, I just . . . I did it almost without *thinking*.'

'Well, you might have to do it again soon if the elves keeps on comin',' Nanny said briskly. 'We're witches, Tiffany. We has the power for a reason. We just 'as to make sure as it's the right reason, and if there's an elf comin' through and hurtin' a baby, take it from me, that *is* the right reason.' She paused. 'If'n people do wrong things, well, why would they be surprised if bad things then happen to them. Most of 'em knows this, you know. I remember Esme tellin' me once, she was in some hamlet or other – Spickle, Spackle, somewhere like that – and people was tryin' to string up this man for killin' two children and she said as he knew he deserved it; 'pparently 'e said, "I did it in liquor and it ended in 'emp".' She sat wearily down, allowing Greebo to clamber onto her ample lap. 'Reality, Tiff,' she added. 'Life *an'* death. You knows it.' She scratched the tomcat behind what *might* be described as an ear by someone with *very* poor eyesight. 'Is the child all right?'

'Yes, I took her back to her parents but they . . . can't . . . won't . . . look after her properly.'

'Some folk just don't want to see the truth, even when you points it out to 'em. That's the trouble with elves, they will keep comin' back.' Nanny sighed heavily. 'People tell stories about 'em, Tiff,' she said. 'They make 'em sound fun – it's as if their glamour hangs around after they've gone and stays in people's heads, tellin' 'em that elves is no problem. Just a bit of mischief.' Nanny sank further into her chair, knocking a small family knick-knack off the table beside her. 'Feegles,' she said. 'They're mischief. But elves? Elves is different. You remember how the Cunning Man crept into people's heads, Tiff? How he made people *do* things – *awful* things?'

Tiffany nodded, her mind replaying horrible images while her eyes still focused on the knick-knack on the floor. A present from Quirm from one of her daughters-in-law, and Nanny *hadn't even noticed she had knocked it over*. Nanny. Who treasured every small object her family gave her. Who would never *ever* fail to notice if something was damaged.

'Well, that's *nothin'* to what them elves might do, Tiff,' Nanny continued. 'There is nothin' they likes more than watchin' pain and terror, nothin' that makes 'em laugh more. And they loves stealin' babbies. You did well to stop them this time. They will come again, though.'

'Well, then they will have to die again,' said Tiffany flatly.

'If you are there . . .' Nanny said carefully.

Tiffany slumped. 'But what else can we do? We can't be everywhere.'

'Well,' said Nanny, 'we've seen 'em off before. It was hard, for sure, but we can do it again. Can't that elf of yorn help?'

'Nightshade?' Tiffany said. 'They won't listen to her the way things are right now! They threw her out.'

Nanny pondered a bit, then appeared to come to a decision. 'There *is* someone they might listen to . . . or at least they *used* to listen to 'im. If he can be persuaded to take an interest.' She looked at Tiffany appraisingly. 'He don't like to be disturbed. Though I have visited him before, once, with a friend' – her eyes grew misty at the memory* – 'and I think Granny and he may have had words in the past. He likes ladies, though. A pretty young thing like you might be just his cup of tea.'

Tiffany bristled. 'Nanny, you can't be suggesting—'

'Lordy, no! Nothin' like that. Just a bit of . . . persuadin'. You are good at persuadin' folks, ain't you, Tiff?'

---

* Nanny's friend on that occasion had been Count Casanunda the lowwayman – a highwayman who carried a stepladder on his horse, on account of his being a dwarf, and was most gallant towards the ladies he encountered.

'I can do persuading,' Tiffany said, relaxing a bit. 'Who do you mean and where do I go?'

The Long Man. Tiffany had heard a lot about the Long Man, the barrow that led to the home of the King of the Elves – mostly from Nanny Ogg, who had gone into the barrow and met the King once before, when the elves had been getting unruly.

The professors would have said that the King lived in a long barrow from ancient times, when people didn't wear clothing and there weren't so many gods, and in a way the King himself was a kind of god – a god of life and death and, it seemed to Tiffany, of dirt and ragged clothing. And men still sometimes came to dance around by the barrow, horns on their heads and – usually – a strong drink in their hands. Unsurprisingly, they found it hard to persuade young women to go up there with them.

There were three mounds to the barrow, three very *suggestive* mounds that no country lass who had watched sheep and cows in action could fail to recognize – there was always a lot of giggling from the girls training to be witches when they first flew over it and saw it from the air.

Tiffany headed up the overgrown path, pushing her way through thorns and trees, untangling her witch's hat from a particularly insistent bush at one point, and stopped by the cave-like entrance. She was strangely reluctant to duck under the lintel, past the scratched drawing of the man with horns and down the steps she knew she would find once she had pushed aside the stone at the entrance.

I cannot face him just by myself, she thought with terror. I need someone who can at least tell people how I died.

And a wee voice said, 'Crivens!'

'Rob Anybody?'

'Oh aye. We follow ye all the time, ye ken. Ye are the hag o' the hills and the Long Man is a big hill.'

But, 'Wait by the gate please, Rob, I must do this by myself,' she said, suddenly filled with sureness that this was the right choice. She had killed the three elves; now she would face their king. 'This is hag business, ye ken.'

'But we knows the King,' said Rob. 'If'n we gae along wi' ye, we can fight yon scunner in his ain world.'

'Oh aye,' added Wee Dangerous Spike. 'A big laddie, ye ken, but I'll gi' the bogle a face full of Feegle he'll nae forget.' He experimentally nutted one of the entrance stones, bouncing his head off the rock with a satisfying *clunk*.

Tiffany sighed. 'That's what I'm afeared – I mean, afraid of,' she said. 'I want to ask the King for his help. Not anger him. And I know the Feegles have history with him . . .'

'Aye, that's us,' said Rob proudly. 'We is *history*.'

'Nae king, nae quin, nae laird!' roared the assembled Feegles.

'Nae *Feegles*,' said Tiffany firmly. A sudden burst of inspiration hit her. 'I need you *just here*, Rob Anybody,' she told him. 'I have to do my hag business with the King without anyone disturbing me.' She paused. 'And there are elves afoot. So if any should come seekin' their king, I want *you* – Rob Anybody, Wee Dangerous Spike, all of ye – to stop them coming down after me. I need you to do this for me. It's *important*. Is that *understood*?'

There was a bit of grumbling, but Rob had brightened up. 'So we can gi' them scunners a guid kickin' if they shows up here?' he asked.

'Yes,' Tiffany said wearily.

This was met by a cheer. 'Nac Mac Feegle, wha hae!'

She left them there, squabbling over who should guard which part of the Long Man, Wee Dangerous Spike bashing his head enthusiastically against the entrance stones again as a sort of warmup for what he hoped was coming, and she walked into the stinky darkness, clutching the small crowbar she had brought with her, along with a horseshoe. She put one hand into her pocket and held tight on to the shepherd's crown – her ground, her turf. Let's see if I am truly the hag of the hills, she thought, and she gripped the big stone blocking the entrance.

It rose up gently, no crowbar necessary, the stone crackling as she raised it higher and higher, revealing the steps beyond. The path inside led her deeper and darker, spiralling round and round, taking her into the heart of the barrow.

Into a pathway between the worlds.

Into the world of the elven King, where he floated between time and space in his land of pleasure. It was stifling, though there was no fire – the heat seemed to be coming out of the earth.

And it stank. It reeked of masculinity and unwashed clothing, of feet and sweat. There were bottles everywhere, and at the end of the hall, naked men were wrestling, grunting and groaning as they twined and twisted with their opponents, their bodies greased as if from a bucket of lard. There were no women to be seen – this was a land where men indulged themselves with no thought for the other sex. But when they saw Tiffany, they stopped and put their hands over their essentials – as Nanny Ogg would have said – and Tiffany thought: Ha, you big strong men, your meat and two veg hanging out, you are frightened, aren't you? I am the maiden – and I am also the hag.

She could see the King of the Elven Races. He was just as Nanny Ogg had described, still stinking of course, but somehow hugely attractive. She kept her eyes on the horns on his head, trying not to look at *his* meat and veg, which were *huge*.

The King sighed, stretching out his legs and tapping his hooves against the wall, an animal scent like that of a badger in heat rising from him and curling towards her. 'You, young woman,' he said lazily, his voice an invitation to romance, to wickedness, to pleasures you had not known you wanted until that moment. 'You come into my world. Into my entertainments. You are a witch, are you not?'

'Indeed I am,' said Tiffany, 'and I am here to ask the King of the Elves to be a proper king.'

He moved closer and Tiffany tried not to blanch as the stench of him thickened. He smiled lasciviously, causing her to think, I know who you are and what you are, and I think Nanny Ogg must have liked you . . .

'Who are you?' he queried. 'By your garb, you seem indeed to be a witch, but witches are old and somewhat wrinkled. You, girl . . .'

Sometimes, Tiffany thought, I am so *fed up* with being young.* My youth has got his attention, but what I need is his *respect*.

'I may be young, my lord,' she said firmly, 'but as you see, I *am* a ha— a witch. And I come to tell you that I have killed three of your people.'

That should do it, she thought, but the King merely laughed. 'You interest me, my girl,' he said, stretching languorously. 'I do no harm,' he added lazily. 'I simply dream, but my people, oh dear, what can I do? I must allow them their delights, as I do myself.'

'But their delights are not to *our* taste,' said Tiffany. 'Not in *my* world.'

'*My* world?' chuckled the King. 'Oh, you have pride, little girl. Perhaps you would like to be one of my ladies. A queen needs pride . . .'

'The Lady Nightshade is your queen,' said Tiffany firmly, her legs shaking at the invitation in the King's words. *To stay here? With him?* her mind shrieked. She gripped the shepherd's crown more firmly. *I am Tiffany Aching, of the Chalk*, she said to herself, *and I have flint in my soul*. 'Nightshade is my . . . guest,' she added. 'Perhaps you did not know, my lord, that your

---

* A thought that she would most certainly grow out of, assuming she survived long enough.

queen has been thrown from Fairyland by the Lord Peaseblossom?'

A lazy smile spread across the King's face. 'Nightshade . . .' he mused. 'Well, I hope you enjoy her company.' He spread his legs, making Tiffany gulp, and leaned forward. 'You begin to tire me now, girl. What do you *want* from me?'

'Get your elves to see sense,' said Tiffany. 'Or there will be a reckoning.' Her voice almost wobbled on the last bit of this, but it had to be said, oh yes.

There was a huge sigh, and the King yawned as he lay back again. 'You come to my abode and you *threaten* me?' his voice caressed. 'Tell me, mistress, what care should I have for those elves who play in your lands? Even the Lady Nightshade? There are other worlds. There are *always* other worlds.'

'Well, *mine* never was a place for elves,' Tiffany said. 'It was *never* yours. You just latched on to it – a *parasite* – and took what you could. But once again I have to tell you these are the days of iron – not just horseshoes, but iron and steel forged together in great lines across the land. It's called a *railway*, my lord, and it is spreading across the Disc. People are interested in mechanical things, because mechanical things *work*, while old wives' tales mostly just don't kill them. And so people laugh at the fairies, and as they laugh, so you will dwindle. You see, nobody cares about you any more. They have the clacks, the railways, and it's a new world. You – and your kind – have no future here now other than in *stories*.' She said the last word contemptuously.

'Stories?' the King mused. 'A way into the minds of your peoples, mistress. And I can wait . . . the stories will survive when this "railway" you speak of is long gone.'

'But we will not stand by to see small children taken as playthings for elves any more,' Tiffany said. 'I and others will burn those who take them. This is a warning – I would like it to be friendly but, alas, it seems this is not possible. You are living in railway time and *you should leave us be*.'

The King sighed again. 'Perhaps . . . perhaps,' he said. 'New lands to discover could be entertaining. But I have told you, I have no desire to visit your land in this time of iron. After all, I have all the time I wish for . . .'

'What about the elves who have already come through?'

'Oh, just kill them if you wish.' The King smiled again. 'I may remain here until the end of time, and I don't think that you would want to be there. But I have always liked the ladies, and so I will say that if elves are stupid, they deserve my censure and your wrath. My dear Mistress Aching – *and yes, I do know who you are* – you clasp good intentions to you like a mother clutches her young. Now, should I even let you leave? When I am looking for . . . entertainment.' He sighed. 'I do so desire new amusements sometimes – perhaps to tinker with something, to discover new interests. And one new interest could be you. Do you think that I will let you leave my home?' His heavy-lidded eyes caressed her.

Tiffany swallowed. 'Yes, your majesty. You will let me leave.'

'You are so sure?'

'Yes.' Tiffany wrapped her hand around the shepherd's crown once again, and felt the flint at its centre give her strength, draw her back to her own land, to her land above the wave. She stepped backwards slowly.

And nearly tripped over something on the floor behind her.

The King was staring too. It was a white cat and she heard the King's voice, surprised for the first time: 'You!'

And then there was an end to it, and Tiffany and You spiralled back the way they had come, and the Feegles were outside, patrolling up and down and enjoying the happy opportunity of fighting a tree or two, since no elves had turned up, but these trees were still right scunners, stickin' their barbs as they did into Feegle heads and beards. They *deserved* a guid kickin'.

'Well, I'm not sure that did any good,' Tiffany said to Rob as she emerged from the tunnel.

'Weel,' said Rob Anybody, 'let them come. Ye will always have your Feegles. We Feegles are everlasting.'

'Everlasting if there is enough to drink!' Wee Dangerous Spike added.

'Rob,' said Tiffany firmly. 'Right now, not one of you needs a drink. We need a *plan*.' She thought for a moment. 'The King will not help – yet. But he is looking for new entertainments. Perhaps if we offer him something of that ilk, then he will think more kindly upon us and at least leave us alone?' Leave us to kill his elves, she thought to herself. He did say he wouldn't mind. Would he change his mind?

'Ach, nae problem,' said Rob proudly, confident of his ability to find a PLN. 'That King of the Elves, he needs somethin' tae do, ye say.'

'Like the men of Lancre!' Tiffany said suddenly. 'Rob, you know how Geoffrey has them all building sheds ... Well, you built a *pub* once. How difficult would a shed be?'

'Nae trouble at all, right, lads?' said Rob, happy now. For he had his PLN. 'Let's offski.' He looked down at You. 'How come your pussycat follows you around, mistress?'

'I don't know,' said Tiffany. 'She's a cat. They can go anywhere. And after all, she was Granny Weatherwax's cat and that means quite a lot.'

But Rob wasn't listening. Not now. He was thinking of his PLN. And the following day, at the mouth of the Long Man there was a shed replete with everything a gentleman could require, including fishing line and every tool you can think of, all made of wood or stone. Tiffany thought that might make the King of the Elves happy. But she did not feel it would get his help ...

Lord Peaseblossom lounged on a velvet-covered couch in Fairyland, idly fingering the ruff of feathers around his neck, swigging from a goblet of rich wine.

Lord Lankin had just entered the chamber. He

bowed before his new king, a glorious red broom of a tail slung casually round his neck, a memento of a recent raid. 'I believe, my lord,' he said lazily, silkily, 'that our warriors will soon wish for . . . greater enjoyments in the human world. The barriers seem weak, and those of us who slip through to hunt are finding no real opposition.'

Peaseblossom smiled. He knew that his elves had been testing the gates, some skipping through the red stones of Lancre whilst others had gambolled near the villages of the Chalk, wary only of the little red-haired men who liked nothing more than a fight with an elf. The elves were like the Feegles in one respect – if there was nobody to fight, they would fight amongst themselves. And squabbling was *de rigueur* in Fairyland – not even cats were as bad.*

And elves could take umbrage. They loved umbrage, and as for sulking, that was a top entertainment. But everywhere they had been, they had stirred up little pockets of trouble, being nuisances, causing damage for damage's sake. Stealing sheep, cows, even the occasional dog. Only yesterday Mustardseed had gleefully snatched a ram from its flock on the hills and then loosed it in a small china shop, laughing as it had lowered its horns and – yes – *rammed* the shelves.

But there was no rhyme nor reason to it. They needed to show what they could *really* do. Perhaps, Peaseblossom mused, the time was afoot to lead his

---

* It has in fact been said that elves are *like* cats; but cats will work together – for instance, when sharing a kill – while elves squabble and fight so that a third party may go home with the food.

elves on a raid that all elves would sing about for a long time to come.

A smile flickered across his thin, sharp face, and he waved a hand in the air, changing his tunic instantly to one of leather and fur, a crossbow tucked into his belt.

'We will put a girdle of glamour around their world,' he laughed. 'Go, my elves, go make your mischief. But when this still-bent moon swells to her full glory, we will go together in force. That land will be ours once more!'

In her father's barn, Tiffany was watching Nightshade wake up. She had mixed up a new tonic for her yesterday: a good strong dose of reciprocal greens* which had made the elf sleep deeply for a whole day, giving her body a chance to regain its strength.

And, incidentally, giving Tiffany a chance to go round the houses without worrying about what the Feegles might do in her absence. I might even have time to fly to Lancre and check on Geoffrey if I do it once more, she thought. She knew the Feegles would never hurt a sleeping elf, but one awake? Well, their instincts might just take over if Nightshade should put a single dainty finger wrong. And, of course, she didn't trust the elf either . . .

'Time for a walk,' she said as Nightshade stretched her limbs and looked around her as she woke. 'I think it is time you saw a few more humans.' For how else

---

* It looked a rather poisonous green before it was heated up, but in most cases the end certainly justified the greens.

could she teach Nightshade about how this world worked if Nightshade mostly only saw the inside of the barn and a few ready-to-boil-over Feegles?

So she took Nightshade down into the village, past the pub where the men were sitting looking glumly at their beer, fishing the occasional barrel gushie out of it, past the small shops, picking her way carefully over the debris outside Mrs Tumble's Plates for All Seasons, down the road and back up into the downs. Tiffany had asked her dad to let people know she was trying out a girl to help mix her medicines, so nobody really looked *directly* at her, but Tiffany had no doubt that they would all have taken in every single detail as she passed. It was why she had insisted on Nightshade's dairymaid's dress being toned down, so there were now no bows, no ribbons, no buckles, and a decent pair of boots rather than dainty slippers.

'I have been watching humans,' said Nightshade as they were clumping back up the road. 'And I can't understand them. I saw a woman giving an old tramp a couple of pennies. He was nothing to do with her, so why would she do that? How does it help her? I don't understand.'

'It's what we do,' said Tiffany. 'The wizards call it empathy. That means putting yourself in the place of the other person and seeing the world from their point of view. I suppose it's because in the very olden days, when humans had to fight for themselves every day, they needed to find people who would fight with them too, and together we lived – yes, and prospered. Humans need other humans – it's as simple as that.'

'Yes, but what good would the old lady get from giving away her money?'

'Well,' said Tiffany, 'she will probably feel what we call *a little glow*, because she has helped someone who needed help. It will mean that she is glad that she is not in his circumstances. You could say that she can see what his world is like, and – what can I say? – she comes away feeling hopeful.'

'But the tramp looked as if he could do a job of some sort, to earn his own pennies, but nevertheless she gave him hers.' Nightshade was still struggling to understand the human concept of money – the elves, of course, could simply make it appear whenever they willed.*

'Well, yes,' said Tiffany, 'that sort of thing does happen, but not always, and the old lady will still feel she has done the right thing. He may be a bit of a scamp but she tells herself that she is a good person.'

'I saw a king in your land before – Verence – and I watched him and he didn't tell people what they should do,' Nightshade continued.

'Well, he has a wife to tell him what to do,' laughed Tiffany. 'That's what humans are. Right up to our kings and queens, our barons and lords. Our rulers rule by consent, which means that we like having them as rulers, if they do what we want them to do. There were a lot of battles long ago, but there again

---

* It disappeared pretty quickly too, as anyone given fairy gold soon discovered. Usually by the morning, which often meant a lively evening in the pub. And an even livelier evening the following night if visiting the same establishment.

everyone finally realized that it was better to work peacefully with everyone else. For one person alone cannot survive. We humans definitely need other people to keep us human.'

'I notice that you don't use magic very much either,' Nightshade added. 'Yet you are a witch. You are powerful.'

'Well, what we witches have found is that power is best left at home. Magic is tricky anyway, and it can turn and twist and get things wrong. But if you surround yourself with other humans you will have what we call *friends* – people who like you, and people you like.'

'Friends.' Nightshade rolled the word, and the idea, around in her head and then asked, 'Am I your friend?'

'Yes,' said Tiffany. 'You could be.' She looked at the people passing by and said to Nightshade, 'Look, try this. There's an old woman trying to carry a very heavy basket up the hill. Go and help her, will you, and see what happens.'

The elf looked horrified. 'What do I say to her?'

'You say, "Can I help you, mistress?"'

Nightshade gulped, but she crossed the road and spoke to the old woman, and Tiffany listened and heard the old woman saying, 'What a kind girl you are, thank you very much. Bless you for helping an old lady.'

To Tiffany's surprise, Nightshade carried the basket not only over the hill but also along the next stretch of the road, and she heard her ask, 'How do you live, lady?'

The old lady sighed. 'Little by little. My husband died years ago, but I am good with the needle and so I make things. I don't need charity. I get along and I have still got my home. As we say, worse things happen at sea . . .'

As Nightshade watched the woman go away, she said to Tiffany, 'Can you give me some money, please?'

'Well,' said Tiffany, 'witches seldom have money about their person – we don't live in that kind of world.'

Nightshade brightened up. 'I can help then,' she said. 'I'm an elf and I am sure I could get into a place where the money is.'

'Please do not try that,' said Tiffany. 'There would be a lot of trouble.'

She ignored a grumble from the side of the road, 'Nae if you don't get caught.'

'We is guid at gettin' intae places, ye ken,' another Feegle muttered.*

Nightshade paid the Feegles no heed. She was still puzzling. 'That old woman had absolutely nothing, but she was still cheerful. What did she have to be cheerful about?'

'Being alive,' said Tiffany. 'What you are seeing, Nightshade, is someone making the best of things, which is something else humans do. And sometimes the best of it is good.' She paused. 'How did it make you feel?' she asked. 'Carrying that basket.'

Nightshade looked puzzled. 'I'm not sure,' she said

---

* Very true, though getting out again was sometimes trickier, especially if there was strong drink about.

slowly. 'But I'm not sure I felt like an elf should . . . is that a good thing?'

'Look,' Tiffany said, 'the wizards tell us that in the very, very olden days, humans were more like monkeys, and being a monkey was a very clever thing to be as monkeys like to see into everything. And then the monkeys realized that if one monkey tried to kill a large wolf, he would soon be a *dead* monkey, but if two monkeys could get together they would be very happy monkeys, and happy monkeys create more happy monkeys so they would have lots of monkeys, which chatter and gibber and talk all the time until, in the end, they became *us*. So too could an elf change.'

'When I get my kingdom back . . .' Nightshade began.

'Stop there,' said Tiffany. 'Why do you want your kingdom back? What good has it done you? Think about it, for I am the human who has looked after you, the only person you might call a friend.' She looked seriously at the elf. 'I have told you that I – we – would be happy if you were to be Queen of the Elves again, but only if you can truly learn from your time here. Be prepared to live in peace, teach your elves that the world has changed and that there is no space for them here.'

There was hope in her voice now, a hope that human and elf might be able to *change* the stories of humans and elves.

A princess doesn't have to be blonde and blue-eyed and have a shoe size smaller than her age, she thought.

People *can* trust witches, and not fear the old woman in the woods, the poor old woman whose only crime was to have no teeth and to talk to herself.

And perhaps an elf could learn to know mercy, to discover humanity . . .

'If you learn things,' she finished softly, 'you might find yourself building a different kind of kingdom.'

CHAPTER 16

Mr Sideways

The old boys in the villages around Granny Weatherwax's cottage had swiftly taken a liking to Geoffrey. They respected Nanny Ogg and Tiffany, of course, but they really *liked* Geoffrey.

They would taunt him sometimes; after all, he was in a woman's business, but when he got on his broomstick – sometimes even with his goat perched behind him rather than harnessed to its little cart – and whizzed away to the horizon, they were speechless.

Even when he was really busy, he always had time to stop and chat and there was always a brew on in any shed when he came by, and a broken biscuit for Mephistopheles. The old boys were fascinated by the goat, but wary nonetheless after the day when someone gave it a drink of ale just to see what would happen and, to their astonishment, Mephistopheles danced like a ballerina and then kicked a young tree so hard that its trunk split in two.

'It's like those folk who do mushi,' said Stinky Jim.

'I don't think that's the right word,' said Smack Tremble. 'Ain't mushi something you eat? Out in . . . foreign parts.'

'*You* mean One-man-he-go-up, he-go-down,' Captain Makepeace said. 'A way of fighting.'

'That's it!' said Stinky Jim. 'There was a fellow at the market in Slice who could do that.'

'There's a *lot* of people in Slice who can do that kind of thing,' Smack Tremble added with a shiver. 'Odd place, Slice.'*

They sat and thought about Slice for a moment. You could find anything at Slice market if you looked hard enough. Famously a man once sold his wife there, where the phrase 'bring and buy' was taken literally, and he went home with a second-hand wheelbarrow and felt he had the best of the bargain. Then they looked at the remains of the sapling and agreed that Mephistopheles was indeed a remarkable goat, but perhaps it would be best to leave his diet alone.

The remarkable goat himself stoically chewed his way through the long grass by the pub fence as though nothing untoward had happened and then trotted off to find Geoffrey.

On this particular fine morning, Geoffrey was at Laughing Boy Sideways's house. Tiffany had been treating a particularly troublesome bunion of his

---

* Quite correct. As the common joke says, most inhabitants of Slice are more than one slice short of a loaf.

which had resisted her ministrations for weeks. She had been considering breaking her rule and using magic on the thing, just to be done with it, when Geoffrey decided to pop in to see Mr Sideways on a day when Tiffany was away at the Chalk. He found the old man by the back door of his cottage, just about to hobble down the path to the old barn. Instead of heading back into the cottage as he would have done if Tiffany had called, Mr Sideways beckoned to Geoffrey to follow him down the path towards the rickety barn. And it was as Geoffrey watched the old boy struggling painfully along in his old army boots that he noticed something very wrong.

'Well, dang me!' Mr Sideways said when Geoffrey prised the offending hobnail from his left boot. 'If I'd known that was what the trouble was, I'd have dealt with the bugger meself!' He looked at Geoffrey with bright eyes. 'Thank 'ee, lad.'

Old Mr Sideways lived on his own and had done so for as long as anyone could remember. He was meticulously dressed and in the city might have been described as 'dapper'. Apart from his work overalls, which were washed regularly but were streaked with paint and oil, he was always spick and span. So was his little cottage. The living room, which he kept immaculately tidy, had paintings of people in old-fashioned dress on the wall – Geoffrey assumed these were portraits of Mr Sideways's parents, although he never spoke of them. Everything the man did he did carefully. Geoffrey liked him, and even though he was a very private man, he had taken to Geoffrey.

The shed Mr Sideways had constructed adjacent to the old barn was also immaculate. Every shelf was neatly stacked with carefully labelled old tobacco tins and jars. His tools were hung against the walls, neatly ranked by size. They were clean and sharp too. Tiffany had never been allowed beyond Mr Sideways's living room, but Geoffrey had soon been welcomed to share a mug of tea and a biscuit in the shed by the barn.

Each one of the sheds Geoffrey visited on his rounds of the old boys was different, expressing the personality of the occupant, unfettered by female intervention. Some were chaotic, with piles of scrap and half-made objects scattered about; others were tidier – like Captain Makepeace's shed, which was full of paints, brushes and canvases, but still had a clear sense of order.

But no one was as tidy as Mr Sideways. And then Geoffrey noticed something missing. All the other sheds had at least one work in progress visible, whether it was a half-made bird table, or a stripped-down wheelbarrow with a new shaft, but there was nothing like that to be seen in Mr Sideways's shed. And he evaded the question when Geoffrey asked what he was working on.

'What are you up to, Mr Sideways?' Geoffrey asked. 'You look like a man who has been thinking, and I know you are a canny man at that.'

Mr Sideways cleared his throat. 'Well, you see, lad, I am building a machine. I've no interest in bird tables or mug trees and the like. But machines now . . .' He paused, then looked carefully at Geoffrey. 'I've been thinking that it might be useful, what with the troubles folks are having.'

Geoffrey sat calmly, waiting for the old boy to finish his tea and reach a conclusion. Eventually Mr Sideways put down his mug and stood up, brushing the crumbs off his lap. He swept them up with a small pan and brush he clearly kept just for that purpose, washed out the mugs, dried and stacked them neatly on a shelf, then opened the door.

'Would you like to see, lad?'

While Geoffrey drank his mug of tea with Mr Sideways in Lancre, over in the Chalk Letitia, the Baroness, was sipping tea daintily with Magrat, the Queen of Lancre, who had arrived unexpectedly on her broomstick – a broomstick flying the pennant of Lancre, the two bears on black and gold, just to make sure that nobody could be in any doubt that this was a royal visit. She had arrived bearing a bunch of roses from the castle, throwing Letitia and her staff all in a tiswas and Letitia flapping about the cobwebs, some of which she had even managed to get tangled in her hair.

Magrat had smiled at the rather shaky-looking Letitia, and said, 'I'm not here as a queen, love. I am here as a witch. I always have been one and always will be. So don't worry about all the pomp – you know how it is, it's just expected. A bit of dust here and there is nothing. Some parts of my castle are full of dust, I am sorry to say. You know how that is too.'

Letitia had nodded. She did indeed know what it

was like. And as for the plumbing . . . well, she did not want to even *think* about how old-fashioned the castle was. The ancient privies had a habit of gurgling at the wrong time, and Roland said that if he had the time, he could create an orchestra from the bangs, gurgles and clankings that sometimes followed his morning visits.

She had rallied the troops, though, and now the two ladies sat side by side in the castle hall, breathing in the peaty fumes from the fireplace – it was always, always cold there, even in the summer, which was why the fireplaces were so big and ate several small trees at a time. The kitchen staff had brought out a hasty tray with tea and little snacks – and yes, the sandwiches *did* have the crusts cut off to make them appropriately dainty for the two noble ladies. Magrat sighed – she really hoped Letitia at least asked for the crusts to be given to the birds.

There was also a plate of rather wobbly cupcakes.* '*I* made those,' Letitia said proudly. 'Yesterday. From a recipe in Nanny Ogg's new cookbook – you know, *A Lot of What You Fancy Makes You Fat.*' She coloured a little, and her hand crept self-consciously up to her bodice, where it was clear that when curves were being handed out, Letitia had been at the end of the line.

Magrat took a cake by its little case rather carefully. Some of Nanny Ogg's recipes could include . . . unusual ingredients, and she already *had* three

---

* It appears to be a fact of life that if two or more well-born ladies should gather together, cupcakes are *essential*. Otherwise the ceiling might fall on them.

children. She nibbled at the little cake, and the two ladies exchanged the usual pleasantries, with Magrat admiring a watercolour Letitia had painted of the chalk giant up on the downlands. It was surprisingly detailed, especially in the No Trousers area. Nanny Ogg would definitely have approved, Magrat thought.

Then she got down to business. 'Well,' she said, 'I'm sure I don't need to tell you, Letitia, but up in Lancre we've had enough of the elves. Something must be done.'

'Oh dear, I'm sorry to say that Roland is about to write to Mistress Aching about the wave of elf raids and ask her what she's proposing to do about them. There have been an awful lot of complaints, you know, and he's out inspecting the damage.' Letitia sighed. She understood that her husband looking at the damage comprised more than just inspecting the aftermath and saying, 'Tsk, tsk,' and 'How long has this been going on?' – it needed to include other things to make his tenants feel that someone was doing something about it. And Roland's wife had impressed on him that this was not just a matter of being seen, but that rolling up his sleeves and getting stuck in alongside his men was good for morale. Even better if he bought a round in the pub when the day's work was done and became not just the boss but almost a friend. 'We've got men enough here, no doubt about that,' she added, 'but most of the time they are working on the farms. It would be appreciated if other witches could help.'

'And unfortunately, that means us,' Magrat said smartly, with the emphasis on the *us* part.

Letitia looked embarrassed. 'I'm not a proper witch, you know.'

Magrat looked at the Baroness. There was something terribly *soggy* about Letitia, as if you could pick her up and wring her out. But witches came in all shapes and sizes. Both Nanny Ogg and Agnes Nitt, for instance, were decidedly plump* while Long Tall Short Fat Sally went up and down according to the tides – and there was no doubt that water could be powerful. 'My dear, you are selling yourself short,' she said. 'And I know what it is. I believe, my dear, that you are frightened that you wouldn't make the grade as a witch. We all went through that – girls normally do. Tiffany has told me all about you, you know. As for me, I don't know what I would be like in a house with a screaming skeleton. Were you not the girl who gave a headless ghost a pumpkin to carry around? And handed a teddy bear to a screaming skeleton for comfort? You don't think you are a witch, but every part of my soul says you are. I wish I'd had your opportunities when I was a girl.'

'But I am the Baroness. I am a lady. I can't be a witch.'

Magrat made a sound like 'hurrumpf', and said, 'Well, I am a queen. That doesn't stop me being a witch when needs must. This is the time, my dear, when we stop thinking about ourselves and who we are and get down and dirty. Tiffany cannot fight the

* A very *kind* term for Agnes, used only by her friends.

elves on her own, and this is a war – and it will keep on going unless everyone pitches in.'

Her words flowed in and filled Letitia. 'You are right, of course,' the young Baroness said. 'Naturally Roland will agree with me, as he always does. Count me in.'

'Good,' said Magrat. 'I have got some chainmail which I think is your size. And now, how soon can you leave for Lancre? I believe we are meeting to discuss the situation. Can you ride a broomstick or do you need a lift?'

Tiffany straddled her broomstick. She had heard in the village that old Mrs Pigeon was near her time, and a wave of guilt had flooded through her. Yes, she had two steadings. Yes, she had to work out what to do with Nightshade. Yes, she had no time to rest. But she hadn't seen the old lady for over a week, and in a week an old lady could fall through the cracks of life.

Nightshade was perched behind her, her sharp eyes noting everything. Noting how the Pigeon family had only the smallest plot of land, with soil so poor it was a wonder they got a crop out of it at all, their fortunes depending mostly on the little flock of sheep they had in their field by the stream.

Sid Pigeon, the youngest son, was there, looking much smaller somehow without his shiny railway uniform. To Tiffany's surprise, he had brought a new work friend home with him.

Nightshade recoiled. 'A *goblin*! In their house. Stinking . . .' she said with distaste.

Tiffany felt like kicking her. 'A very *respectable* goblin,' she said smartly, though it was true that she could smell the goblin as soon as she went into the house, even over the layers of other smells happily living in that very dirty home. She nodded to the goblin, who was sitting with his feet up on the table, eating what looked like a chicken leg that others – possibly the cats – had had a go at before him. 'Sid's *friend*.'

'Of Piston the Steam, mistresss,' the goblin said cheerfully. 'Works with the iron and steel, I doess—'

'Tiffany,' Sid said urgently, 'have you come to see Granny? She's in bed upstairs.'

Old Mrs Pigeon was indeed in her bed, and it didn't look to Tiffany as if she was likely to be getting out of it ever again. The old lady was little more than a wrinkled set of bones, her twiglike fingers clutching at the edges of a faded patchwork quilt. Tiffany reached out and held one of her hands and . . . did what she could for the old lady, calling the pain out of the shrunken body—

And all hell broke loose downstairs.

'Sid! Them pesky fairies or whatever – they've only gone and fouled the stream. It's all yeller! And there's dead fish floatin' in it! We've got to move the sheep – now!' Mr Pigeon sounded desperate as he called to his son.

As a thunder of boots left the house, Tiffany held her concentration, drew more pain from old Mrs Pigeon. And then Nightshade was at her side.

'I don't understand,' she said. 'That . . . goblin went with the humans.'

'It's called *helping*,' Tiffany said smartly, still trying to hold on to the pain she had taken from old Mrs Pigeon. 'Remember?'

'But goblins and humans don't like each other,' Nightshade continued, puzzled.

'I told you, Of Piston the Steam is Sid's *friend*. But this isn't about *liking*,' Tiffany said. 'It's about helping each other out. If the goblin camp was on fire or something, the humans would help *them*.' She looked down at Mrs Pigeon; the old lady was falling into a sleep now. 'Look, I need to go outside for a minute,' she said. 'Stay with Mrs Pigeon, would you? Let me know if she wakes again.'

Nightshade was horrified. 'But I can't – I'm an elf! I've already carried that basket. I can't . . . help *another* human.'

'Why not?' said Tiffany sharply. 'Of Piston the Steam just did. Are elves less than goblins?' But she had no time to waste, so she headed downstairs and threw the pain out into a pile of stones laid ready for building into a wall.

It made a rather unfortunate loud bang – there had been quite a *lot* of pain – which is probably why, when she got back upstairs, Mrs Pigeon had woken up. Woken up and asked for a cup of water.

The old granny was staring up at Nightshade, a smile on her gummy face as she reached out for the cup. 'You're a good girl, you are,' she was saying weakly. 'A good girl . . .'

A good girl? A good *elf*?

Nightshade put her hands to her stomach. 'I think

it is beginning . . .' she said softly, looking up at Tiffany.
'I feel a sort of warm spot. Here, in my stomach. A
little *glow.*'

Tiffany smiled, laid a gentling hand on Mrs
Pigeon, and then took Nightshade by the arm. 'I need
your help,' she said. 'Elves have put this glamour on
the stream and it runs past several farms . . . can you
put it right?' She paused. 'As your *friend*, Nightshade,
I am asking for your help. The Feegles can help with
the sheep, but to remove the glamour? This is something only one of your kind can do.'

Nightshade stood up. 'A glamour from Peaseblossom?' she said. 'This will be no trouble to remove.
That elf is *weak*. And yes, I will help you, Tiffany.
You are my . . . friend.' The word sounded odd in her
voice, but there was no doubt that she meant it.

So she went down into the fields with Tiffany, past
the skittish sheep in the yard – some of whom, courtesy of the ever-present Feegles, had just broken the
county record for stream-to-yard time, one young
lamb actually doing so *on one leg* – and down to the
boiling water.

Where she did indeed put it right.

And the tiny little glow inside began to
smoulder . . .

The old barn behind Mr Sideways's shed was full of
miscellaneous weaponry, souvenirs from many con-
flicts, lovingly oiled and meticulously labelled.

'I've been collecting them,' Mr Sideways said
proudly. 'Every campaign I bin in and more besides.

You should always keep your weapons handy. I mean, I don't say anything bad about the trolls and the dwarfs, but we fought them more'n once and so I say, you always have to make sure. Somebody says something and before you know it, we're knee-deep in dwarfs. They give you the up and under. You can't trust 'em with the up and under.'

Geoffrey looked around the walls of the barn in astonishment. The machinery of death was everywhere, if you looked at it properly. And there he was, this smiling old man with whom he'd just been sharing a cup of tea, eyes sparkling, ready to face the foe, especially if it wasn't human. And he was known as *Laughing Boy*? What would he have been like if he had been known as *Scowling Boy*?

'I can turn a lathe as good as anybody,' Mr Sideways said.

'A lathe,' said Geoffrey. 'You get swarf, don't you?'

'Oh yes, terrible stuff if it gets in your eye.' He smiled. 'And it could be useful for something.' There was a moment when he almost led Geoffrey back out again, but then he could not hold it in any longer – he *had* to show the boy what he had been working on. 'Come, lad,' he said. 'Have a look at this. It was going to be a secret until it was finished, but of course I can tell *you*.'

At the back of the barn there was a huge shape covered with a tarpaulin. Mr Sideways led Geoffrey over to it, reached up and gave the tarpaulin a tug, and as it fell away Geoffrey gasped.

The machine looked like a great metal grasshopper, with a counterweight at one end, and an enormous leather sling at the other. As he gazed at the machine in astonishment, Geoffrey realized that he had seen something similar in the books Mr Wiggall had shown him at home. He said, 'This looks dangerous.'

'I hope so,' said Mr Sideways. 'I've always wanted one of these, ever since I saw them in action. The dwarfs had ones a bit like this which could throw a troll flat on his back. Those dwarfs know a thing or two, I must say, and I'm very big on gnome defence.' He coughed. 'Got the idea to build one after I'd been watching the lads down the pub do the Stick and Bucket dance.'*

'So I see,' said Geoffrey.

'Captain Makepeace is very impressed,' Mr Sideways added. 'So me and the boys are going to try it out tomorrow, but nowhere anyone can see us.'

These old gentlemen have certain qualities, Geoffrey thought. Just because they are old doesn't mean they can't be powerful.

---

* A dance that should only be performed when no women are nearby. If you saw it, you would know why.

CHAPTER 17

An Argument of Witches

Through the unbarred door, Lord Lankin creeps into a crumbling old manor house. Up the creaky stairs, snuffing out the candles in the sconces as he passes, he opens an unbolted door and prowls into a nursery, where a young nursemaid rocking a cradle looks up, gazes into his eyes, and then pulls a sharp pin from her basket . . .

Sitting in the Great Hall at Lancre Castle with their allies and friends, Tiffany and the witches of Lancre contemplated the construction of a battle plan.

It had taken some effort to get everyone there and settled down. Geoffrey had done a marvellous job rounding up reinforcements from all over, flying hours in every direction with Tiffany's message, to every witch she could name.

Even blind Mrs Happenstance and Long Tall Short Fat Sally had turned up, with Mrs Proust from Ankh-Morpork. And there was a group of younger witches too: Annagramma Hawkin, Petulia Gristle, Dimity Hubbub, Harrieta Bilk and others. Under Queen Magrat's watchful eye, Letitia ticked them off Tiffany's list as they arrived.

Having a queen backing you up was a good thing, Tiffany thought, as Mrs Earwig came in and started bossing everyone around – Magrat swiftly put a stop to *that*, for even Mrs Earwig found that she couldn't argue with royalty. But dealing with witches all together was like carrying a tray full of marbles. Witches were very good at rubbing one another up the wrong way, and little feuds turned up and went away and disappeared and started again. It was silly and everybody knew it, but they couldn't help themselves.

Geoffrey came into his own on occasions like this. Whenever bickering broke out, he was there with the perfect word or a sympathetic smile. Seeing his calm-weaving doing its subtle work was a joy, Tiffany thought. You could almost see the calm coming out of his ears.

'Ladies,' Tiffany said, calling the meeting to order. 'Here's the problem. The elves are back again, this time in force. And if we don't stop them soon, things will get very bad indeed. I know some of you have encountered elves before' – she looked at Nanny Ogg and Magrat – 'but many of you have not. They are a formidable foe.'

Nightshade was standing at the side of the hall,

almost too demure in her dairymaid's dress. She didn't *seem* very formidable, but a few of the older witches were eyeing her as though they had just encountered a bad smell.

Mrs Earwig tutted and looked as though she was about to say something, but Petulia got there first. 'Tiff, are you sure that it's wise to have an elf here listening to this?' she asked.

'Don't you worry, my girl,' Nanny Ogg said. 'If our little friend tries anything, there will be fireworks and no mistake. Certainly no more elf!'

'The last time this happened, didn't the King of the Elves intervene?' Annagramma Hawkin asked, looking at Nanny Ogg.

'He did indeed, but he almost didn't. Tiffany's been to see him already, and it seems Old Horny ain't interested,' Nanny answered. 'Can't rely on him in any case.'

'Time moves differently in his realm,' Tiffany explained. 'Even if he did decide to do something, it might be now, or next month or next year.'

'What about the wizards?' asked another witch. 'Why aren't *they* here?'

Nanny snorted. 'Ha! *That* lot. By the time they got a spell ready, the elves would be over the Ramtops and far away.' She adjusted her position and sniffed. 'No, this is *witches'* business. Them wizards have all got their bums on chairs and their noses stuck in *books*.' She said this last word with a sideways glance at Mrs Earwig who was, of course, known for her love of writing.*

---

* Most everyday working witches believed the best use for a book was on a nail in the privy.

Magrat cut in quickly. 'We also have all the support of Lancre that Verence and I can muster.'

'Well, that's my Shawn,' said Nanny with satisfaction. Shawn Ogg *was* the army of Lancre, as well as its bottle-washer, butler, gardener, trumpeter and – a role Shawn would have liked to lose – the man who checked the garderobes and removed all the night waste. 'And I reckons our Jason can provide us with a few horseshoes. Being as he's the blacksmith,' Nanny added for those who might not know.

Geoffrey coughed. 'I've been working on a few ideas with some of the older gentlemen,' he said softly. 'We have . . . something I think might be useful.'

'And there's Hodgesaargh,' said Magrat. Hodgesaargh – the royal falconer – was a surprising asset, since elven glamour didn't seem to work on him, probably because he spent so much time with his beloved birds that a part of his brain *was* a falcon by now, and hence unprepared to share space with any other predator. It was generally believed that this was also what stopped the birds from pecking out his eyeballs.

Mrs Earwig laughed confidently. 'So what is the problem, may I ask? There are plenty of us here. Surely more than enough for a few elves.' She looked scornfully at Nightshade.

Nanny Ogg exploded. 'No, there's *not* enough of us! How many witches have we here?' She looked around the room. 'Ten, twelve mebbe – more if you includes Geoffrey and Letitia, and the young girls still training – but only half of us bein' senior witches what has much real experience. The elves are sneaky.

They'll have the glamour on you afore you knows it. They come quietly – like a silent but deadly fart – and they get you before you can pinch your nose. Even Esme Weatherwax could barely withstand the power. She fought hard, and you all remember what *she* was like. They didn't get past her – but it was a close thing. Ladies, these 'ere elves are *horrible*. We're right to be fearful. They do . . . things to you. Get at you.'

'It happened to me too,' said Magrat. 'The glamour makes you feel small and worthless. Those of us who have faced it before can't warn the rest of you enough.'

'I fear you are exaggerating. There's nothing glamorous about *that*,' Mrs Earwig said scornfully, pointing at Nightshade.

'Well, *you've* certainly never met no fairy. If'n you had, you would have *scars*,' Nanny spat. She had turned an interesting colour and Tiffany intervened quickly before sparks really began to fly.

'Ladies, ladies, I think it would be useful to have a little demonstration of the power of an elf. Nightshade, would you be prepared to give us a taste of your glamour?'

There was a collective intake of breath as the assembled witches realized what Tiffany was suggesting.

'Be careful, Nightshade. Very careful. Those of us who have met the glamour before will keep an eye on you. I sincerely hope that we won't have a problem.'

And Nightshade smiled – not a particularly pleasant smile, Tiffany noticed.

'Ladies,' said Magrat to the others, trying to

prepare them. 'To be a witch is to be full of yourself – and in charge of yourself as well. It would be a good idea to watch one another when the glamour starts to take hold.'

'Tish and pish!' said Mrs Earwig. 'I am my own woman, and always will be. I am a witch, whatever you might think, and I don't deal in fairy tales.'

In a syrupy voice, Nanny Ogg said, 'You just *write* them, Mrs Earwig.'

'But not as reality,' said Mrs Earwig. 'That's allowed.'

Nanny Ogg looked at her face and thought: We will see.

'Ladies,' asked Tiffany, 'are you all ready?' There were some nods and yeses, so she said, 'Nightshade, please show us your glamour.' And she grasped the shepherd's crown in her pocket – this was a moment when she knew she would need to keep a strong hold on her sense of her self. *Yan tan tethera*, she chanted softly to herself. *Yan tan tethera.*

Nightshade began slowly, her foxy little dairy-maid's face filling with a shining light, with beauty, with *style*, and then she was suddenly the most wonderful thing in the hall.

Fantastic.

Marvellous.

Enchanting.

Terrific.

The air was thick with glamour and Tiffany could almost hear the witches fighting it. The inexperienced ones – Annagramma, Petulia and Letitia, Dimity and

Harrieta – suddenly seemed flaccid, their faces like dolls.

Petulia – like many of the other witches – felt a beguiling feeling that the world was all hers, all of it, with everything that was in it. And then, her dream – as did theirs – unravelled. *Who did she think she was? No one liked her, no one wanted her. She wasn't worthy of anything. No one wanted her. Everyone knew she didn't have any skills. It would be so much better if she was dead. Maybe it would be better if she simply let the pigs stamp her down into the mire, and even that wouldn't be bad enough.* She screamed.

Tiffany moved towards Nightshade, and almost like a bubble bursting, the elf let go, and her glamour was all gone. But everyone in the hall looked shaken. Except, Tiffany noticed, Mrs Earwig.

'So, what happened?' the older witch snapped bossily. 'What are you all doing?'

'Mrs Earwig, did you not feel as though you were small, nasty and a waste of space? Totally without redemption?'

Letice Earwig's face held nothing but puzzlement.

Nightshade looked at her, and back to Tiffany. 'It was like hitting a rock,' she said. 'This one has something interesting . . . something missing.' She turned to stare again at Mrs Earwig. 'Are you sure you are not an elf?' she queried.

'How dare you! I am just Letice Earwig. No one can stop me being me!'

'Perish the thought,' said Tiffany. 'But everyone else was affected. And that, ladies, was just one elf.

Imagine what it will be like when we are facing a horde of them.'

'It was like seeing my father,' said Geoffrey. 'I heard a voice telling me that I was no good and I never would be. A mouse, a maggot, no one worth crying for. He was never satisfied about anything.'

His words sang into the room, and the witches' faces showed that each knew exactly what he was talking about.

With the demonstration finished and Nightshade back in her unassuming dairymaid guise, the bickering was almost over.

'Well, fellow witches, there we have it,' Tiffany said. 'We know who we are after and what we have to do, which is to keep the elves away from this world. It's very unlikely that we could kill them all.' She hesitated. 'What we have to do is make them see that dealing with us will not be easy, and it might be a very good idea to go back to where they came from.'

'So,' Queen Magrat said, 'how long do we have to get ready?'

Tiffany sighed. 'We don't know,' she said. 'But they will come soon, I feel.' She looked at Nightshade, who moved now into the centre of the room.

'The *when*,' said the elf, 'will surely be at the full moon. A time of . . . endings.'

'*Tonight*, then . . .' Magrat whispered.

'And if I know Peaseblossom,' continued the elf, 'the *where* will be on every front where the barriers may be weak.'

'What do you think, Tiff?' said Nanny Ogg.

'They've been coming into the Chalk already, right? And they've been up here in Lancre – through the Dancers.'

Nightshade nodded. 'They will come through both those gates,' she said. 'And afterwards fan out.' She shivered.

Tiffany was taking charge now. 'Well, we're going to need to face them on two fronts then. Here in Lancre, and over in the Chalk.' She looked around the room. 'We'll have to split our forces.'

'Well,' said Nanny Ogg, 'you can count on me. I've always been a fighter. You has to be a fighter to be a witch. We don't have to worry – *they* does. If you can get an elf down and kick it about a bit, it's not goin' to be so glamorous as it was. Take it from me, even elves has soft parts which don't like no boot in 'em.'

Tiffany glanced at Nanny's boots. They looked as though they had been built by a blacksmith, and in Nanny's case they probably had been. A kick from one of those and it would be 'So long, elf!' It might not kill them, but you could certainly say that all the glamour would have been kicked out.

'They know where the stone circles are,' she said, 'but by Thunder and Lightning they had better keep away. After all, we know where the stones are as well, and we humans are clever, and we can sometimes be very nasty to boot. When we need to, I suspect.' She turned to Nightshade, who had been watching everyone carefully. 'What do you make of it, Nightshade?'

The elf smiled and said, 'You humans are a strange

people. Sometimes soft and stupid, but also surprisingly dangerous. There are very few of you, and very many of the elves ranged against you. Yet I believe that traitor Peaseblossom has no idea what he will be facing. And I'm glad of that.'

Tiffany nodded. Magrat, Nanny Ogg, the surprisingly strong Mrs Earwig – there was more to Letice Earwig, she realized, than the occult jewellery and fancy outfits suggested – the other witches of Lancre, Mrs Proust, Geoffrey and Mephistopheles. It would have to do.

'I think Lancre will be well served by you all,' she said, looking around. 'But I must go back to the Chalk. It's my land.'

'Who will you have to help you in the Chalk, may I ask?' said Mrs Earwig.

'Well,' said Tiffany, 'there's Miss Tick – a formidable lady, as I am sure you will all agree, who sends her apologies for her absence today.' Or would, she thought to herself, if I could have *found* her again. 'Also Letitia.' She looked at the young Baroness, who was trying to look brave. 'And there's the land itself, of course. But remember, I have some other admirable allies. We are not on our own.' She had been keeping an eye on the pile of broomsticks by the door, and even though they hadn't been invited she could see the face of Rob Anybody, and by the look of it a significant number of his clan. She laughed; they must have come up with Magrat and Letitia, she thought. 'Ladies,' she announced, 'please allow me to introduce . . . the Nac Mac Feegles!'

There was a susurration amongst the witches as the room started to fill with a sea of blue skin and tartan – not all the witches had met the Feegles before. Tiffany heard Nanny Ogg whisper not quite quietly enough to Queen Magrat, 'Put anythin' drinkable in the cellar.'

'Ach, ye are a cruel hag, so ye are, or my name isnae Rob Anybody,' Rob moaned.

Magrat laughed. 'Rob Anybody, you are a war all by yourself, man! Welcome to the palace but please don't drink everything. At least, not until we have won the war.'

'Now ye are talking, lassie – I mean, your queenship. Where there's a war there's a Nac Mac Feegle.'

There was a barrage of cries of 'Crivens' from the clan and Rob Anybody shouted, 'Aye, get 'em doon, and the kickin' starts.' There was another cheer then and Big Yan jumped up and shouted, 'Ye will need to tak' note, ye weans. We dinnae say yes tae Mister Finesse, but we jes' kick 'em.'

Hamish added, 'Whan Morag swoops doon on top o' 'em, her beak 'n' talons'll tak' their breath awa'. And she's a heavy girl.'

'Be happy that they are on our side,' Tiffany said. She looked reprovingly at Mrs Earwig, who had a snooty look on her face. 'It's true that they are rough diamonds, but no better warriors can be found anywhere on the Disc.' And she hoped that Mrs Earwig didn't hear the mumbling:

Daft Wullie. 'What's this? Did we stole any diamonds?'

'It's a manner of speaking, ye daftie.' Rob Anybody.

'But we *got* no manners. We treasure the fact, ye ken.' Wullie, again.

'It's an idiom.'

'Who're you calling an idiom?'

Tiffany laughed to herself. It appeared that the kelda had been seeing to the clan's range of expressions.

Rob waved his claymore in the air, making one or two witches retreat a step or two, and then he leaped up onto a table and glared down the hall. 'Weel, I see the Lady Nightshade is with us the noo,' he said. 'Ach, the big wee hag and the kelda seem tae think that we shouldnae do anything aboot this elf – we are tae leave her alone. Although,' he continued, looking at Nightshade, 'we'll be watching her carefully, verra carefully indeed. Oor kelda is soft, oor kelda, as soft as *stone*, ye ken – she is nae one to let a body break their troth and get away wi' it!'

'Dear sir, Mister Feegle,' said Mrs Earwig. 'This is a council of war, so we should be discussing strategies and tactics.'

'Ah weel, ye can if ye wish, but we are Feegles and we dinnae mess about wi' things like that. It's all aboot usin' yon claymore to best offence. And if ye dinnae get that right, your last resort is to nut 'em.'

Tiffany took in Mrs Earwig's face and said cheerfully, 'Could you do that, Mrs Earwig?'

She was given a Look, and Mrs Earwig said, 'I will nut as I see fit.' And to Tiffany's surprise, the other witches applauded, and for once Mrs Earwig was wreathed in smiles.

'I tell ye, I would nae cross yon carlin,' said Rob Anybody.

'Nae me,' said Big Yan. 'She's as sharp as a she-wolf.'

'So wheer's yon battle, then, hag o' the hills?' Rob demanded.

There was another roar from the assembled Feegles, and a forest of little swords and clubs were thrust into the air.

'Nac Mac Feegle, wha hae!'

'A guid kickin' for the wee scunners!'

'Nae king! Nae quin! We willnae be fooled again!'

Tiffany smiled. 'If Nightshade is right, the elves will ride through this coming night – when the full moon shines in the skies. Ladies – and Geoffrey,' she addressed the assembled witches. 'Go and get some rest. I must fly back to my steading now, but good-night and good luck.'

'Let the runes of fortune guide and protect us all,' Mrs Earwig added portentously, always determined to get the last word in.

Tiffany loved the little room she'd had since she was a child. Her parents hadn't changed anything, and unless it was raining or blowing a gale, she slept with the window open.

Now, weary from the broomstick ride back, tense with the expectation of what the night might bring but hoping to get a few hours' rest, she savoured the atmosphere of the little room, finding strength from its familiarity.

A strength that came from feeling that she was *exactly* where she should be. An Aching.

'I get up Aching, and I go to bed Aching,' she whispered to herself, smiling. One of her father's jokes, and she had rolled her eyes when hearing it again and again as a child, but now its warmth curled over her body.

And there was the china shepherdess on the shelf.

Granny Aching.

And next to it she had placed the shepherd's crown.

Aching to Aching, down the generations.

Land under wave, she mused. That was what the name Tiffany meant in the speech of the Feegles. Tir-far-thóinn, 'Tiffan', the kelda would call her. The sound of her name was magic, real magic from the beginning of time.

It was a soft night. She told herself that she really ought to get some sleep – she'd be no good without some rest – but she lay there, the cat You snuggled up against her warmth, listening to the owls. Hootings were coming from everywhere, as if they were warning her.

Outside her window, the moon was rising, a gloriously full silver orb to light the skies, to lead the elves in . . .

Tiffany's eyes closed.

And a part of her, the soul of her, was in a chalk pit, the shepherd's crown in her hand, its five ridges catching the light of the full moon, and it was glowing, like an aquarium out of time.

Now she could hear the roar of the ancient sea beneath her, its voice trapped in the millions of tiny shells that made up the Chalk.

And she was swimming . . .

Great strange fish were coming towards her, big and heavy-looking with teeth.

At that point, Dr Bustle* floated into her mind and took his cue. '*Dunkleosteus*,' he said as a creature the size of a house floated by. '*Megalodon*' was huge and carnivorous – more teeth than Tiffany had ever seen in one go. Then there were sea scorpions – armour-plated, clawed horrors. But none of them paid any attention to her. It was as if she had a right to be there.

And then there was a smaller creature, an explosion of blue spines that did notice Tiffany.

'*Echinoid*,' whispered Sensibility Bustle.

'That is correct,' said the creature. 'And I am the shepherd's crown. Deep in my heart is the flint. And I have many uses. Some call me the sea urchin, others the thunderstone, but here, now, in this place, call me the shepherd's crown. I seek a true shepherd. Where can a true shepherd be found?'

'We shall see,' Tiffany heard herself saying. 'I am

---

* Part of him anyway, his memories being relocated to Tiffany's mind following an episode early in her witching life. The rather pedantic wizard's knowledge, especially of ancient languages, came in very handy sometimes, like when she wanted to read a peculiar menu in Ankh-Morpork.

Tiffany Aching and my father is a king among shepherds.'

'We know him. He is a good shepherd, but not the best. You must find the king of shepherds.'

'Well,' said Tiffany, 'I'm just a witch, but I will help you if I can. I work hard, mostly for other people.'

'Yes,' said the echinoid. 'We know.'

I'm talking to a creature from under the sea, thought Tiffany. Is that right? First Thoughts, not Second Thoughts, her mind reminded her.

'It is strange,' said the voice of Dr Bustle in her head. 'But not so strange as falling down a rabbit hole with a pack of cards.'

Let me think about it, her Second and Third Thoughts said. If talking creatures from the sea turned up everywhere, we'd all know about it, so this must be something just for me.

The voice came from nowhere, as though it was part of that ocean from Time: *'Tiffany Aching is the first among shepherds, for she puts others before herself . . .'*

And the shepherd's crown was warm in her hand, a golden light glowing from within its depths. An heirloom handed down from generation to generation of Achings – down to Granny Aching, on to Joe Aching, and now to Tiffany herself . . .

Then the sea had gone and she was back in the pit, but the magic was still there, for slowly, oh so slowly, she could see bones pulling themselves free of the chalk, rising to draw together . . . to make two figures . . .

Thunder and Lightning! Granny Aching's sheep-dogs. The best dogs any shepherd could ever have. Dogs for the first among shepherds.

Now they were at her feet, their ears pricked, and Tiffany felt as if she could almost reach out to touch them. *Almost.* But not quite. For if she should touch them, be part of them, would she too be drawn into the chalk, to be bones like them . . . ?

'Come by, Thunder. Away to me, Lightning,' she whispered, the familiar commands filling her with courage.

Then she was suddenly awake, back in her room, You draped across her feet and an owl's huge eyes hanging in the dark of the trees outside.

And someone was tapping on the window.

While the moon shone gloriously full over the stone circles, lighting a path for her wayward children, who rode through in their splendour . . .

CHAPTER 18

The Shepherd's Crown

There was the face of Rob Anybody, and he said, 'The scunners are breaking through, Mistress Tiffany. It's stairted!'

'So cry "Crivens" and let loose the clan Mac Feegle!' Tiffany commanded as a small group of Feegles scrambled out from under the bed, from where they had been watching over her. One of them appeared to have been hiding in her boots . . . he was now punching at the laces with a cry of 'Tak' tha', yer nasty wrigglin' little bogles!'

Boots, Tiffany thought. I wish I had brought Granny Weatherwax's boots to wear for this fight. They would have given me strength. And then she stopped this thought. No. This is *my* land. *My* turf. *My* feet. *My* boots. *My way* . . .

But she still scolded herself as she struggled into her

dress and thought that she should have slept with her day clothes on: What kind of leader are you?

As she stumbled to pull on her boots she felt a weight in the deep pocket of her fine black dress . . . and she pulled out the shepherd's crown, which she thought she had put on the shelf. Had she put it there herself earlier that night? Ready for this moment?

And to the moon she said, 'What is the shepherd's crown? Whom does the shepherd's crown serve?'

And the answer dropped into her head. 'Tiffany Aching, Land under Wave.'

She twisted a thong of leather rapidly around the flint and hung it around her neck. She would go into battle with its power at her heart, she thought. The power of generations of Achings. Of Granny Aching. Of the shepherds of all time.

Then she ran down the darkened stairs and out of the door, locking it behind her, and was not surprised to see You the cat perched on the front of her broom-stick, purring and looking smug, while Nightshade was stumbling from the barn, Wee Mad Arthur at her side.

Then she was flying through the silvery night, the elf Nightshade clutching at her waist, Feegles hanging on to the bristles, and the owls following behind her, a squadron of feathered allies . . .

Over in Lancre, Nanny Ogg was sleeping and her snores could have cut timber. Suddenly there was a mild explosion which might be called a *grumph!* and the cat, Greebo, woke up and sniffed the air.

Nanny *had* been sleeping in her day clothes. After all, she thought, who knew for sure when the elves would come.

She shouted, 'Greebo, ring the castle bell.'

The cat was suddenly not there, but there was a blur of cat travelling at speed up to the castle, Greebo's unmistakable smell lingering in the air behind him, and when the guard saw him coming towards him he ran after him into the bell tower.

And as the great castle bell tolled, light blossomed throughout the castle as candles were lit in every window, followed very shortly by the rest of Lancre Town. The bell! What danger was this?

In the royal bedchamber, Queen Magrat nudged her husband, who was still rubbing his eyes, and said, 'Verence, help me buckle my escutcheon, will you, my dear?'

The King sighed. 'Look, why can't I go with you? It's going to be dangerous.'

Magrat smiled. The smile that you gave loving but occasionally annoying husbands. This was old ground. 'Well, someone has to be left at home,' she said. 'It's like chess, you know. The Queen saves the King.'

'Yes, dear,' said the King and opened the cupboard that contained the armour of Queen Ynci. Ynci had been the most fearsome warrior queen Lancre had ever seen. Well, so the stories said, as she hadn't *actually* existed. But the people of Lancre hadn't let a tiny thing like that stop them adding her to their history, and so a set of armour had been made to go along with a portrait. Magrat had worn the armour the last time she faced the elves, and it seemed only right to wear it again.

As the door opened, Magrat thought she heard a subtle little sound of a call to arms. Queen Ynci's armour had a life of its own and it always shone, even in the dark. Verence helped her buckle on the mail armour – which she secretly thought of as *fe*-mail – then she slipped her feet into the heavy-soled spiked sandals, and topped it all off with the winged helmet. The last piece to go on was the leather baldric.

Verence wanted to embrace her, but he thought, I won't. There were too many spikes, in any case. But he loved his wife to distraction, so he tried again to volunteer himself to be somewhere in the coming fray.

'Magrat, my love,' he murmured, 'it seems so shaming if the King can't fight.'

'You are a very good king, Verence,' his wife said firmly, 'but this is witches' work. And someone has to look after the people and our children.' The Queen – Magrat, as was – staggered under the weight of the armour, and under her breath she whispered a little magic. 'Queen Ynci, Queen of Queens, make your armour light.' And suddenly she felt strong, stronger than she had ever been before.

She picked up a crossbow in one hand, her broomstick in the other, and almost flew down the stairs to the Great Hall where the other witches, who were for the most part en déshabille, stared at her with wild surmise. Wild surmises take on many shapes and every witch, some still in their underwear, stared at the Queen and the surmise each gave her hung there in the rafters.

In the voice of Queen Ynci, Magrat shouted, 'Up, girls, and at 'em. It's started, ladies, so get your heavy-duty knickers on and your sticks ready!' She glared at the only witch to be fully dressed, spick and span in three minutes, to the surprise of all. 'That means you too, Mrs Earwig.'

There was a little commotion at the back of the hall, then a sudden *crash* and a group of witches ground to a halt.

'What's happening?' Magrat cried, still in the voice of Queen Ynci.

'It's only Long Tall Short Fat Sally: she's got two feet down one knicker!' said Mrs Proust. Surrounded by witches, Long Tall Short Fat Sally – small and squat right then, like a low-lying thunderstorm – was swiftly put back on her feet.

Mrs Earwig looked rather smug and said, 'I've been looking at my charts. The omens are good.'

'Well, omens are ten a penny,' said Mrs Proust. 'I've got lots of them. After all, we are all witches.'

And the ghost of Queen Ynci filled Magrat, who said, 'Let us fly.'

In Mr Sideways's old barn, Mephistopheles laid a hoof gently on Geoffrey's sleeping form. Geoffrey jumped out of the straw and discovered that the old boys who had readied themselves for the coming battle by bivouacking in the barn with him were already up and about, creaking a bit, and making their toilet in a bucket.

Geoffrey looked at the old men. They had spent

most of the evening carousing and telling stories of the days when they were all young and handsome and healthy and didn't have to pass water far too often.

They had managed to make their wives give them a ticket of leave, and said wives had been given to believe that their husbands were just in the barn for a few drinks and reminiscences. The wives, as wives do, had festooned their menfolk with big scarves, mittens on strings and woolly hats with, alas, pompoms on the top.

Captain Makepeace – the old boys' acknowledged military leader – said, 'It's time to go and get out Laughing Boy's confounded contraption.'

Geoffrey looked at the captain's warriors and sighed internally. Could they do it? They were old men. And then he thought, Yes, they are old men. They have been old men for a long time, which means they have learned many things. Like lying, and being crafty and, most importantly, dissembling.

'We shall fight them on the mountains. We shall fight them on the rocks. We shall fight them over the hills and down in the valleys.* We shall never surrender!' Captain Makepeace roared, and there was an answering cheer.

'They will not like it up and over 'em!' Smack Tremble called out, waving what looked like a rusty bayonet in the air and, worryingly, living up to his name. 'They will not like it, oh no they won't!'

Mephistopheles grunted as Geoffrey hitched him

---

* There was plenty of all these to pick from in Lancre, so he had a good choice of battlegrounds. As long as they were all up and down.

to his little cart, which the old boys had filled with mysterious bags before drinking the night away, and the two of them followed the old men out of the barn.

Captain Makepeace didn't need to tell his men to be stealthy. They already were. It was running fast that would be a problem. And stealthily they made their way into the wood and further on to where they had hidden Mr Sideways's contraption, camouflaging it with branches.

Geoffrey watched them pull Mr Sideways's project out into the clearing. It stood there looking ominous. Surrounded by the bushes. Waiting its moment. Like a huge insect.

One with a nasty sting . . .

Up by the circle of stones called the Dancers, Lord Lankin was exulting. His elves were dancing around the stones, flitting in and out and metaphorically tweaking the noses of the Piper, the Drummer, the Leaper – the best-known stones. The power of the gate was weak, and the glamour of the elves was . . . *fearsome.*

'They are not even here, waiting for us!' Lord Lankin gloated. 'Stupid humans. If we go down through those woods, we could be out into the centre of Lancre in one great charge. And the moon is full and on our side.'

And in the silver moonlight, the elves, some on horseback, bells jingling and harness tinkling, made their way down the hill towards the woods.

But as they neared the edge of the trees, Lankin

saw a young human boy step out onto the path with an animal by his side. It was a goat.

'Who are you, boy?' he demanded. 'Move aside. I am a prince of the elves and you are in my way. Move lest I show you my displeasure.'

'Well,' said Geoffrey, 'I don't see why I should. My advice to you is to turn round, sir, and go the other way or else it will be all the worse for you.'

Lord Lankin laughed out loud. 'We will take you away, boy, and the things we will use on you when we get you back home will be incredibly nasty. Your torment, for naysaying a prince of the elves.'

'But why, sir? I mean no harm to you. I have no weapons. Can we be calm about this? It would appear that I have made you unhappy, and for this I am sorry.' Geoffrey paused – he was trying to weave a peace between them, but it was like trying to get a rock to agree with a hard place. 'Surely both of us are civilized people,' he finished.

Lord Lankin screeched, 'Now, young man, you have trodden on the tail of the snake.'

Geoffrey calmly said, 'I believe this is not the case. I know you, mister. I know what kind of thing you are. You are a bully. I know about bullies, oh yes I do! I have known them all my life. And believe me, you aren't the worst.'

'You are nothing, boy. We'll kill you anyway. And why a goat, may I ask? They are stupid creatures.'

Geoffrey found his calmness floating away. He was worthless. A maggot. A ne'er-do-well. He felt powerless, a baby again . . . And as the elf spoke, in

Geoffrey's mind an echo came. *Even if I let you live, you will amount to nothing.* This time it was the voice of his father, and he stood there, frozen.

The elf prince said silkily, 'Are you crying, you little baby?'

'No,' said Geoffrey, 'but you might be.' For now his eyes had caught the flash of red fox fur swinging on its leather thong across the lord's chest, and he felt a rage beginning to build. 'We are not here for your . . . *sport*,' he stated, throwing the glamour from his mind with a huge effort of will.

He clicked his teeth and Mephistopheles was on the elf.

It was a ballet with speed. The Mince of Darkness pirouetted to dangerous effect. He used his teeth first, then kicked hard with his legs, and ended by using his horns. Lord Lankin was spinning, kicked and tossed into the air from all directions, and the other elves drew back to keep out of the range of the maelstrom.

And Geoffrey said to the battered prince, 'You are just a trickster. And I have found your trick.' He shouted, 'He's down, gentlemen. Time to put him *out*.'

The branches parted and there was a *twang* as Mr Sideways yelled, 'Keep your hats on, boys, cover your eyes,' and the contraption sang, swinging up into the air, filling it with a twinkle of swarf and terrible death that came from nowhere to shower over the elves.

Smack Tremble cheered. 'They don't like it up and over 'em! Oh no, they don't!'

'Swarf,' said Nanny Ogg approvingly, from one side of the woods, where she and some of the other witches were waiting – prepared for what Captain Makepeace had called a *pincer* movement, with Mrs Earwig and more witches on the other side. 'Pieces of iron,' Nanny told the witches with her. 'Very small. Very clever. Throw it down on elves, and they're in a world of hurt. Tiny bits of iron ev'rywhere. And, I stress, ev'rywhere.'

The Lancre Stick and Bucket machine sang again. And again. And each *twang* was followed by the war cries of ancient battles, rivalling those of the Feegles. On this day of days, the old boys were younger than they thought.

And the elves were, indeed, down and out, screaming from the pain of the terrible metal that stripped their glamour away from them, leaving them writhing. Many dragged themselves away back up the hill towards the Dancers, while any who had escaped the rain of swarf now found themselves sandwiched by the witches.

From one side, Magrat piled in to make life unlivable for those remaining, her armour shielding her from their glamour while her crossbow shot deadly arrows at them, and fire flew from her fingertips, forcing those who had ridden into battle on yarrow stalks to fall from the sky as flame destroyed the stems.

From the other side, the elves were assaulted by Mrs Earwig. And they really didn't know how to deal with her. She was shouting at them like some horrible headmistress – and they couldn't get through to her; she was impervious to their glamour. She also had an umbrella which she had opened, and it was amazing how much of a problem it was for the elves, its metal spokes poking at them, hitting tender spots.

'This lady is *not* for turning,' Mrs Earwig boomed. She rose among them like a whirlwind, and as they were floored, Long Tall Short Fat Sally became very fat and heavy and sat on them, bouncing up and down. While Mrs Proust hurled her novelties – novelties that now worked as advertised – over the elves, trapping them in curls of spells that seized their glamour and took it for their own.

The younger witches were in and out of the mêlée, diving from the skies on their broomsticks, throwing spells at every elf they saw: fire burning them where they stood, wind blowing dust into the horses' faces, madness into their minds, such that the horses reared, throwing their elvish riders to the ground. Then there was the crunching as Nanny Ogg came to the fore with her big, big boots. The ones with nails everywhere.

Petulia was face to face with an elf – and a different kind of battle was going on, as the elf threw its glamour towards her, sparkling shards of glamour shining in the air between them, and Petulia fought back with her soft voice and strong will, her words hypnotic, irresistible, boring the elf as she bored her beloved pigs, lulling it until it dropped dramatically at her feet.

'Hah! Easier than pigs!' was Petulia's response. 'Less intelligent.' And she turned to the next opponent . . .

And in a lull, there was Hodgesaargh, with his favourite gyrfalcon on his wrist – the Lady Elizabeth, a descendant of the famous Lady Jane. He slipped the hood off, and the bird joyfully hurled herself into the fray, hitting the nearest elf between the eyes with her sharp talons. Then her beak got to work . . .

When it came to it, the battle for Lancre was over quite swiftly. Queen Magrat had all the surviving elves brought before her. 'Even the goblins are smarter than you – they work *with* us these days,' she told them, standing tall and strong in her spiked armour, the wings on her helmet silvered in the moonlight. 'We have had enough of this. You could have had it all. Now, go away to your forlorn spaces. Come back as good neighbours – or not at all.'

The elves cringed. But Lord Lankin, his warrior garb now only rags and his body bloodied by the terrible swarf, hissed in defiance at them as he crawled away. 'You may have won this battle,' he snarled, 'but not the war. For our Lord Peaseblossom will yet make this world bow down to us.'

And then they were gone.

Nanny Ogg said seriously, 'It seems to me, girls, that it goes like this. We fight the elves at every turn, and they is always comin' back. Perhaps it might be a good thing? To keep us on our toes, to stop us from gettin' lazy. To put us on the anvil, so that we remembers how to fight. And at the end of time, living *is* about fightin' against everything.'

She laughed, however, when she heard the old gentlemen coming up the hill, singing, 'There was a young lady from Quirm, whose thighs were exceedingly firm . . .' And the rest of the song helpfully disappeared as the captain remembered just in time how that verse ended.

Captain Makepeace leaned over to Nanny Ogg and said, 'They came through the Dancers, right? Let's put a ring of swarf all around the stones. That would be the end of their fun. They would be locked out for ever.'

'Well, I reckons it would be a good start,' said Nanny.

But Lord Lankin had one thing right. The elves might have lost the battle in Lancre, but the war was not yet over. For, many miles rimwards, Lord Peaseblossom had indeed ridden through the stone circle on the Chalk, with a band of elite warriors at his back.

The Feegle mound was one big scuttle as the Nac Mac Feegles turned out of every nook and cranny to fight. Everywhere was heat and noise. You could call it something like an overgrown termite mound – not in front of the Feegles, unless you liked picking your teeth up from the ground – but there was the same bustling. It could even be said that the vanguard was steaming along, but these being Feegles, there were squabbles in the ranks which, as everyone knew, was just the way of the clan.

When Tiffany arrived at the mound with Nightshade, the throng spread out in the direction of the stones.

The gateway had fallen to the elves.

Who were now heading towards them, a glorious band of lords and ladies, resplendent in the moonlight. The air was thick with their glamour.

Miss Tick was waiting. A Miss Tick with a board propped up on a few sticks she had handily knotted together to create a trestle. And on the board was written PLN. With a teacher's determination not to let anything interrupt her in the midst of any kind of lesson, her insistent voice was demanding the younger Feegles' attention as she tied a strange net, a tangle of intricate, carefully woven knots and loops, to her broomstick.

'Remember, I want you to keep it *in one piece*,' she was saying sternly.

Then, within minutes, it was a mêlée. In fact, a mêlée of mêlées. There was a sting in the air and Tiffany recognized the surge of static electricity. How could the elves be so stupid, she thought, as to attack in the midst of a storm? Did they not remember how she had used thunder and lightning to defeat them before? The sky was crackling. The hairs on her head tingled. She could see signs of a coming downpour happening everywhere, could recognize the build-up to an enormous storm.

As Awf'ly Wee Billy Bigchin's mousepipes screeched out a battle hymn, pitched perfectly to assault the elven ears, there was a distant scream from a train at Twoshirts. A roar of iron and steel, a bellow that shouted: This is no world for elves!

Feegles and elves were fighting now, with no quarter given on either side. Tiffany could see that the Feegles were dealing with things in their own special way – which included getting into the elves' clothing and fighting them from within. If there was something that an elf really hated, it was to have their clothing torn, and a black eye didn't do much for the image either. You can't be suave with a black eye, Tiffany thought.

She suddenly burst out laughing. It had been a long time since she had set eyes on Horace the Cheese,* but now she saw him rolling heavily over every fallen elf, and when they were flattened the younger Feegles got to work as well, mostly with their heavy boots, but also with their double-the-fun clubs that curled in the air, clonking elves on the head and then coming joyfully back for another go. And yes, there was Maggie in their midst – a Feegle daughter fighting alongside her brothers! And indeed fighting even more furiously than her brothers. Tiffany thought, She's like a small Ynci. The Feegle maid had been waiting for something like this to prove herself, so woe betide any elf who got in her way. It was one small step for a Feegle lassie – but a giant step for all Feegle womenfolk!

Miss Tick was flying overhead now, the strange rope-net hanging beneath her broomstick filled with young Feegles. As she pulled at one knot after another, the Wee Free Men were tumbling out to fall smack on the heads of the elves below. *Crash! Whack! Crump!* Followed by *Aargh!* from the elves.

And the witch had small bottles with her too – concoctions mixed in her caravan that she was now gleefully emptying over the heads of the elves' horses as she swooped above them. There was a moment's

---

* Horace was a cannibal cheese, an adopted member of the Feegle clan.

pause as each horse absorbed the mixture, then its eyes crossed, followed rapidly by its hooves, and it toppled to the ground, losing its footing, hurling its rider onto the earth to be quickly covered by Feegles.

Letitia had arrived now, summoned by Hamish, and was tumbling from her horse, determination in her face, borrowed chainmail over her dress. She somehow *flowed* through the elves – there was a certain magic to it as if she were some goddess of water, streaming everywhere: no thought to it, but no stopping it either. Suddenly the elvish horses still standing were bogged down in a quagmire, and the Feegles were there on hand to keep them in the mire.

Nevertheless, it looked as if the Feegles, Miss Tick and Letitia were really not getting the better of the elves. Despite the Wee Free Men's pouring into elvish underwear and tearing it up, Tiffany realized that the Nac Mac Feegles were actually in danger of losing.

Nightshade pointed out Peaseblossom sitting on a black charger, and Tiffany flew down to confront the leader of the elves. His minions scattered as she arrived – they had seen the expression on Tiffany's face.

Peaseblossom was laughing. 'Ah, the little country girl. How pleased I am to see you!'

She felt the tug of his glamour but rage was a useful tool, and she hated that grinning face. It was so self-centred. It loved itself beyond any other thing.

'Peaseblossom is a very stupid name for an elf of your size,' she said rather childishly.

And then, suddenly, the elf had sprung from his

horse to stand before her, a sabre in his hands, and his laughter was gone, only evil in his eyes.

A voice said, 'Don't touch her, Peaseblossom.'

And Nightshade was stepping forward, her glamour fully restored and shining gloriously, her hair streaked silver with the moonlight, her new wings resplendent. She held herself like a queen again, her gaze slowly moving over the warriors behind her treacherous lord, and such was the power of her presence that even the Feegles paused in the frozen silence.

'Why do you follow this . . . perfidious elf?' the Queen demanded of the elves. '*I* am your rightful queen, and I say that you do not have to do this. There are . . . other ways.' She spun on the spot, her velvet robes spiralling around her slim body. 'I have learned this. And this girl' – she pointed at Tiffany – 'is my *friend*.'

Tiffany couldn't stop what happened next.

'Friend?' Peaseblossom spat. 'There are no *friends* for elves.'

He raised his arm and his sabre tore through Nightshade with a terrible swishing sound. The elf Queen fell, crumpling to the ground at Tiffany's feet, where she writhed for a moment that seemed to last a lifetime, myriad faces and shapes appearing and disappearing, flickering in and out of substance, before finally lying still, a forlorn heap. Tiffany reeled back in shock. *Peaseblossom had killed the Queen of the Fairies!*

Worse, he had killed her *friend*.

Peaseblossom, revelling, turned to Tiffany, his face sharp and merciless. 'You have no friend now!'

Suddenly the air was full of ice. 'You killed one of your own to get to me, you cursed elf,' Tiffany said, her voice cold, red-hot anger boiling inside her. 'She wanted to explore a new way, an alliance of humans and elves, and now you have killed her.'

'You stupid little girl!' Peaseblossom taunted. 'You think you can stand against me? What a fool you are! We elves knew well of the witch who once walked the edges of this world . . . but you, you are just a *child*, filled with pride because you were once lucky against a failing queen' – he glanced contemptuously down at the little heap that had once been the Queen of Fairyland – 'and now I will see you dead, alongside your *friend*.' He spat out the last word, and his glamour snaked towards her, creeping into her head, into her thoughts.

Tiffany recoiled, a memory of Nanny Ogg's voice suddenly saying to her: *Granny Weatherwax said to me as you is the one who's to deal with the future. An' bein' young means you've got a lot of future.* Well, it looked like Granny Weatherwax might have been wrong. She *didn't* have much future to come.

She had failed everyone.

She had tried to be the witch for two steadings. And let everyone down . . .

She had gone to see the King of the Elves. He had turned her away . . .

She had made a friend of Nightshade. Now the elf Queen was dead . . .

She was facing a powerful elf lord who would kill her . . .

She deserved to die . . .

She was alone . . .

Then it came to her. She did *not* deserve to die. And she was *not* alone. She never would be. Not while her land was beneath her boots. *Her* land. The land of the Achings.

She was Tiffany Aching. Not Granny Weatherwax, but a witch in her own right. A witch who knew exactly who she was and how she wanted to do things. Her way. And she had not failed, because she had barely begun . . .

She stood tall. Frosty. Furious. 'You called me a country girl,' she said, 'and I will see to it that the *country* will see you dead.'

The land was speaking to her now, filling her up, throwing the glamour of the elf lord aside as though it were nothing, and the air crackled like lightning. Yes, she thought. Thunder and Lightning. The two dogs were long gone, buried in the hills alongside Granny Aching, but their strength was with her.

And she was standing firm, her feet on the turf, the murmur of the ancient ocean below swelling through her soles. Earth. Water.

She raised her arms. 'Thunder and Lightning, I command you.' Fire and Air. As she drew on the power of the two sheepdogs, there in the air was a flash of lightning, a rumble of thunder. The shepherd's crown glowed golden on her breast – at the heart of it all, the soul and centre of her being – the golden light rising from the apex to surround her, protect her, add its energy to her own.

And the sky broke in half.

Never had there been such a storm. It was full of vengeance and the elves were running, or rather trying to run because the Feegles were in their way and the Wee Free Men had no liking for the elves. In the carnage and the shouting, it seemed to Tiffany that she wasn't in charge any more. She was just a conduit for the wrath of the Chalk.

The land under her feet was trembling, shaking like a wounded animal on a leash, yearning to be free. And the shepherd's crown was shining like a living thing in front of her.

A shepherd's crown, not a royal one.

A crown for someone who knew where she had come from.

A crown for the lone light zigzagging through the night sky, hunting for a single lost lamb.

A crown for the shepherd who was there to herd away the predators.

A crown for the shepherd who could work with the best sheepdogs any shepherd could possibly have.

A *shepherd's* crown.

And she heard again that voice: *Tiffany Aching is the first among shepherds, for she puts others before herself* . . .

A king of shepherds.

No . . . a *queen*.

She felt she needed to apologize to the crown, apologize for letting these elves come through and threaten this land, and so she said in a whisper, 'I am

Tiffany Aching and my bones are in the Chalk. Let the Chalk be cleansed!'

And the world changed.

In the city of Ankh-Morpork, Hex spat out a calculation for Ponder Stibbons – and he saw that an answer was underlined . . .

A prayer wheel spun in the monastery of Oi Dong, and the monks bowed down in gratitude . . .

While a little boy took his mother's hand in the travelling now, and said, 'Mummy, big nasties all gone . . .' He had a wooden train in his other hand, and a little backpack of tools over one shoulder. Perhaps he will be an engineer in this new world when he grows up, his mother thought.

And in Fairyland, there was a sudden *twang*, as if a strand connecting the two worlds had suddenly snapped . . .

There was fighting still going on – it was hard to stop the Feegles once they got going – and Tiffany walked through it as if in a dream. The elves were trying to get away now, but the ground seemed to hold them down and she whispered, 'I ask the Chalk, deliver to me the King of the Elves!'

The heavy dance of the land now had a different tempo.

Dust flew out, and there came suddenly the King of the Elves – the stink and his long hair and antlers were unmistakable. Oh, that stink! It had a life of its own. But in a way, Tiffany thought, it was a male stink of life.

The huge body loomed over her. 'How now, Mistress Tiffany. I can't say, "Well met again,"' said the King. 'But I must confess to . . . surprise. You surprised me before,' he mused, 'with the gift you left me. A . . . shed. What do you humans *do* with this place you call a shed?' He sounded intrigued.

'It is a place for . . . interests. Where the future can be founded,' Tiffany said. 'And a place where those who have lived many years may remember.'

'I have many memories,' said the King. 'But I did not know that you had the power to offer me new entertainments, to draw me to new pleasures. Very few in this world or others are able to do so.'

And now, Tiffany thought, the King of the Elves did see her as more than a young girl. At this meeting she had respect. But he deserved respect too, so she bowed her head towards him, just a little.

'May I apologize for the hotheads in my kingdom,' he continued lazily, his voice smooth and delicious. 'I find them a large annoyance. Quite possibly as you do.' He glared at the quivering Peaseblossom, and then at the corpse of Nightshade. 'You, elf, you killed my queen, my lady Nightshade, just for spite,' he growled. And the King of the Elves brought himself upright and smacked Peaseblossom with a hand that killed, leaving the carcass just lying there, his careless and casual use of violence shocking Tiffany, despite all she knew of elves. 'I'm sorry I had to do that,' he said, 'but they don't understand anything else. The universe turns, alas; it turns and we have to accommodate change or move on. This is a good world we had here, mistress,' the King said now. He shrugged. 'It's a shame about the iron. But perhaps as the universe turns, Mistress Tiffany, we might meet again, on a different turn and in more happy circumstances.'

'Yes,' said Tiffany, 'we might. Now, begone from my land.' Her voice was hard. And in the air there was the piercing sound of a whistle, with an answering screech as the early-morning train left Twoshirts station. 'Listen, your majesty. That is the song of the five twenty-five for Lancre, and that is your future, my lord. A lifetime of metal if you stay.'

'These mechanisms are interesting. There are tools in my shed, and I wonder if such "trains" could perhaps be made . . . *without* iron,' said the King, adding wistfully, 'I am a man of magic, so I should be able to have anything I want.'

'But you can't,' said Tiffany. 'The railways are not for you.'

And it seemed to her, as he left, that the King of the Elves was looking thoughtful.

As the final elves slipped away to limp back to their land, she turned to Rob Anybody. 'Rob, let us bury the Lady Nightshade here, where she fell,' she said quietly. 'I will mark the spot with a cairn of stones. We will remember this day. We will remember her.' Then she added softly, almost to herself: 'We *need* to remember.'

CHAPTER 19
Peace

As the morning flowed into the day, the Feegles were settling down to a feast of drinking, eating and more drinking and telling tales, some of which were bigger than the Feegles themselves.

Rob Anybody looked at Tiffany and said, 'Weel noo, mistress, the field is oor ain! Come on doon intae the mound. Jeannie would love tae see your sonsie face.'

And Tiffany slid into the mound, which seemed bigger than when she had seen it last. The great hall was full of leaping figures and flying kilts as the Feegles danced their reels – Feegles loved a reel at any time; the slap of boot on earth was like a challenge to the universe. Then, of course, every Feegle wanted every other Feegle to know how well they had conducted themselves against the elves.

Every single one of the younger Feegles was

wanting Tiffany – their hag o' the hills – to know how brave he had been. As they gathered around, she said, 'What are your names, boys?'

Wee Callum, a little bit tongue-tied, said, 'I'm Callum, mistress.'

'Pleased to meet you,' said Tiffany.

'Aye, mistress, and this is my brother, Callum.'

'Two of you?' she said. 'Isn't that difficult?'

'Och no, I know who I am and he knows who he is and so does our other brother Callum.'

'And how did you like the fighting?'

'Och aye, we smited them weel enough. The Big Man is a hard task master, ye ken. He sees to it that we can handle the mace and the spear and the axe. And, of course, the feets. And when the three of us got one of they scunners doon on the ground, that's what oor boots was for.'

The old boys were marching down the lane.

And they had a new song now, one that began: 'Ar-sol, ar-sol, a soldier's life for me!' And with each verse, and each step, they were standing straighter and stronger.

> 'Ar-sol, ar-sol, a soldier's life for me!
> For King, for King, for King and Constabulary,
> We wee, we wee, we weaken the enemies,
> For they don't want it up 'em, don't want it up 'em, don't
>   want it up and over!'

And those who had wives kissed them – the wives hadn't seen their husbands so frisky for years – and then they set off down to the pub to tell their mates all about it.

With a pint resting happily in his hand, Captain Makepeace sat on a milestone outside the pub and declaimed, 'People of Lancre. We happy few, we extremely elderly few, have scorned the horrible elves. They say that old men forget, but we won't. Not by a long chalk. We thought we were old – but today we found we were still young.'

And then it was time for another round of drinks. And another, with everyone wanting to stand the old boys a round, until standing was no longer an option. And still the shout went up: Was there time for another flagon?

As the moon rose to herald the hours of darkness the following day there was Geoffrey on his broomstick, which was once again hovering in the air. Tiffany shouted over at him, 'I still don't know how you can do that!'

'No idea, Tiffany – can't everyone?' he replied. 'Let's ask, for here comes everyone.'

And indeed, now the other witches were arriving, led by Nanny Ogg and Magrat. It was time to look to the future once again – a future not now filled with elves. But the present, well, the present was filled with the chattering and gossiping of witches as the tales of the two battles were shared.

Rob Anybody had set fire to a beacon and Tiffany watched the last witches circling until there was space, then coming in to land one after the other. Not one left her stick hovering, though – it seemed as if Geoffrey was the only one who could make his broomstick do that.

'I wonder if they're goin' to sneak back,' said Nanny Ogg after a while. 'You can't trust Old Hairy. He was tryin' to charm you, Tiff, by what you say.'

'I know, but I am not charmed,' said Tiffany. 'Not since the one elf who tried to be a good elf is now dead. We marked the spot where we buried her, Nanny, you know. And if they do try to come back, we will be ready for them. We can put iron on the stones here on the Chalk, like you've laid swarf all around the Dancers in Lancre.' Her voice hardened. 'There is iron in my soul now. And iron in dealing with them should they dare ever to return.'

'Well,' said Magrat the Queen, 'we've knocked them down so often now that I think he means what he said. I think it's unlikely they will come back.'

'I'll drink to them not coming back then,' said Nanny Ogg.

'Ladies, while we are gathered,' said Tiffany, 'I want to talk to you about Geoffrey. He has been a great strength to us – and I know you all saw how he made the old men of Lancre into a fighting force. He is clever and cunning and careful. He knows how to listen. And he has a kind of magic.'

'That's true,' said Nanny. 'Everybody likes Geoffrey. Somehow he seems to understand everybody. Believe me, even some of them old girls would be quite happy to have him deal with their aches and pains and worse. He calms people. You all know that.

He is calm itself, and the calm stays even when he has left. He doesn't just jolly people up. After he is gone, they are somehow much better – as if life was still worth havin'. People like that, like Geoffrey, well, they makes the world, well, better.'

'I totally agree with you,' said Mrs Earwig.

'*You* agrees with *me*?' said Nanny Ogg, almost speechless.

'Yes, my dear, I do.'

And Tiffany thought, At last, we will have peace. 'Thank you, Geoffrey,' she said under her breath. 'Now we are all here,' she said aloud, 'I must tell you that I can't manage Granny's steading. I'm not going to sleep in Granny's bed any more. Because I'm not her.'

Nanny grinned. 'I wondered if'n you would do that, Tiff. You has to be your own woman after all.'

'My roots are in the Chalk and the Chalk is my strength,' Tiffany continued. 'My bones will be part of these hills just like those of my Granny Aching.'

There was a murmur from the witches. They had all heard of Granny Aching by now.

'And I have some very good boots too. Just as I cannot sleep in Granny Weatherwax's bed, I cannot wear her boots either.'

Nanny chuckled. 'I'll collect 'em when I'm next up at the cottage, Tiff. I knows Esme's boots, knows a young witch they'll do very nicely for.'

'Talking of young witches,' Tiffany added, 'Miss Tick has found me some girls with potential. May I send them up to the mountains to begin their training? I will have need of help in the Chalk in the future.'

The witches were nodding. Of course. For it was the way it was done: the young girls – Nancy Upright and Becky Pardon – would spend time with the senior witches and learn the beginning of their trade.

Tiffany took a deep breath. 'And what I suggest is that Geoffrey be allowed to look after Granny Weatherwax's cottage and steading for me,' she said, looking at Nanny Ogg as she said that and getting a wink in return.

She glanced at Mrs Earwig and was surprised to see her nod and say, 'He's a very nice decent young man, and we have seen him at work, and now we live in the time of the railways so perhaps we should change our ways. Yes, I believe Mister Geoffrey should take care of Granny's – *Tiffany's* – steading in Lancre. He's no witch, but he's certainly much more than the *usual* sort of backhouse boy.' And Tiffany could see Mrs Earwig's mind working, and she felt certain that the next time she saw the witch, she would have a lad somewhere around her establishment.

Out loud, Nanny said, 'What did you call him, Tiff? A calm-weaver? Shall we leave it at that for now?'

But Magrat wanted her say too. 'Verence heard of what he did for the old men,' she said. 'He believes he should have a reward. And I think I know exactly what would suit . . .'

And thus, a few weeks later, Lord Swivel was most surprised to see his third son riding proudly up his long, long drive, a herald at his side* and a pennant

* Shawn Ogg, in another of his royal duties.

with the royal insignia of Lancre fluttering in the breeze. The same insignia was also on a velvet coat over the flanks of Mephistopheles.

'May I announce His Royal Ambassadorship Geoffrey Swivel,' proclaimed the herald, breaking into a few notes on the trumpet he held.

Geoffrey's mother sobbed with delight, while his father – a man on whom no calm-weaving would *ever* work – boiled inside with fury as he had to bow to the son he had treated as a nobody. But no one argued with the power of a crown.

There was a purpose to this visit, though. After the usual bowing, scraping and general knee-bending any royal emissary took as his due, Geoffrey grinned around at the assembled company and said, 'Father, I have exciting news! Those of us in the country may oft feel neglected by those in the big city but let me assure you, this is not the case. There have, in fact, been important developments just recently in the field of . . . *chicken runs.* Some young people in Ankh-Morpork . . . young people whose parents have the power to indulge their wishes' – and he tapped his nose with a finger to show that he expected his father to know these important parents – 'feel that it may no longer be necessary to hunt sly old Mister Reynard to protect our chickens.' He beamed. 'They have come up with a new chicken run which is *totally impervious* to foxes. And you, Father, are the lucky, lucky landowner who has been chosen to test this new design.'

As his father spluttered, and his brother Hugh shouted 'Hurrah!' for no particular reason except that it felt like someone should, Geoffrey looked around. He could see his mother's face. Normally she looked like someone the world had trodden on so many times that it was almost an invitation to tread on her yourself, but now she stood tall, her chin high.

'Harold. Our son has worked wonders, and here is a king honouring him and treating him as a friend,' she said proudly. 'Don't you look at me like that, Harold, for today I have spoken. And the Queen of Lancre has invited me to come and visit her,' she added with satisfaction.

There was a bleat from Mephistopheles, and as Geoffrey's father turned to stamp away, the goat turned its back and aimed a square set of devilish hooves right onto Lord Swivel's rump. Followed by a raucous fart that almost – but not *quite* – covered up the noise of the man falling flat on his face.

'A most usefully offensive goat,' Geoffrey murmured to McTavish, who had come to stand by his side.

The old stable-lad looked around. '*And* one your father cannot touch,' he said with a wink. 'Not with that fancy coat on its back.' He sniffed. 'My word, though, Mephistopheles isn't easy on the nose – he whiffs even worse than I remember.'

'Yes,' said Geoffrey, 'but he can climb trees. *And* use a privy. Even count. He's a strange creature; he can turn a dark day into a clear one. Look into his eyes sometime.'

And McTavish looked, and then hastily looked away.

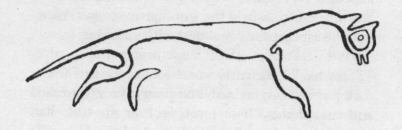

EPILOGUE

A Whisper on the Chalk

Two days after the battle, Tiffany led one of the farm horses up to the hills above the farm. It was a perfect early autumn's day. There was a wonderful cerulean sky, buzzards screaming overhead and a clear view towards the distant mountains of Lancre, their tops still covered in snow even at this time of year.

There were always a handful of sheep up in this part of the downs, whatever the weather. At this time of year there were half-grown lambs kicking their heels and chasing about while the ewes grazed nearby. Here was a well-known landmark for those who knew. A special place for sheep and farmers alike. The place where Granny Aching now lay beneath the turf.

Only the iron wheels of her hut and the old pot-bellied stove with its chimney were still visible, but

315

the ground, the ground was holy: Tiffany came to look at it every time she felt the world grinding her down, and here, where the wind never stopped blowing, she felt that she could deal with anything.

With the help of the horse and a strong rope, Tiffany hauled the rusty wheels out of the turf where they had been embedded, and painstakingly greased and coaxed them back together. Rob Anybody had watched her for a while after she had rebuffed his offer to help, then departed with a puzzled look on his face, muttering about geases, and what he'd like to do to them.

The following day, Tiffany went to visit old Mr Block, the local carpenter. He had once made her a doll's house when she was a little girl; now she had a bigger home in mind.

He was pleased to see her but was startled when he discovered what she wanted from him.

'Mr Block, I would like you to teach me to be a carpenter. I am going to build myself a hut – a shepherding hut.'

The carpenter was a kindly man and offered to help. 'You are a witch,' he said. 'I'm a carpenter. A little hut like that wouldn't take me long. Your granny was very good to our family and you helped my sister Margaret. I'd be happy to do it for you.'

But Tiffany was very definite. 'That's nice of you,' she said, 'but all the work on this hut must be done by me. It will be mine, from top to bottom, and I will pull it to where the larks rise. And I'll still be a witch when anyone should call. But there I will live.' On my own, she thought to herself. For now, anyway, for who knew what the future might bring . . . And her hand crept to her pocket, where she had Preston's latest letter to savour.

And so Tiffany learned carpentry every evening after her day's work was done. It took her some weeks to finish it, but eventually there was a new shepherd's hut stationed close to Granny Aching's grave.

There were three steps up to its wooden door, a horseshoe and a tuft of sheep's wool – the sign of a shepherd – already nailed in place there, and the roof arched over a small living space into which she had built a bed, a little cupboard, a few shelves and a space for a wash basin. From the bed, she could see out of a small window – see clear across the downs, right to the horizon. And she could see the sun rise, and set, and the moon dance through its guises – the magic of everyday that was no less magic for that.

She loaded up the old farm horse again with the bedding from her little room in the farmhouse and her few possessions, said goodbye to her parents and headed up the hill in the late afternoon sun.

'Are you sure, jigget, that this is what you really want?' said her father.

'Yes, it is,' Tiffany replied.

Her mother cried and handed her a new quilt and a freshly baked loaf of bread to go with the cheese Tiffany had made that morning.

Halfway up the hill, Tiffany turned to look down at the farm and saw her parents still arm in arm. She waved and carried on climbing without looking back again. It had been a long day. They were always long days.

Later that evening, once she had made her little bed in the hut, she went out to collect some kindling. The white cat, You, followed close behind.

The little tracks of the Chalk were very familiar to Tiffany. She had walked along them with Granny Aching years ago. And as she reached the wood at the top of the rise, Tiffany thought she saw somebody walking through the dusky shadows under the trees.

Not just one person alone. There seemed to be two figures, both strangely familiar. Beside them, alert to every gesture, every nod, every whistle, trotted two sheepdogs.

Granny Weatherwax, Tiffany thought. Side by side with Granny Aching, Thunder and Lightning at their heels. And the little words in her head came unbidden: *You are the shepherd's crown, jigget. You are the shepherd's crown.*

One of the figures looked over and gave her a brief nod, whilst the other paused and bowed her head. Tiffany bowed back, solemnly, respectfully.

And then the figures were gone.

On the way back to the hut, Tiffany looked down at the cat and, on a sudden impulse, spoke to it.

'Where is Granny Weatherwax, You?'

There was a pause, and the cat made a long *meow*, which appeared to end, '*Meow . . . vrywhere.*' And then purred, just like any other cat, and rubbed her hard little head against Tiffany's leg.

Tiffany thought of the little spot in the woods

where Granny Weatherwax lay. Remembered.

And knew that You had been right. Granny Weatherwax was indeed here. And there. She was, in fact, and always would be, everywhere.

There was a long stream of visitors to the shepherding hut once it became known that Tiffany was back on the Chalk for good.

Joe Aching came up to deliver some messages – and a new letter, from Preston! – and bring Tiffany some things her mother had decided she needed. He looked around the neat little hut with approval. Tiffany had made the space very comfortable. He looked at the books on the shelf and smiled. Tiffany had left Granny Aching's *Diseases of the Sheep* at the farm, but both *Flowers of the Chalk* and *The Goode Childe's Booke of Faerie Tales* had their place by the little shepherd's crown he had given her. On the back of the door was a wooden peg on which hung her witch's hat.

'I reckon ye'll find some use for this too,' her father said as he took a bottle of Special Sheep's Liniment (made according to Granny Aching's recipe) out of his pocket and placed it on the shelf.

Tiffany laughed and hoped her father hadn't heard the cry of 'Crivens!' from the roof of the hut.

He looked up as some dust fell down from where Big Yan sat on Daft Wullie to silence him. 'I hope ye haven't got woodworm already, Tiff.'

She laughed again as she gave him a hug to say goodbye.

Mr Block was an early visitor too. He puffed his way up the hill and found her settled in with You the cat sitting on her lap while she sorted rags.

Tiffany watched nervously as the old carpenter looked around and under the hut with a professional eye. When he had finished, she gave him a cup of tea and asked him what he thought.

'You've done well, lass. Very well. I have never seen a boy apprentice take to carpentry as quickly as this, and you are a girl.'

'Not a girl,' Tiffany said. 'I'm a witch.' And she looked down to the little cat beside her and said, 'That's so, isn't it, You?'

Mr Block looked at her suspiciously for a moment. 'So did you use magic to make the hut, miss?'

'I didn't have to,' said Tiffany. 'The magic was already here.'

The End.

AFTERWORD

The Shepherd's Crown is Terry Pratchett's final novel. It was written in his last year before he finally succumbed in early 2015 to the 'embuggerance' of posterior cortical atrophy. Terry had been diagnosed back in 2007, the year that he wrote *Nation*. At that time, Terry thought he might have less than two years to live and that brought a new urgency to his writing. He had never been a slouch in this respect but now things were measured by the cost in writing time. If demands for his presence took him away from writing, it had to be really worthwhile, such as feeding the chickens or attending to his tortoises. He had so many more books he wanted to write.

It says a lot for Terry's resilience and determination not to go down without a fight that he wrote five more full-length bestselling novels between *Nation* and *The Shepherd's Crown* (as well as collaborating with Stephen Baxter on five *Long Earth* novels). And Terry was still developing new ideas for books right up to his final few months.*

Terry usually had more than one book on the go at a time and he discovered what each was about as he went along. He would start somewhere, telling himself the story as he wrote it, writing the bits he could see clearly and assembling it all into a whole – like a giant literary jigsaw – when he was done. Once it was shaped, he would keep writing it too, adding to it, fixing bits, constantly polishing and adding linking sequences, tossing in just one more footnote or event. His publishers often had to prise the manuscript away from him, as there was always more he felt he could do, even though by then he would be well into the next story which was tugging at his elbow. Eventually the book was sent to the printer, and reluctantly Terry would let it go.

Terry had been thinking about the key elements in Tiffany Aching and Granny Weatherwax's last story for a few years. He wrote the pivotal scenes while he

* We will now not know how the old folk of *Twilight Canyons* solve the mystery of a missing treasure and defeat the rise of a Dark Lord despite their failing memories, nor the secret of the crystal cave and the carnivorous plants in *The Dark Incontinent*, nor how Constable Feeney solves a whodunnit amongst the congenitally decent and honest goblins, nor how the second book about the redoubtable Maurice as a ship's cat might have turned out. And these are just a few of the ideas his office and family know about.

was still writing *Raising Steam* and then re-wrote them several times as he shaped the rest of *The Shepherd's Crown* around them.

The Shepherd's Crown has a beginning, a middle and an end, and all the bits in between. Terry wrote all of those. But even so, it was, still, not quite as finished as he would have liked when he died. If Terry had lived longer, he would almost certainly have written more of this book. There are things we all wish we knew more about. But what we have is a remarkable book, Terry's final book, and anything you wish to know more about in here, you are welcome to imagine yourself.

Rob Wilkins
May 2015
Salisbury, UK

ACKNOWLEDGEMENTS

Despite the effects of his Alzheimer's disease, Terry wanted to keep writing as long as possible and was able to do so not least through the assistance of his fine editorial team. Lyn, Rhianna and Rob would most especially like to thank Philippa Dickinson and Sue Cook for their tireless help and encouragement that kept the words flowing.

A Feegle Glossary

adjusted for those of a delicate disposition
(A Work In Progress By Miss Perspicacia Tick, witch)

Bigjobs: human beings
Big Man: chief of the clan (usually the husband of the kelda)
Blethers: rubbish, nonsense
Bogle: see *Schemie*
Boggin: to be desperate, as in 'I'm boggin for a cup of tea'
Brose: porridge with a drop of strong drink added – or more than a drop. Be warned: it will put hairs on your chest
Bunty: a weak person
Carlin: old woman
Cludgie: the privy
Corbies: big, black burdies known by most people as crows

Crivens!: a general exclamation that can mean
anything from 'My goodness!' to 'I've just lost my
temper and there is going to be trouble'

Dree your/my/his/her weird: facing the fate that is in
store for you/me/him/her

Een: eyes

Eldritch: weird, strange; sometimes means oblong
too, for some reason

Fash: worry, upset

Geas: a very important obligation, backed up by
tradition and magic. Not a bird

Gonnagle: the bard of the clan, skilled in music and
stories

Hag: a witch, of any age

Hag o' hags: a very important witch

Hagging/Haggling: anything a witch does

Hiddlins: secrets

Kelda: the female head of the clan, and eventually the
mother of most of it. Feegle babies are very small,
and a kelda will have hundreds in her lifetime

Lang syne: long ago

Last World: the Feegles believe that they are dead.
This world is so filled with all they like, they
argue, that they must have been really good in a
past life and then died and ended up here.
Appearing to die here means merely going back to
the Last World, which they believe is rather dull

Mowpie: furry animals with white tufts as tails,
making them easy to spot. Sometimes called
rabbits. Good to eat, especially with a dab of snail
relish on the side

Mudlin: useless person

Pished: I am assured that this means 'tired'

Schemie: an unpleasant person

Scuggan: a really unpleasant person

Scunner: a generally unpleasant person

Ships: woolly things that eat grass and go baa. Easily confused with the other kind

Spavie: see *Mudlin*

Special Sheep Liniment: probably moonshine whisky, I am very sorry to say. A favourite of the Feegles. Do not try to make this at home

Spog: a small leather bag at the front of a Feegle's kilt, which covers whatever he presumably thinks needs to be hidden, and generally holds things like something he is halfway through eating, something he'd found that now therefore belongs to him, and whatever he was using as a handkerchief, which might not necessarily be dead

Steamie: only found in the big Feegle mounds in the mountains, where there's enough water to allow regular bathing; it's a kind of sauna. Feegles on the Chalk tend to rely on the fact that you can only get so much dirt on you before it starts to fall off of its own accord

Waily: a general cry of despair

VISIT THE WYRD AND WONDERFUL

TERRY PRATCHETT

WEBSITE

VIDEOS

FORUM

COMPETITIONS

NEWS

AND SO MUCH MORE ...

www.terrypratchett.co.uk
It's out of this world!